THE HUNTRESS

SKY

SARAH DRIVER

EGMONT

To Granny, for inspiring me to rove the great wide
and knowing the sea like you were Sea-Tribe.

EGMONT
We bring stories to life

First published in Great Britain 2017
by Egmont UK Limited
The Yellow Building, 1 Nicholas Road, London W11 4AN

Text copyright © Sarah Driver, 2017
Illustrations copyright © Joe McLaren, 2017
Additional interior illustrations by Janene Spencer

ISBN 978 1 4052 8468 4

www.egmont.co.uk

A CIP catalogue record for this title is available from the British Library

Printed and bound in Great Britain by the CPI Group

65149/1

Hackles

1. The long hall
2. The Protector of the Mountain's draggle throne
3. The forge
4. The armoury
5. Ice-boulders
6. Cells
7. The sawbones' nest
8. Down to draggle caves
9. The pantries

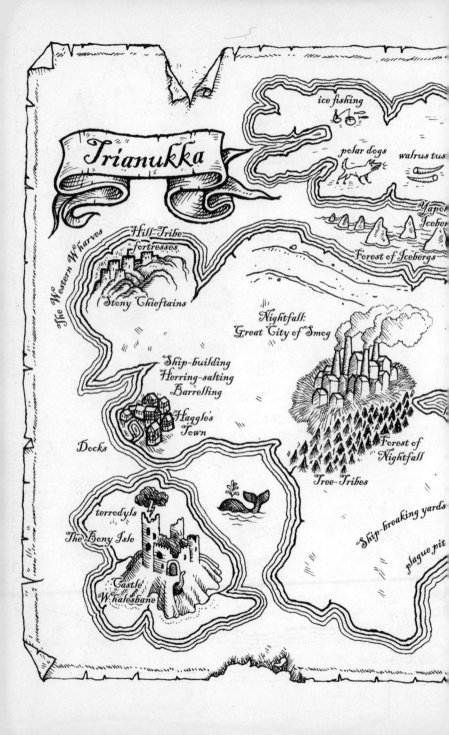

Skybrary

1. Sleeping loft
2. Hammocks
3. Skating slope
4. Cage and winch
5. Bookshelves
6. Snoozing Skybrarian
7. Squishy old chairs
8. Hearth
9. Wish-tea

PART 1

The Great Wide

1
Sea Urchins

I stand on the deck of the Huntress, blinking snowflakes from my eyelashes. In the palm of my hand rests a green jewel. When I peer inside it, my own grey eyes stare back, jolting ripples of shock through my chest in time with the oarsman's drum.

The jewel turns cold, wet and blubbery. Then it grows a spotted skin, like a whale shark. Gills wheeze open in its surface, oozing foam.

I know, sure as the Sea-Tribe blood in my veins, that I'm holding the Storm-Opal of the sea.

And I know I have to protect it, with every stitch of me, but the burden presses on my shoulders, heavier than the beat of the drum.

The jewel splutters and a speck of saltwater prickles my lips. It needs the sea.

We need the sea.

I raise my arm to throw the Opal overboard, its gills struggling against me, but freeze when an urgent voice coils through the roots of my mind, like fog.

Keep this hidden, Little-Bones. I cannot return, there is grave danger. Seek the scattered Storm-Opals of Sea, Sky and Land, before an enemy finds them and uses them to wield dark power. Take them to the golden crown before all Trianukka turns to ice, trapping the whales beneath a frozen sea. Remember the old song? The song will make a map. Keep your brother close by your side, and know you're never alone. I will find you when I can. Da.

A ragged breathing makes my skin shiver, as though spiders are tiptoeing along my spine. As I turn my head towards the noise, my ship begins to shift – until her deck is slick with blood and her flanks are studded with huge, fire-spitting guns.

A face blurs into focus. The eyes dark and full of rage, the brows heavy and black, the thin lips pulled into a sneer.

The face belongs to the murderous-false captain; the man in a red cloak and boots with brass buckles, the navigator who stole our ship. The one who took Grandma away.

Stag.

Even in the dream-world my muscles squirm to run from him.

A stooped man in a cloak of purple lightning appears by Stag's side. Stag whispers in his ear. Then the two of them raise their arms slowly to point at the Opal in my hand.

I close my fingers around the jewel and tuck it close to my heart. My bones feel scalded. I wish their greed-filled eyes never touched the Opal.

There's a flurry of movement and when I look up Stag's pointing a gun out towards the plank. My eyes follow his to a bundle of rags huddled there.

Grandma.

Before I can move, or shout, or anything, fire explodes from the gun and the grey world is streaked with splashes of red. The sky blinks, and the edges of the dream wobble like air above a flame, and then my hand's empty. And the loss makes me stagger. The Opal spins away and suddenly it's in Grandma's eye socket. But she's falling, crashing into the sea, wrenching out my heart as hers drowns.

Mouse!

The pull to her is oar-strong but when I strain to reach her, hands hold me back.

I'm hollow. Cold and numb. I'm too small. My voice is trapped under layers of ice. I'm frighted. I can't get to Grandma. She's gone.

The hands loosen and I'm sprawling on the deck. I run, painful slow, then pitch fast off the plank, diving through the sea, stretching my fingers into the blackness. She should be here. Where is she? Grandma!

For the first time ever, the sea is a dead place where naught lives. A crust of ice shuts out the light from above.

Do you remember, when the sea, lay, still, in wait for me? drifts a voice.

Don't you remember?

I thrash, reaching for the surface. The dream pinches my brain. I struggle in the grip of the dream-sea, fighting the water, clawing until my muscles scream . . . then finally rising up, up, up, through ice that thickens with every thump of my heart.

My spirit thuds into my body and I jolt awake, gasping, neck stiff and sore.

I'm slumped over a creature's back, and my legs are hanging in thin air. As I scrabble to clutch onto something solid, my fingertips scrape a scaly hide – and the memory of where I am seeps through me.

The young terrodyl streaks through a sky fat with snow. *Fastestfastestfastest*, gabbles his beast-chatter. *Fastest beast of all!* I dig my knees into his bristles to keep from falling off. My little brother Sparrow's arms are wrapped round my waist and his head's pressed against my back. Hunched behind him is Crow, the ship-wrecker boy who I still ent heart-certain we can trust, though he helped me rescue Sparrow from Castle Whalesbane.

I remember flying all day; over a sea, a forest and a smog-shrouded city. Then I must've dozed off. Now the sun's barrelling for the horizon again.

Dream fragments are still thudding around my head like trapped moonsprites. The Sea-Opal! I quickly pat down my pockets, whistling in relief when I feel the bump of the gem through the cloth. But my dream-dance has left me drained and hollow. I remember for the thousandth time that Grandma's dead, and it's the same sharp, sick pang, followed up with guilt that I ent told my brother yet – and I don't know how.

'*Finally*, the rat awakes!' calls Crow. 'Any clue where we are?' He snorts loudly and then spits into the air.

I twist round to reply, and wince as the bandage on my face pulls at the wound that slashes down my right cheekbone to the corner of my mouth. 'I don't know,' I shout, as a fresh wave of pain sears through me. 'Happens the world's a flaming bigger place than even a Sea-Tribe girl could've guessed!'

'Ain't it just,' Crow bellows.

The terrodyl thrashes his head from side to side. *Where go where go now?* he rasps.

I tell the beast what I've been telling him since we took flight. *All I know is we have to fly as far and fast as we can from Castle Whalesbane.* My tongue wraps itself around the raw, earthy words, tasting the wildness of my beast-chatter.

Castle my nest home. Not bad place!

I suck in a deep breath. *Stag was controlling your nest-mates and sending them after us. And the mystiks there wanted to hurt my brother!*

Where go? chatters the terrodyl. The fearsome-foul stink of his breath hits me right in the face.

I bite back a wave of impatience. *Hang on. I need to think.* I chew my cheek, trying to rid my brain of the last dream-tangles. The beast is right to ask – we need to head for somewhere, cos we can't just fly forever. But we can't go back to my ship either, cos it's just as dangerous as the castle.

Seek the scattered Storm-Opals of Sea, Sky and Land . . . remember the old song?

Da's message floats into my mind again. When my brother sang the old song, his notes stirred the message into a magyk map that showed me the three Storm-Opals. Now one is safe in my pocket, and I wish I could check the map again, but now it's in Stag's grimesome clutches. I just have to hope he won't unlock the magic of the Opals himself. All I know is there's an Opal waiting somewhere in the realm of Sky . . . could we reach it, somehow?

'I need to pee,' snuffles Sparrow, breaking into my thoughts.

'*Gods*, what I wouldn't give to stretch my legs!' grumbles Crow.

'Pipe down, would you?' I shout. 'I'm trying to think.'

'Should we make a plan?' calls Crow. 'You don't have to do all the thinking by yourself, you know. Are you telling this thing where to fly?'

8

I hunker closer to the terrodyl's skin, against the wind. Should I tell Crow about the Opals?

Before I can gift him a reply he tuts and I feel angry spikes throbbing from him. 'You still don't trust me, do you?'

This boy's even more impatient than me. 'Course, I just—'

'Whatever!' he snaps. 'Just keep us away from your ship, for the time being.' Then he yawns. 'Anyway, now you're awake I'd say it's my turn to catch a few winks.' He falls silent, and soon enough his breathing's sleepy-soft.

We zoom further and faster through the sky. Ice-cold snot is stuck to my lips, and I keep 'em moving so they don't freeze shut. 'My name's Mouse,' I mutter. 'I'm thirteen Hunter's Moons old.' My teeth chatter. 'The *Huntress* is our ship. The home of our Tribe. And we'll claim her back from Stag.'

My sea-hawk, Thaw-Wielder, snoozes between my belly and one of the terrodyl's spines; a warm bundle of sleek feathers. She's grown again, but she ent realised she's got to be more gentle when she lands on me – I'm still sore from the last time her huge claws thudded into my shoulder. I rub her head, feeling the delicate bones of her skull beneath her feathers. Then I pull my hand back as a shock stabs into my fingers – the Opal in my breeches pocket has made Thaw puff up into a ball, crackling with heat and smelling like the sky before a storm.

I scan the horizon. On the shore, stretched from east to west, a beach of black sand wears a skin of ice, and beyond glints a dark sea hissing and pluming into jets of water that are fighting not to freeze solid.

I hum under my breath. *You must remember what waits there, you'll find it at the point high in the air.*

Then I stop, cos the song brings my dream-dance crashing back over me like a wave. Thaw stirs and stretches out a brown and white wing, uncovering her eyes and watching me curiously. *Remember how that line of the old song once gifted us the idea of searching at Whale-Jaw Rock, Thaw?* I say when I can breathe again. *It's east of here, and marked by a great plume of water, that looks like a whale breathing through its spout.*

Sea-breather, she babbles, eyes glinting.

I nudge the terrodyl's right side with my heel. *We should bear east!* I call.

My gut lurches into my mouth as the creature twists in the air to change direction. He chuckles. *Long-flying since asked crawler where go. It answers almost at end of world!*

I grin at the beast's cheekiness, and turn back to Thaw. *Reckon we'd better find the place soon,* I tell her. Cos the world's ready to crunch up our bones and spit us out if I don't get all three Opals to the golden crown.

She blinks slowly at me, a shiver rippling through her feathers. *Remember home,* she warbles softly. *Remember name. Tell Thaw feather-truth, bone-truth.* The fierceness in her eyes gifts me the heart-strength to dredge my truth from the depths of my bones.

My name is Mouse. I'm thirteen Hunter's Moons old, I mutter between chattering teeth. *Sometimes my Tribe call me Little-Bones. I love to howl and dive for pearls and shoot arrows from my longbow. There's fire-crackle in my heart,* Grandma always said. *There's fire-crackle in the hearts of all my Tribe. It's a fight that blazes inside.*

Thaw gurgles a quick battle-squawk and puffs up her feathers.

My home's been thieved, and now I'm out in the wild. My Tribe are in danger. I need my fire-crackle more than ever. Cos the fight's only just begun.

2
Bragful Boastings

We fly east, the sea curving from our left and spilling into the distance ahead. The wind buffets the terrodyl and tries to claw off our skins. I'm watching for the *Huntress* without even meaning to, cos my heart pangs whenever I glimpse movement below.

I picture my friend, chief oarsman Bear, battling furious waves and shivering at his post. Forced to be one of Stag's oar-slaves, chained and half starved. I have to make things right and claim our ship back – there ent a beat to lose. *Can you keep watch for the geyser – the sea-breather?* I ask Thaw, as we fly over a landscape of cracked brown earth, abandoned dwellings and ripped out trees that lie on the ground, roots grasping for the sky. My belly twists like I've swallowed a nail – seems like the world is brimming with chaos.

Thaw-Wielder flicks open one bright yellow eye. *Thaw watches!* She hops out of my lap onto the terrodyl's head and fans out her striped wings, shaking the frost from them. Then she huddles down, head twitching to right and left as she watches for the flicker of the geyser.

Heart-thanks, Thaw, I tell her. Then I cough, cos my beast-chatter always comes from the very back of my throat, and I'm proper parched to boot. Long icicles hang from the terrodyl's wings. Wonder if I could snap one off for drinking water?

I stretch out my arm, eyeing an icicle, but then a fizzing finger of lightning stabs from the sky into the black sand below, exploding black arrows up into the air. The terrodyl hisses and swerves away from where the lightning struck. Then a sparkle catches my eye, and when I glance again we've crossed the shoreline and a glittering forest has opened up below us.

A forest of shapes.

Scores of towering blue icebergs shoot upwards from the sea. Glowing balls of blue zip between the bergs. I squint down at them and then my chest riots. 'Berg owls!' The feathery bundles thud into caves they've burrowed in the ice. 'We're flying over the great Iceberg Forest of the Wildersea!'

When I turn to grin at the others, a slip of moonlight skitters out of Sparrow's tunic pocket and streaks silver footprints up his neck, over his ear and onto my shoulder. *Where where what-huh-what black-hair chatters?* Thunderbolt chimes eagerly. The moonsprite swings from my earlobe with a tingle-cold grip.

I chuckle. *Icebergs. You can't miss 'em. It means we're flying over the border of the Wildersea! Now all we need to do is follow the icebergs east towards the Bay of Thunder, and I'll know how to find Whale-Jaw Rock from there.*

She gifts me a short chirrup of approval before zipping back to Sparrow. Not so long ago me and the sprite couldn't stomach the sight of each other, so I'm heart-glad she still wants to be friends.

'What d'ya reckon, Sparrow? Ent these bergs something?' Then I remember he can't see much, cos of the creeping white film on his eyeballs, and I chew my tongue.

'I'm thirsty.' That's all he says, and proper quiet.

'Don't worry, we're on the right path, so we won't be flying much longer. And I've got an idea,' I call to him, eyeing the icicles on the terrodyl's wings.

'Can I have a story, too?' he whimpers. 'My nightmares are more stronger. They keep giving me the brain-aches.'

I squeeze his hand. 'S'alright, they'll soon stop now we've got you away from that place.'

'But I feel like something bad's gonna happen.' He bangs his head against my back. 'I dreamt a golden lightning bolt shot us down.'

'We've left the bad stuff behind, too-soon,' I tell

him softly, panicking inside about what to do if he has more shaking fits. 'How about that story?' I clear my throat. Stories grow twisted over time, especially if you tell them without story pictures etched in bone to guide you. But I remember one so well that I can taste the words, ready to spill out. The story everyone knows, but I never knew the heart-truth of when I used to tell it before. Now the truth of it rattles through my marrow.

'One hundred moons and suns ago, long after the first oarsman beat his drum, the last King of Trianukka had an ancient golden crown and three powerful Storm-Opals.' As I tell the story, I feel Sparrow relax against me the tiniest bit. I clutch the terrodyl's spine tightly as it navigates the Iceberg Forest. 'The Opals were to be set in the crown, to heal the trouble between all the Tribes of Sea, Sky and Land and let them live in peace together. The first Opal held a foam of sea, the second a fragment of sky, and the third a fracture of land. But before the gems could be set in the King's crown, it got gobbled up by a great whale. The Opals had to be kept safe, so the crinkled old molluscs—'

'You mean mystiks!' murmurs Sparrow.

'Aye, same difference. The *mystiks* of the Bony Isle guarded them, deep within the walls of Castle Whalesbane, where the King dwelt. The King blamed the Sea-Tribe captain, Rattlebones, for hiding the crown in the whale's belly, and that brought a hundred years of war, and gifted all the power to the land.'

That's where the story always ends but now I've got more to tell. 'Sparrow, we can hammer in our own iron rivets, can't we? How about this?' I sniff away the sticky ice inside my nose. 'Somehow, after moons and moons, the three Opals were thieved from the castle and scattered, setting grave danger loose on the world. Sneaking ice tiptoed ahead of the winter, and the seas threatened to freeze and trap the whales. Trianukka was at risk of ripping apart altogether. But heart-luck was waiting to save the day, in the form of a girl. One Hunter's Moon, this girl – who was the best at longbow shooting, amongst other things—'

'No bragful boastings!' yelps Sparrow.

'– aye, she'd packed most skills under her belt as it happens. Well, she found a note telling her to find the scattered Opals and to take them to the golden crown before the world turned to ice. *And* – get this – the girl found the Sea-Opal, right under her nose.'

Crow splutters. 'I think boasting might be putting it mildly, mate.'

My heart clangs, *whooshing* blood into my cheeks – I'd reckoned him still asleep, and I ent certain if I want him to know all that stuff yet. Grandma always did say my big mouth would be the end of me. 'Shut it, you.'

'Interesting how you make everything about you, ain't it? And you do realise the whole thing's just a kids' bedtime story?' He sniffs loudly.

'You're wrong, I reckon!' pipes Sparrow.

Crow scoffs.

I tug my cloak tighter around me and will Sparrow not to utter another word. If the wrecker boy thinks it's just a story, I'll let him think that, for now.

But Sparrow thumps my arm weakly. 'When you gonna tell the bit of the story that's about me?' he croaks.

Mememe, croaks Thaw-Wielder, feathers trembling with wanting to be part of the story, too.

Then one of the icebergs looms through the sea-mist and the terrodyl dodges, then pulls higher into the sky. Some of the bergs are so tall their heads are lodged in the clouds.

'Hold tight!' I scream. I grab Sparrow's hands and pull his arms tighter around my waist. When the terrodyl's finished climbing his wings settle again into a steady, whooshing beat. The air's thinner up here and my lungs suck at it greedily.

We keep flying east, taking it in turns to nap, until another thin, wintry dawn cracks the sky from black to grey to white.

I stare down at the last iceberg, on the very edge of the forest. Then it's behind us and there's just a blend of grey-white sea and sky, before clouds seal us in. My belly gurgles loudly. Me and Crow ent munched a morsel or glugged a drop since we sailed to the Bony Isle to save Sparrow – and the gods only know when *he* last filled his boots. Then a low rumbling spreads through the terrodyl.

Hungerhungerhungerrrrr, empty belly, he chatters mournfully.

Maybe we could land, and Thaw and the terrodyl could catch some fish for us all? *Fear-Beast, Thaw-Wielder, land to catch food?* I ask. Thaw hoots her approval.

First time Crawler not utter soft-shell babblings. The creature's spines ripple happily as he starts to drop lower in the sky. Through a cut in the clouds I glimpse a flash of dark, rocky earth.

'I can't be doing with those weird noises that bubble outta your throat when you talk to the thing,' Crow calls. 'What did you say to it?'

I roll my eyes. 'He's a *he*,' I shout back. 'Least I think he is. He ent a *thing*, anyway. He's gonna catch some fish to eat.'

'Why's it going to bother doing that, when it can just crunch us up and spit out our bones?' he yells.

I twist to look at him, laughing. 'Calm your fright-blubber, this one's just a bab.'

Crow glares at me with contempt so thick it's like

he's slapped it on with a tarring brush.

Sparrow's hands feel cold and sweaty. Keeping hold of them tightly in one of mine, I lean right, along the terrodyl's hairy wing. I reach out slowly, towards the icicles hanging underneath it, until I can touch one of them with a fingertip.

'What d'you think you're up to?' bellows Crow.

Ignoring him, I lean out a smidge further, wrap my first two fingers around the ice . . . then fright tingles in my chest as Sparrow's hand starts slipping from my grasp.

'*Sparrow!*' I lurch back into my seat, making the terrodyl sway and flap for balance, and grab Sparrow's arms with both hands. 'Nonononono! Don't you dare fall!' His filmy eyes roll back as he passes out and slumps over the left side of the creature's back.

I swing the other way off my perch, too fast, grabbing hold of the spine in front of me just before I topple into thin air. Blood rushes to my head as I hang almost upside down.

'You'll get our bones smashed to splinters!' Crow yells.

'*Shut your face* and grab Sparrow!'

He gives me a stare like death, but he stretches to grab my brother.

'Don't let him slip out of his cloak!'

'I *know!*'

Sparrow's arm drops from my waist. I grab his hand, but he slithers further to one side, eyes sunken and blackening. '*No!*'

Thunderbolt squeals, plucking strands of his hair in her fists.

We're all leaning heavily over the terrodyl's left side. Sparrow's hand turns hot in mine, and a smell of burning weaves into my nose.

'Pull him back into the middle!' shouts Crow.

'What do you *think* I'm trying to do?' I hiss through gritted teeth, fighting not to let go of my brother as painful shocks zap into my palm. I squeeze my knees hard against the terrodyl and clench my belly to stay on its back. Purple lightning flickers at the ends of Sparrow's fingers. Last time I saw it, he was having a shaking fit. Hell's teeth – *please* don't let him have one now!

The beast panics, flapping in circles. *Crackle-bolts throw off throw off get to nest-home!*

Steady, steady, brave beast! I yell.

The lightning stabs into my wrist and I curse, moving my grip from Sparrow's hand to his arm.

It's the one he's been cradling since we rescued him. There's a loosening, and a gruesome *crack-thunk* as the arm flees its socket. Sparrow slides heavily off the terrodyl's back and I grab for his other hand but miss. My blood thrums in my ears as I fight to keep hold of his arm. I hate the world for letting this happen when I'd almost got my brother safe. I swore to Ma that I'd always protect him, and I ent about to break my promise now.

The terrodyl flails wildly, plunging lower in the sky. I haul at Sparrow as hard as I can. Crow wedges a hand into his armpit and slowly starts lifting him up.

Sparrow's almost back in the middle. The terrodyl rights itself, grumbling. It's gonna be all right. It's gonna be fine.

I've just let out a pinch of breath when a golden beam slices through the air, thumping into one of the beast's huge wings. The wing crumples with a sickening *crunch*.

Then we're plummeting; one screaming tumble-blur of arms, wings, teeth and legs.

The beast is falling.

Falling.

The world drops away.

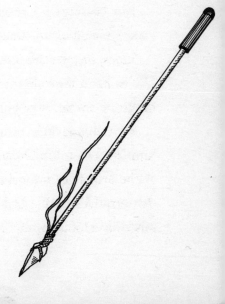

3

The Dread

Purple lightning splurts from Sparrow's fingers into the sky, shocking him awake. I reach for him but the force of the wind thieves my strength. I can't get us back onto the terrodyl, and the broken wing flaps loose as a sail.

My belly pulls free, lands in my throat. Nails tear at my wrist. Thaw-Wielder shrieks, digging her talons into my hair. Her chatter is torn by the falling and I can't catch her words.

The terrodyl's scream rips the world apart. He scrabbles at the air with claws like daggers.

It was a spear. My brain rings dully with knowing. We've been shot down. And now we're falling into death like none of what's happened even matters.

Everything turns oddly slow-but-fast, like the world's rushing forwards and backwards in a sickly tangle and we're strung up in the middle of it. A heavy silver mist settles, and a storm of spooked birds cranks through it towards us.

Bloodseekerssharptoothhuntershuntersfleefleequick! gabble the birds. *Shouldbenestingnestingnesting!*

I try to move but it's like I'm stuck in a nightmare and my muscles don't work.

Crow stretches his fingertips through the air and brushes my cheek. His mouth shapes words, but the wind punches my ears too hard for me to hear.

Mother, screams the terrodyl's beast-chatter. *Brothers. Nest-home. Wing hurtful, don't let me go, get me home!*

With the word *home*, all the sound in the world fades, in one heartbeat, like an explosion of nothing.

Are we dead?

The silver mist darkens into a pulsing shadow. A foggy tendril snakes away through the sky. Then the world speeds up again in a stuttering rush and our terrodyl crashes through the cloud. We plunge after it. A scream surges up my throat and the wind peels my eyelids back and I pedal my legs in the air and

SLAM.

I smash into a mess of sticky webbing that flings me up into the air with a sharp, wrenching jolt. I somersault

once,

twice,

then finally land sprawled on my front inside the mist-shadow. I scrabble to my knees as Sparrow and Crow plunge, shrieking, from the sky. I grab my brother and hold him still while the sticky mist hurls Crow up again before he tucks into a ball and rolls to a stop. The shadow seals shut over our heads, blinking out the sky.

Shock-waves judder through my body as I stare at a dark, throbbing world of cold and damp, its edges tightening around us. We're caught in some kind of springy net. I touch the wall, then jerk back my hand. It's like the whole thing is made of hard, sticky clumps of wet, spinning pearls.

My blood leaps. It's woven from raindrops.

The walls close in until we're hanging in the sky, tangled together in the bottom of the net, the raindrops pressed against our faces. Crow curses, flailing and jabbing me with elbows sharp as knives.

'*What* – how is – it's *raindrops*!' I gasp.

'Some vicious magyk, don't touch it—' babbles Crow over my words.

'How can I not touch it, kelp-brain?'

We tumble around like seastones, and I keep Sparrow close, my feet almost slipping through gaps in the bottom of the net.

The Opal falls from my pocket and a spear of panic stabs my gut until Thaw snatches it in her beak and drops it in my hand. She folds herself into my cloak.

Ugghhhh, foulness, she warbles, feathers quivering.

Horror clutches at my chest. Whose path have we stumbled into now?

Far below comes a *thud* and a splintering *crack*. I peer through the spinning raindrops to see our terrodyl sprawled across a rock, his beast-chatter filled with hurts. A trickle of inky blood fizzles from his crumpled wing and gnaws holes in the snow. Guilt stings me like a ray, cos the beast's just a bab and I lured him from his home to help us escape.

Sparrow weeps, curled in a trembling ball, his moonsprite trilling inside his pocket. My gut clenches. If I hadn't let go of one of his hands, he wouldn't have slipped and maybe we would've been too quick for that spear. It's *my* fault something bad happened – again. I thought I could grab one of them icicles, thought I knew best, but I *didn't*.

Suddenly the net starts moving. Crow stares at me. 'What is this thing? What's going on?' he whispers.

I shake my head. 'I don't know.' I shut one eye and peer through a tiny gap between the drops of water. The net is dragging towards a brown smudge that's growing bigger and bigger. I squint. My belly squirms. It ent one smudge – it's a gathering. A flock. 'Sparrow,' I whisper. 'Crow.' I try to swallow but my throat catches. 'Look!'

Crow puts his eye to the wall. 'What are they?' he asks, voice half choked.

'How would I know?' I grip the net in my fists and the raindrops wriggle against my palms. 'How about we stop gabbing and get ready to fight?'

But my fire-crackle dims to embers as the smudges slice the sky, closer, closer, filling the world, until we can see what we're facing – a flock of giant, shaggy beasts. Between each one's wings sits a proud-faced warrior. They wield golden bows, blades and spears. I tear my gaze away and stare down at Sparrow's tangled yellow hair, a howl of fright and heart-sadness brewing in my chest.

'They look like huge winged foxes,' says Crow, squinting and then twisting to look at me.

I force myself to look again. They're more like . . . *bats*, but with the orangey fur and long muzzles of foxes. 'Whatever they are they're proper frightful.'

The creaky *slick-click* of their skins and bones mixes with the beat of their wings against the wind, like a war-drum.

Huntsaltbloodfish? Dragcatchriptaste! HuntHuntHunt – BITE – tongueraspslithertear!

Their beast-chatter is ravenous. Their teeth snap against the metal bits in their mouths, and lanterns swing from poles fixed to their heads.

The warrior at the front clutches a spear in one hand, and in the other a staff with a tendril of the raindrop net wrapped around it. All the warriors' faces are draped in gleaming mail – as the net drags us closer, I realise their armour's forged from raindrops, too.

'But . . . the Sky-Tribes are dead!' I stutter.

'They look dead to you?' murmurs Crow. He clenches and unclenches his fists.

When we're within spitting distance of the warriors, the net stops moving and sags in the air, making us stumble. The staff clutched by the leader keeps us skyborne – but what if she lets go? My fingers fumble for the amber amulet hanging around my neck; the one that Bear gifted me for protection.

Scores of accusing eyes pierce the raindrop mail. My voice feels trapped, deep inside. I pull my face away from the wall and stare at my hands – they're shaking. I curse, biting my nail, and press my eye to the gap again.

The leader stands with her feet planted strongly on her bat's bare back. She points her staff at the net and jerks it and we're whipped into a dizzying circle that makes us snatch for each other's hands. When the net is still again, the top of it has unravelled to join the silver tendril wrapped around the staff.

Ten riders crowd the open net, staring down at us. Their bats' wings slice the night, stirring a breeze of greasy flesh and dung.

'The birds were fleeing from you,' I breathe. A flicker of fright shudders up and down my spine.

The leader's blue eyes narrow. She peels back her raindrop headdress. It melts into a loose cowl around her neck, revealing a white-haired girl of about fifteen moons, with a mean, neat face and a gold ring through her nose like she's a bull. Black eye-paint slashes down from her brows to her jaw. She lifts her pointed chin. 'We are much feared.' Her thick, knotted accent is brushed through with disgust.

I struggle to my feet in the net and stand as arrow-straight as I can. Thaw pokes her head out of my cloak, ice-crusted feathers bristling with fury, but before she can bolt I clutch the cloak tighter, muffling her chattered protests. Ent no way I want this lot laying their mitts on my sea-hawk.

A second rider folds back their raindrop armour, swiftly becoming a girl with dark red hair, a big chin and widely spaced brown eyes. 'These creatures stink of seaweed and fish guts,' she says, wrinkling her forehead. 'My draggle was the first to sniff them on the wind.' She leans down to stroke the thing's ear and it clicks an oily purr. Her words are laced with triumph and there ent a thing I wouldn't give for the chance to knock her sideways into thin air.

'Well scented, Pangolin,' says the white-haired girl,

squinting at me like I'm a speck of grot. 'The Protector of the Mountain will reward you.'

The girl gifts her a snaggle-toothed grin. 'Thanks, Lunda.'

'Who are you?' Crow glares at them through matted locks of hair.

The rider called Lunda twirls her spear, knuckle-rings flashing. She stares, a tight smile curling her lips but never touching her eyes. '*I* ask questions. What are you doing here? Were you sent to perform witch-work?' The other riders flinch and write symbols on their chests with their fingers.

Me and Crow swap looks. *Witch-work?*

She sighs, then barks a sudden command. 'Take them to Hackles. The Protector will sentence them for their crimes, whether they speak or not.' Her draggle's wings carve the air as it swirls away from us.

'What *crimes?*' I yell. 'And what's Ha—'

Crow reaches up and tugs my cloak.

I stumble, glance down at him and my brother, and fear stabs through me. 'Sparrow!' He's lying limp as a gutted fish.

Crow rubs Sparrow's arm. 'Wake up, little mate!'

Sparrow's breath is ragged and when I shake him and call his name he won't wake. A chewed-up cry worms through my lips before I even know it's brewing.

'You have to help us!' I shout. I keep my hands on Sparrow's shoulders, squeezing the tender part like Grandma showed me, to make pain and wake him up. But naught happens. I look up towards the flock of riders and they're blurring cos my tears are falling fast.

When I look back down Sparrow's lips are tinged blue and that's when I notice the way his arm lies, the angle of his elbow all crooked. Beads of sweat stand out all over him and his forehead burns under my touch. His arm must've had what Grandma called a 'skinny break'. That loosening I felt was the arm breaking good and proper.

'Riders!' I call. 'You get over here and help me. My brother won't wake up!' The salt of my tears prickles on my tongue.

I lift my chin and *howl*, like I'm warning my Tribe of danger.

And somewhere, in the distance, a creature howls back.

4
Witch-work

The howl leaves a gloopy silence in its wake.

Startlement stretches my eyes wide. That howl pulled at my chest like it knew me.

Lunda halts her draggle and twitches her head this way and that, alert and ashen-faced. 'They're coming,' she mutters.

'Who?' asks Crow, jaw flickering as he grinds his teeth.

Riders fidget, a crackle of fear passing between them. Lamplight glances off the rings in their noses, making them look like a tangle of stars. Their whispers crowd the air, until the wind fizzes with one word.

'*Wilderwitches!*'

Then the howl comes again. Closer. It cracks the sky like a throatful of death and rings eerily off the distant icebergs. I hunch low, digging my nails into my palms, breath tattered. *This* must be witch-work.

'They're pack hunting again!' shouts Pangolin.

'Shushhh!' orders Lunda.

Pack hunting? I turn to Crow. 'Have you heard of Wilderwitches? Are they sky-hunters?'

But Crow's answer is knocked from his mouth when a rider *thwacks* him in the back with the butt of their spear. He opens his cloak, presses his face inside and lets out a muffled stream of growls and curses. Then he sits with his hood pulled up, glowering face shielded by folds of cloth.

Lunda steps along her draggle's back as easy as I would in the rigging. 'Which direction are they coming from?' she hisses.

Pangolin glances around. I watch her face; all the tiny workings of her muscles, the tenseness.

Then I spit. 'Help me, right now, or I'll summon that thing closer!' I say it with all the bluster I've got, cos I ent the foggiest whether I can summon it or whether I'd want to, but if this Tribe *think* I can, maybe they'll help my brother.

'You will not summon anything!' Lunda thunders. 'You are the Protector's *prisoner*!'

'Ha! You try and stop me.' I check Sparrow again – his breath comes weak and flutter-quick, but it's there.

Then I stand. My howl's brewed hot and stormy so when I send it up it's the fiercest I've ever howled, and proper loud.

The horde of riders *flinch* in their saddles, and Lunda guides her draggle towards the net, raising her knuckle-ringed fist.

Crow moves to shield me but he stumbles, nearly stepping on my brother, so I shove him out of the way and he curses at me, eyes like fire-arrows.

Before I can gift him a sorry, the strange witch-howl comes a third time, closer still. It rattles through my marrow and cloaks the threats Lunda hurls at me. A deep hush follows it, like falling snow. Lunda freezes, her fist still raised.

In the silence I duck low again and put my face close to Sparrow's mouth, feeling a tiny hot flutter of breath touch my cheek.

'Lunda, we need to hide,' says Pangolin, two spots of heat blooming in her round cheeks. 'We cannot outpace them.'

'No.' Lunda smiles, white hair wispy-wild. 'We will smash them for daring to threaten us – we were *made* for this fight.'

Riders whisper and write symbols on their chests with their fingertips again. Pangolin's breath gushes out like she's winded. 'But there aren't enough of us. We'll be dragged to our deaths!'

DeathdeathdeathdeathDEATH! screeches one of the draggles, and fright bolts through the flock. They jostle, the riders grapple with the reins and Lunda's thrown face down on her draggle's back. She scrabbles to grip the staff holding our net, almost dropping it. Before I can stop myself, I'm staring down at the snow, stained black with terrodyl blood.

Lunda jerks to her knees, spitting out a mouthful of orange fur. 'You *idiot*!' she gasps at Pangolin, purple-faced. 'You've spooked them!' She uncoils a black whip from her waist and starts furiously lashing her beast to try and control it. The others do the same, but still the creatures buck and writhe in the sky. The net judders and Crow groans, clutching his belly.

Finally Lunda gets her draggle turned around. 'Pangolin has forced us into a cowards' escape, despite the fact that this is *our* rightful sky-territory!' she calls. 'We must get the sea-creepers to Hackles before the Wilderwitches swoop. Douse the lamps and follow the stars!'

Pangolin's draggle wobbles for a beat, and she fights with the reins until it steadies. Then she pulls her raindrop cowl over her tear-stained face and vanishes from sight.

The riders smother their lights. A velvet darkness snuffles close.

Are the Wilderwitches a Sky-Tribe, too? What kind of Tribe hunts and howls like wolves? My mind soars, fast as a hawk. Until now I'd reckoned there were no Sky-Tribes at all.

The riders flit after their leader. The wind bites my hands and face as we're pulled through the air, the opening in the top of the net sealing again as the tendril unravels from the staff.

A damp mist begins to rise. It presses against the net. 'They're coming closer!' yells a voice.

My ears fill with the sharp cracking of whips. I squint through the raindrop net and watch the mist thicken. It bristles like fur, then separates into ghostly shapes that streak through the air, uttering yips and howls. I croak Crow's name but my voice is drowned by the yells of the riders.

'Hurry!' one cries. 'The sky-wolves are almost upon us!'

We're flying fast, too fast for me to try to help my brother, and the mist is a stew-thick fog that the riders try to brush from their eyes. 'Faster!' shouts Lunda. 'Don't swallow even a wisp of this witch-fog!'

When the howl comes again it's splintered into a hundred fragments that throb all around us and set my teeth rattling. I clamp my eyes shut.

When I look again, the fog has furred and toothed and clawed itself into an army of wolves, some with white or grey fur, others black or red. I wrap my arms around myself and think of bolting along the *Huntress*'s deck, her salt- and snow-dusted boards crunching under my boots, sunlight dancing in Da's hair. I will us home with every stitch of blood and bone, but naught happens.

'There's summat fearful wrong about these wolves,' mutters Crow.

I raise my ice-stiffened brows. 'They're prowling through the flaming *sky*, for one thing.'

'It's more than that,' he snaps. 'Their faces are more human than animal.' He stares at the wolves as they race closer and closer. 'Can you hear their – what do you call it?' He flails for the words.

I squint at him impatiently. 'Beast-chatter?'

'Aye. That's the one.'

I listen again, hard, but there's a silence. I shake my head.

'That's what I thought,' he whispers. 'They're shape-changers, not wolves.'

I stare at Crow as his words wash a memory over me – when he was Stag's spy, hiding aboard our ship in bird form. If I listened for his beast-chatter there was just emptiness, cos he weren't really a beast at all.

We lock eyes in the gloom and I quickly look away, watching the sky-wolves for as many beats as I dare while Crow's gaze burns my skin.

The fog's closed over us like a shroud, poking up our

noses and worming into our lungs. Far below, slices of land and sea chink through it, then vanish again. Our path curves to the right, towards a wall of blackness. Storm clouds? My gut twists, but soon we're close enough to see that it's not cloud at all.

We're headed for a bulk of pure, solid mountain.

A mountain range that makes me know that others I've seen were just hills. This mountain is a place so huge, of so much old power, that I've never felt so small in all my life.

The wolves howl, one by one, 'til their voices join into a long, throaty wail. They lope through the sky, snouts carved open into eager snarls. Their eyes are a mix of blues and greens and greys. Human, like Crow said.

Suddenly one lunges from the mist to the right and snatches a draggle and its rider clean out of the sky. The rider plummets towards the valley below with a strangled scream, and the sky-wolf shakes the draggle by the wing, like a rag doll. The rest of the flock shrieks and swerves, and I'm dimly aware that I'm screaming with them. Crow reaches for my hand. His cheeks are blotched red with fright.

Just as another sky-wolf springs, a bone-splitting BOOM throttles the sky and echoes off the mountain, almost shaking my spirit loose.

'Riders, low! Hackles is spewing!' yells Lunda. The

draggles swoop suddenly and our net falls through the air for a beat.

Then huge ice-boulders *slam* overhead. They smash the front ranks of the sky-wolves to pieces of mist, leaving only the splintered ghosts of their howls.

The sky-wolves fall back, becoming a grey, snarling wall behind us. And when another marrow-shattering boom rocks the sky, they turn tail and race away, the rear ranks torn apart by massive clumps of ice. Shock tugs at my mouth.

We're dragged higher and higher still, until we're level with the clouds. Crow turns grey and cradles his head in his hands.

The mountain looms.

Sparrow moans, soft as a bone pipe, but when I call to him he don't open his eyes and shakes wrack his body.

'Stay in the waking world, too-soon,' I murmur in his ear. My little brother was born before he was baked proper. I ent letting him leave me too soon as well.

The mountain is a black wall blotting out the world beyond. A great wound in its side oozes ice. A churning sound buzzes in the air, and I can feel a bowstring-tenseness that tells me it's waiting to spew again.

We dip and swerve to the right, towards a chink in the rock. Behind us, ice boulders *thunder* through the air, spat out by the mountain range.

Then we're hovering, trapped between the ice-bombs behind and the bleak cracked mountain ahead. The gap in the rock is packed with raging winds and swirling snow.

Lunda and the other riders shout into the wind and raise their arms high. They urge their draggles through the gap in the mountain. I squeeze Sparrow's hand as we fly between two of the mountain's jags, through a mass of cloud.

We're only halfway through when the cloud begins to freeze around us, tightening, icing our garb to our skin, squeezing . . .

Up ahead, the riders shout panicked words that are lost in the storm.

Then we're through the gap and the storm's behind us and we can breathe. When I look back, there's just a broiling mass of lightning, fog and frozen cloud.

The mountain echoes with the high shrieks and open-throated grunts of eagles. Inside my cloak, Thaw hisses.

There's no trace of the world we came from.

5
The Mountain

We plunge downwards. My belly flips. I peek through a gap in the raindrop net and the ground is rushing closer. Closer. *Closer.*

I squeeze Sparrow tight and tuck my face into his neck, bracing for the hit. Crow grabs onto Sparrow too, and our wide eyes fasten together in panic.

Snow squabbles in the air. A snowflake pastes onto my eyeball – I scrub it away – and when I look through the net again there's a smoky shape pressing up through the snow. My heart clambers into my throat.

The mountain is a jagged, ring-shaped fortress surrounding a settlement, like a bristling beast squatting gleefully over a kill. Spiny turrets are chiselled into the rock.

We thud into a snowdrift that guzzles sound. The net sags heavily onto us, sticking to our faces. I reach up to push it off, scraping my scar, and curse, sucking my teeth against the pain. Wind rushes overhead, snagging the raindrops in its grip, as the draggle flock glides past to land nearby. 'Did the storm-barrier keep them out?' calls a fretful voice.

'Of course!' snaps Lunda.

Crow wrestles with the net. 'Help me get this thing open.' He pushes his fingers between the raindrops and wrenches open a small hole.

As soon as he's made it the hole shrinks, so I tug a merwraith scale out of my pocket and try to snick a proper cut. The raindrops buzz and rush to knit back together. 'Bleeding cockle dung,' I mutter.

I take Sparrow's face in my cold-numbed fingers, whispering to him. He moans, but he won't wake up. I tighten his cloak around him and pull his hood over his face. Then my ears twitch, and a prickle spreads up my neck. Boots are crunching through the snow.

I nuzzle my face close to the tough web of clamouring raindrops, and through the drifting whiteness a long-limbed girl has appeared, swamped in a cloak of brown feathers.

Her copper hair is bundled on top of her head like a tangled nest and her long red skirts billow around a pair of fur-trimmed boots. There's something bare about her gaunt face; the flash of raw hope she wears is the only light on the mountain.

She steps nearer, then catches herself and glances around sharply, face turning dull and closed. She fits wooden snow-goggles over her eyes and melts into the snowstorm.

Lunda scrunches towards us. The raindrops slowly unravel into a thread that slides away along the ground and *slurps* into her staff.

Me and Crow thrash upright, pulling up our hoods, and watch as the riders leap off their draggles and hurry towards a row of statues etched into the rockface. Reckon they must be likenesses of their sky-gods – human-bodied, eagle-headed, terrodyl-clawed. The riders kneel, muttering prayers.

Other figures battle through the snow to unsaddle their beasts. Then the draggles wheel around and soar into the air. *Huntsniffbloodquickscurrytheybitetheywait heartsbeatbeatbeat*, they whisper, lips stretched into gruesome grins. Their huge shadows pass overhead, together with the sweet, damp stink of their fur.

'*Don't* tell anyone your name!' I whisper to Crow. He nods.

'What happened back there, Spearsister?' a man calls to Lunda, as he turns from muttering his prayers.

'Cloud-freeze is not part of the barrier,' says another. 'We could have been frozen to death!'

'We must make more appeasements to the flicker-

42

gods,' says a woman, twirling her blade in her fingers.

'When did you last see their lights? Even the gods have turned their backs,' retorts the first man, lifting his gaze to the scrap of sky pinched between the mountain's leering jags. More tribesfolk pipe up, their grumblings swelling louder.

The flicker-gods? I think of the white and green sky-fire that my Tribe call the fire spirits. Instinct makes me tip back my head to look, but there's no sign of life.

Lunda glares a warning look. 'Everything is under our control,' she hisses. One by one, the tribesfolk fall silent.

'Welcome to Hackles,' says Lunda, hand on hip as she watches us along the length of her pointed spear. A gloat bubbles onto her face. I tense my muscles to run, though there's nowhere to go.

Other riders prowl to join her, staring at us with narrowed eyes.

I show Lunda the quiet and stormy look Grandma said could seek out all a person's secrets. Grandma would take no nonsense from these slither-wings, so I hold tight onto the heart-strength that she stitched into my bones and shine it out at the girl. For a beat, Lunda's fierceness is startled away.

Then she snarls, knocking me over the head with a spiny knuckle ring. I crouch, cursing and clutching my head.

Pangolin unwraps her raindrop headdress and stoops to touch Sparrow. I leap forwards with a growl but Crow grabs my wrist.

'Arm's broken,' says Pangolin, brushing back her knot of thick braids. She watches Lunda's face like a mongrel begging for scraps.

'A pantry-squidge could tell that much, Pangolin!' snipes Lunda, making the other girl flush. She straightens and peers around. 'Pika! *Hey!* Over here! *Pika!*'

I follow her stare. To our right is a stone hut, smoke huffing from its chimney. Up ahead a run of steps is carved into the mountain, leading to a set of wooden doors crowned with two crossed spears. A tall boy with white hair and cinnamon skin unfolds himself from the steps and slouches towards us. 'I heard you.' His dark eyes sweep Lunda's face. 'Half the mountain's heard you. Think an avalanche must be brewing.'

'Stopper your beak,' declares Lunda. 'Take the cripple to the sawbones' nest while me and Pang get the other sea-creepers to their cells.'

Crow scowls.

'You ent taking him anywhere without me!' I hiss.

'The draggles are hunting.' Pika folds his arms wearily. 'I have to be ready to stable them when they return, and the caves are a mess after you left in such a clamour.'

'Do not defy me, apprentice, or I'll have you mucking out the draggle-dung well past midnight!' Lunda spits, flicking her stubby white braid off her shoulder.

The boy snorts but he does as she says. He bends to pick Sparrow up and my brother's head lolls like his neck's gonna snap. He looks smaller than it's even possible to be.

'Don't take him! We stay together!'

'Mouse,' mutters Crow. 'Just let them help him.'

'*Help* him? You seen this place, slackwit?'

He wipes his sweaty brow with the back of his hand. 'She told that boy to take Sparrow to the sawbones – that's another word for healer. Know any other healers round here?'

The heart-truth of his words melts away my fight. But when the boy turns his back to carry my brother away, a hollow pit tears open inside me. 'I'm coming with him!' I shout. Then a wave of sky-sickness makes me so dizzy I can barely stand.

I pull away from Crow and bend forwards, gulping for air, as Sparrow's carried towards the stone steps in the mountain. I straighten in time to see him vanish from sight.

Then there's just all these pairs of strange eyes fixed on me. And no friend but Crow; a boy who not so long ago I couldn't trust a stitch. Feels like my blubber's been turned inside out.

Crow's telling me something but his face swims before my eyes and his voice is stars away. Then everything blurs, and hands grab us. Thaw-Wielder pokes her head out of my cloak and nips at a rider.

'Oohhch!' the rider squeals, sucking the blood from her finger. 'I think we'll be having you, hawk-sister!'

Hah! Bad-blubber not have Thaw! shrills my hawk, dodging and spiralling off into the sky.

We're forced apart. Crow's fighting, I'm hurling threats, but we're lost in a tangle of fists and spears and shields. 'Mouse!' Crow bellows. The wind roars, *slashing* snow into my eyes, and when I can see again he's being shoved under the crossed spears and through the wooden doors.

I'm pushed to the right, towards a doorway etched into the hulking flank of the mountain. Shivering figures shovel snow, others snap icicles from overhanging rocks and there's a *clatter-clang-clatter* as they drop them into cauldrons for melting. One lingers to warm his hands over the steam, and a rider cracks a whip, knocking him to the ground.

I'm dragged through the door and up a spiral stairway cut straight into the rock. Then I'm pushed forwards and made to climb higher, higher, higher into the mountain. 'Please, tell them my brother gets shaking fits,' I gasp in the thin air.

Hot breath burns my frozen ear. 'Were you given leave to speak, sea-creeper?'

'*Please!* Just tell them!' It gets even harder to breathe, cos now the thin air stinks of rotting eggs, musty pelts and damp. 'We made a potion of violet root but I didn't get the dose right and—' I'm shoved into a crooked stone passageway, my words *oofed* away into the bitter cold.

Grubby moon-lamps are strung along the ceiling, dimly showing how the passage weaves around a bend and out of sight. Moonsprites wail inside the smeared glass, making the lamps flare.

Letoutletouttrappedtoolong! Grrrrrrfizzlefearhelphelphelp!

Our footsteps ring against the stone. The cold stabs up through the soles of my boots. I stumble, and the tip of a spear digs into my back, jolting me forwards. The anguished cries of strangers echo from inside the walls.

Soon it feels like we've walked so far into the mountain that we're gonna fall off the other side of the world. 'Where've you taken my crew?' I wheeze.

My captors don't answer. I look back and glimpse a long, serious face and lips purple with cold, but then the spear-tip finds me again and I stagger forwards.

We reach a thick wooden door. One of the riders wrenches at it, scrabbling with her fingernails, but the door is stuck. 'The ice has sealed this one shut, too.'

In the end she gets it open by lighting a torch and heating the lock, while I twist and kick in the other's vice-grip.

Then I'm jabbed hard in the back and sent sprawling into a freezing cloud of sour air.

I stumble to my knees on a damp, grimy floor. The door slams with an echoing *clunk*, like the sealing of a tomb.

6
Hackles Rising

I throw my weight against the door. Sickness has robbed my voice, so when I try to scream, nothing comes. What if Sparrow shakes, or they see his lightning? What if they use his powers like the mystiks did? And – I fight the thought, but it moulds tightly over me. What if he dies?

I'm trembling, and my head swirls like there's a storm of fog and snow blundering through my brain. This weren't meant to happen. We should've reached Whale-Jaw Rock by now.

On the other side of the door, boots scrape against the frost, moving away.

I cough and rasp another empty breath. The sickness that started as we climbed higher in the sky squeezes my belly in an iron grip. I'm frighted for Thaw too, but I ent got the strength to yell for her.

I stare around the murky stone turret. There's a straw mattress on the floor and one thin, grime-streaked blanket. Through a star-shaped hole at the top of the wall, the wind screeches in a thousand broken voices.

It hits me, in a sickening drum-boom – I ent going anywhere. I can't look for the Opals. A picture of Da floats before my eyes – on the storm-deck, watching the sun skim the waves, his eyes smile-crinkled.

I reach into my pocket and curl my fingers around the little wooden carving of the *Huntress* that I made for Da so long ago. Some time between leaving our ship and disappearing he added sails to the carving, and wrote a message on them – a message to tell me what I've got to do. And to tell me he'll find me when he can. The message gifted me heart-strength. And when Sparrow's song turned it to a magyk map that showed me the Opals hope sparked in my veins. But the map couldn't magyk the thing me and Sparrow really wanted – Da.

And now I ent even got the message. Stag's thieved it, just like he thieved Grandma's life and my ship.

My ship. When I close my eyes, I can almost smell her joyous stinks of fish and birch-smoke and tar.

'Tell me we can get some rest, now?' pleads a thin voice, startling me out of my thoughts. It's throbbing from frosty metal pipes that criss-cross the wall.

'We can't,' answers another. 'There are trials.'

I scuttle closer to the pipes to listen.

'I am bone-weary,' gasps the first. 'Have you any food?'

'No.' There's a scrape and a clank and the voices are almost drowned out.

A sob rattles the pipe. 'My sisters are not growing as they should – I need to give them more.'

'Shhh! The Protector provides . . .'

Their voices fade. I shiver. Then a distant wolf howl pierces the night and I drop into a crouch, staring up at the hole in the wall.

My heart beats twice before the turret quakes. I cover my head with my arms and feel the explosion in my chest as the mountain spews more ice-bombs. What is going on in this Sky realm?

As the sound dies away, the Opal's wild power sparks through my cloak pocket. I pull it free and wince as it singes my eyebrows. I can feel the gem longing for its kin, the same way I long for mine. The ache in my chest turns to a painful yearning for my Tribe. It feels like the stitching of my life has come apart at the seams, so I hardly know who I am any more.

I press my back to the wall and slide down until I'm huddled on the ice-glittered floor of the turret, arms wrapped around my knees, chin pressed into the bloody rips in my breeches.

If I don't get the Opals back together and find the golden crown, the sea's gonna freeze solid.

My thoughts fly and scatter and drift. I wonder if

these draggle-riders – or the Wilderwitches – know the legend of the Storm-Opal Crown. I can't believe there are two Sky-Tribes left! I remember seeing the ruined Sky Path at the Tribe meet on Dread's Eve, lost to vines and thorns. Being in a hidden Sky realm would make for a tale my Tribe would love to guzzle. It's like I'm living one of Grandma's stories. But all I can feel is the heaviness of my quest.

My eyes cross and numbness steals over me. I feel my spirit pushing the edges of my skin.

I'm slipping into a dream-dance and the Opal in my hand seems to breathe, turning clammy and blubbery, just like the last time.

But the rotten stink of this place creeps into my nose, making me gag. I grind my teeth together, dig my nails into my palms. The sky-sickness hits harder and I retch bile onto the straw, then fall to the grubby mattress and drag measly lungfuls of air through my bleeding lips. Then I sneeze, spattering my wrist with black snot.

There's a tangled wail in the sky outside. I look up, sickness spins the room and I have to get my head down again. A sorrowful beast-chatter floats into the turret.

Wherenowwherenow? Home, lost, Thaw heart-sore for her two-legs!

My sea-hawk's searching for me! *Thaw*, I croak uselessly, feeling a growl of fury build in my belly. Heart-sad homesickness carves up and out of my throat, spilling hot tears onto my cheeks. The *Huntress* slices through my thoughts, calling me home. My ship plucks at me until an invisible cord, connects us.

Man gone, hisses a sudden beast-chatter, somewhere in the pipes. *Flew low, low, low. Scribble scrap scribble scrap.*

But the beast-chatter rolls off my skin like a bead of water, as the Opal grows fluttering gills and my spirit *squeezes through layers of bone, muscle and skin, then sneaks through the hole in the wall, into the raging night.*

7
The Dredging

I'm a ragged ghoul in the wind, high above the mountain fortress. The Opal pulses against me. Even though I've left my body behind I feel a smile tugging for the fun of flight.

I'm struggling to dive towards the sea when the wind catches me in its jaws. I'm flung across the edge of the mountain. The world falls away.

Across the mountainsides below streak the gleaming dream-spirits of reindeer, mountain goats and wild horses.

Swirling storm-clouds gather and skinny lightning spears the sky. Stooped red trees paint the mountain like a river of old blood, where the leaves of autumn froze before they could fall.

I fly faster and finally through the smoky fog I glimpse the sea and the jagged icebergs. Another sliver of lightning slashes down and cracks into a berg, sending blocks of ice tumbling into the water.

A coastline looms. I trace its craggy edges with glowing dream-fingers. Huge cauldrons of oil bubble on the cliff edges.

I can sense my home in a rich dream-stink of tar and iron rivets. She's pulling me closer, but where is she? The further I tumble the closer I get to a fleet of ships. My spirit pangs.

The Huntress is one of them.

I strain my spirit into the wind, wiggling like an eel, feeling a pull between my body and my ship. Panic jangles from me into the night air, sizzling a flurry of ghostly sparks. The air thickens with the grey, moaning spirits of whales and the cold vast depths of the sea flood into my mind; the depths that swallowed Grandma. I shrink back from the whale spirits, fighting the memory.

The ship's anchored over the spot where the great warship from the Icy Marshes, Frog Witch, is said to have sunk ten moons ago. The sea is slicked with a thick cloak of ice that crunches as she tries to throw it off.

I drop through the sky, treading air like it's water. Below, Stag stands on the storm-deck, bellowing at the crew. His voice stabs into my dream, making me growl. Polar dogs sprawl beneath the rail. Their chains clank as they twitch their muzzles to the sky and whine, spooked.

Thingthingthingnomarrow? *chatters one.*

Nofoodhungryhungrywhatit?Deadthinglurking!*replies* a pack-mate, snotcicles hanging from its snout.

Stag glances at the dogs. Their white clouds of breath puff into the air and his narrowed eyes follow them, until he's looking right at the spot where I'm hovering, my dream-toes

bathed in dog breath. My spirit flares, turning jagged and spiny with horror.

Can he see me?

But then he turns his attention back to the deck, and my spines of fright retract.

'Heave!' commands Stag. There's a creaking of ropes and a strange squealing noise. Then a huge bone claw winches into the air, trembling like a held breath.

'Shipwrecks mean merwraiths. And merwraiths mean riches.' Cold mirth curls the edges of Stag's voice.

Merwraiths? No. He can't!

My nerves stretch tauter than a bowstring, but still I glide closer to the ship. Cos even with evil lurking, I can't waste the chance to glimpse chief oarsman Bear.

The tar-blackened ropes that tether the dredging claw snake down in front of me. The crew lower the claw towards the sea. When the waves gulp it, dread bites me.

'It's reached the seabed!' someone cries.

'Hold steady!'

One of Da's sayings fills my head. 'Are we not all the gods' little creatures?' My sluggish dream-blood simmers. I'm voiceless, but I wish I could roar. I flutter towards the deck and the polar dogs tense, then riot, thrashing against their chains, gifting rough barks to the sky as they watch me shimmer.

The claw shudders from the sea, spitting a clatter of long, curved whale bones across the deck. I know I should look away. Terror squeezes my throat. I don't want to watch.

But I have to.

Tangled on the claw's bony barbs are three merwraiths, the scales of their long, drooping tails flashing bright. One's got a tail of rusty bronze; the others gleam storm-cloud grey. Sodden flame-red hair is plastered to their heads, and pearly globs of fish eggs web their fingers and lace up their arms, chests and throats. My mind flits to Rattlebones, the ancient Sea-Tribe captain who turned to merwraith long ago. My guiding ancestor. These wraiths are our kin. Once they proudly strode their decks, fire-crackle in their hearts.

The merwraiths' eyes are glazed behind a foggy layer of film. But they're awake, and they're frighted.

I whimper, my voice trapped in the space between the worlds, ringing off the masts and round my brain. The horror turns to bony fingers that wring my belly until I gasp.

The merwraiths begin to wither. Their hair becomes seaweed, their fish eggs turn to strings of black slime that drip onto the deck. Only their scales stay bright. The crew snick their knives open.

Get away from them! I scream, but no one hears me 'cept the polar dogs. They howl, frenzied, until Stag blasts a gun into the air, forcing silence.

I flutter, tangled in the ropes, a ghost filled with heart-fury. The face of one of the merwraiths crumples and the eyes fall out – now plain grey seastones that roll about the deck. A shriek rips from her lips before she shrivels into a pile of weeds, slime and rocks, and only her gleaming scales remaining. Sobs rake my chest, and in the tiny gaps in between I sense another mourner. Bear, huddled at his oar, his tears turning to chips of ice on his cheeks.

Missing him and wanting to be in his arms carves my chest into a gaping hollow.

The merwraiths lie sprawled in a heap. Crew fall to their knees beside them and prise dark, rusted scales off with their blades, the two metals scritch-scraping.

Stag watches, smoking his pipe. Course he ent dirtying his own hands. My scorn pushes me towards him, until I'm hovering in the drifting fog by his side. He puffs out smoke rings, and I think of Da's message. Does Stag have it still? I flex my dream-fingers, imagining grasping the message and pulling it back with me. Could it be possible?

I dip into his pockets, but I can't feel anything and frustration coils around me like a tentacle.

A polar dog lunges at me, snapping starving jaws. Get back! snarls Stag in beast-chatter, kicking out at the dog.

I zoom away, making for Bear, but I'm caught in the wind, flung upwards, bashed against spangle-cold icebergs. A fright-tattered voice reaches me. 'You are his weakness! You must help us!'

It sounds familiar. Knowing spreads through me. The voice belongs to one who has guided me.

Rattlebones!

*Ancient blood sparks in my veins and I feel the link
between us glowing bright and golden.*

*She's the only captain I know who can show me the path,
except this time she needs my help.*

Help you how? I mouth, but I don't know how to talk in a
dance and the wind plucks my words away. *Why?* I try harder
to force words out and finally they come, clumsy and thick.
'Where are you?'

When the wind's grip loosens I dive down through the air
and skim out across the churning water. Above the sea I dip
my fingers through a skin of ice, watching the surface like a
looking glass.

A soft old face appears, wrinkled like the map of a long-
ago life.

'You're safe!' The words plink into the water.

'Aye,' says Rattlebones. 'For this time.'

The word *time* sloshes strangely through my mind.

'What's happening to my home?' I ask.

Her blind eyes stare into my marrow, and pictures begin to
flash inside my head.

I see Grandma's medsin-lab crushed to slivers of glass and
splinters of wood. The armoury has swelled to twice its size,
filled with unfamiliar weapons. The door to the Hoodwink
where the sea-hawks nested has been wrenched off, leaving an
empty socket in the mizzen-mast.

'Evil prowls,' whispers Rattlebones. 'The false captain hunts whales and wraiths, making deals with greed. He seeks supporters among the lonely and the bitter, the desperate and the greedy. When he has used your ship he will break her apart. He wants to keep the Tribes at war, brew vicious battles and crown himself King.'

My spirit splinters apart and jolts back together. 'What about Grandma Wren? Have you seen signs of her in the wraith-world?'

Heart-sadness floods Rattlebones's voice. 'None.'

Last hope drips from me into the water like spots of blood, and washes away.

'There is a stillness where I try to sense her. But Little-Bones, where is your own life-blood? Why are you so long a ghost?'

She puts another picture in my head – my sleeping body, dusted with frost on the floor of the turret cell at Hackles. Then she fades – down, down, down into the depths – leaving me alone.

I fly fast as I can towards the aft-deck hatch, even though I can feel my dream-dance rubbing thin. I need to find Da's message.

Before the hatch I reach a pulling point, where I feel like the cord between my spirit and my body is gonna snap. Maybe I've been a ghost too long, like Rattlebones said. Fright clangs through me and though I ent ready to give up I'm suddenly rushing through the night, terrorised, away from my ship, spirit-belly brushing against rock.

That's when I see it – a shimmering spirit snagged on a tree root on the side of the mountain.

My dream-eyes widen 'til they feel like hollow pools. Another dream-dancer? I flit closer to it.

But this spirit is unrestful and it wails wretchedly into the wind. Every mote of my being prickles in shock. I've never seen another human spirit dancing free of its body. This one looks stuck. Its eyes snap onto me, huge black holes of loss. My heart is awash in darkness! it calls. It reaches out spindly-silver fingers and brushes my cheek.

I turn away but the fingers curl around my ankle. I twist to look behind and the spirit wrenches itself free from the tree root, then streaks past me. I soar quick quick quick towards the prison in the sky, where my body waits. Dimly I can hear my brother singing.

The lost spirit squeezes through the hole in the wall but I zip after it and grab a fistful of its scraggy hair. We struggle; a storm of force and feelings, slamming against each other. It thrashes away and then pings towards my body. The amber amulet of protection begins to glow in the hollow of my throat – it's proper strange to see my own body from above. The spirit tries to pull the amulet over my head but I shove it away and my feet slip into my sleeping self and I wake up tasting blood. I'm on my back on the floor in the dark cell, shouting and cursing and crying with a voice strangled by the mountain.

My voice is the thing I could always make bigger and louder when I felt too small. Now the sky's shrunk it.

When I've raked a breath the truth presses hard on my shoulders. My body ent safe when I dream-dance. That thing just tried to thieve my bones.

Crow warned me at Castle Whalesbane that things might get in while I'm dream-dancing, or I might not be able to get back. He said I needed a binding – some kind of spirit anchor.

I start to shudder, scanning the air for signs of a spirit, but nothing's there that I can see. The Opal is still in my hand and my fingers are cramped from holding onto it so tightly. I fold into a ball, dragging the thin blanket over me.

I unlock each stiff, sore finger from around the Opal. The gem is warm against my palm and if I focus I can almost feel a pulse inside it. Then I snatch my breath. The Opal is casting swirling patterns of light on the grey blanket, a miniature dance of the fire spirits, just for me. My hair crackles with charge.

Golden flecks twist and flutter under the Opal's skin. They settle my bones and help me remember. Rattlebones told me the merwraiths and my Tribe need my help.

But – *you are his weakness.* What did the old wraith mean?

There's a sudden rustle and the sound of something scraping over the stone floor. I gasp and pull the blanket off my face. In the foggy moonlight my breath is a white cloud.

And near the far wall, another cloud steams.

Something is in here with me.

8
Sawbones

I scramble into a crouch, every muscle tensed. My pulse booms in my ears as I remember the thing that tried to steal my body, and I grip Bear's amber amulet.

Something rushes towards me, so I whip a merwraith scale from my pocket and tuck it between my knuckles. I raise my fists. 'Stay back!'

'Noooo, shhh, oh the gods, no fretting,' a girl husks. Her words have a sweet, songlike tilt to them. 'I stole you a mug of hot goat's milk, from the Protector's own night-cauldron—'

'Not that *flaming* Protector again!' I splutter.

'I'll spice the milk,' she begs. 'And let you have the last cheese and garlic pancake on the mountain. But please be calm!' Her breath has puffed closer, and the shadowy outline of a tall figure lurks behind it.

My head's stuffed with confusion, and my wound throbs, dull-*sharp*-dull. Why is this shadow garbling on about pancakes? 'Who are you?' My lips bleed when I move them, and my teeth chatter. 'What are you doing here?'

'They left you with nothing to keep you warm – you could have frozen to death. I snuck in to watch over you. But what do I find?' Her voice sharpens. 'That you've been night-flying.' She speaks like I've done the stupidest thing in the world, but her words are snagged with envy, too.

'How do *you* know?' I snap, before I can guard my tongue.

'When you fly, the smell sticks to you. The memory of flight is tell-tale.'

She can *smell* my dream-dancing?

She strides closer. Her arms are full of shaggy white goat skins that she dumps next to me. I grab one and tuck myself into its musty folds. The warmth shocks tears of relief into my eyes.

The girl squats in front of me. She closes her eyes, a smile spreading over her face.

I shrink away from her. 'What you doing?' In the weak moonlight all I can see are snow-goggles and a headful of messy braids.

She lifts the goggles onto the top of her head. Her green eyes slant up and out like a cat's. She's the girl I saw when we landed – the one garbed in a cloak of feathers. 'Remembering,' she answers, weary sadness weighing down her voice.

Then comes another wrenching *crack-crash-BOOM-roar-rush-splinter* as Hackles spews more ice. I bury my face in the goat skin.

'Our stronghold is more agitated than usual,' says the girl thoughtfully, when the turret stops rattling.

I swallow. 'Aye. There's something making the world wild—' I stop myself cos I don't know a thing about this girl.

She lunges close and grabs my wrist. 'Yes. Every beat that the draggles' wings brought you closer, the weather raged fiercer. Something is stirring.' Her light brown face is covered in splodgy rust-coloured freckles and she's got the same gold bull-ring through her nose as the others. 'Where did you fly?' she asks urgently. 'What did you see? What is it *like*?'

I stay silent, watching her. Part of me wants to tell her how it's like there's two of me – the me in this world, and the me in the world of shadows. She stares back and takes a breath to say something more but I cut her off, a whip-stroke of defence burning my insides. 'Don't know what you're babbling about.'

The girl cocks her head and looks at me like I'm denying the tide will come in. Then she shrugs and plucks a moonsprite from her pocket.

I curl my lip, remembering the heart-sore sprites held prisoner in the passageway lanterns. But the girl's long fingers are gentle as she drops the sprite into a cracked glass jar.

Lamp-snoozings, it gargles, throbbing a silvery glow into the cell that shows the girl more clearly.

She's oak-tall – might've gathered about sixteen birth-moons – all knees and elbows, garbed in a long scarlet dress stitched with stars and moons, and draped in the feather cloak. A bright half-band of gold circles her neck and stripes of gold paint flash on her face, from the middle of each lower eyelid down to her jaw.

'What's that paint on you?' I ask.

'It means I am a sawbones; a curer. I can only wear it when my mother isn't watching, mind.' She gives a low chuckle.

I flood my eyes with scorn. 'Don't need no healer.'

'Would you prefer to let the rot hunker down in that wound, and eat away half your face?' She shudders. 'Trust me – I've seen it happen. Though lately, injured prisoners disappear before I can even sneak a check of their wounds.'

A flurry of arrowheads storms my blood. 'Wait – if you're a healer, have you been helping my brother, too?' I blurt. 'Did the guards tell you about his shaking fits, like I asked?'

Her smile gutters out. 'I have not been allowed near him. But I listened at the pipes – your message was delivered. He has a broken arm, and a fever.' She holds up a hand and signals for me to wait. 'He may not wake for some time, but they are treating him with success. He is safe, for now. In fact, his sickness is what protects him. She wants all her prisoners well enough to be tried.' She gabs it all in a rush, like she's been waiting moons and moons for someone to talk to.

'*What?* I ent letting some loon woman put him on trial!'

'Be quiet!' she hisses, fright tightening her face. 'Hackles has ears. The Protector of the Mountain is not *some woman*. And all three of you will be judged. If she finds you guilty, the punishment will be – severe.' She looks away and stands up.

I don't wanna think too hard on what *severe* might mean. 'But we ent done nothing!' Then I fall forwards and put out a hand to catch myself on the stone floor, bile rushing into the back of my throat. When I've finished retching I look up and the girl's watching me with a face full of sorrow.

'I don't need your pity,' I bite out, wiping my mouth.

She chinks a tiny smile. 'I have something better than pity.' She rummages in her pocket and pulls out

68

some yellow petals. 'You have the mountain-sickness. These will help calm it.'

I twist my mouth and don't move, but she holds them closer to me. One of her hands is sprinkled with fine white scars, and the knuckles are bloody. On the other she's wearing a dark grey glove. 'Take them,' she says gently. 'They will make it better.'

I blow the air out through tight lips and reach for the flowers. The petals are cool and smooth between my fingers. When I crunch them a bitter, earthy taste fills my mouth.

'Heart-thanks,' I stutter, mouth ash-dry. Then a thought squirms in my belly. She's gifted me kindness. Maybe I can get her to help me escape.

'Oh!' she exclaims, making me startle. Then she winces at her own noise. 'I almost forgot your milk,' she whispers. 'Hope it's not bone-cold.' She searches the floor behind her, then presses a steaming clay mug into my hands. A delicious warmth spreads through my fingers, all the way up my arms.

'Wait, it's better with this mixed in.' She takes a vial from her pocket and pinches some rust-red powder into the cup before I can snatch it away. 'Don't worry,' she says quickly. 'It's nutmeg and cinnamon – I'm not in the business of poisoning! You should be glad of a little flavour. These days it's just goat's milk, goat's cheese,

69

tough old goat's meat and bog myrtle.' She ticks them off on her fingers. 'We're on lock-down. No trade, because of the war.' She speaks fast and tight, like she's afraid someone's gonna spring out of the shadows and gag her.

'Ent never met someone before that can babble faster than me.' I take a sip of the drink. It warms me from chest to toes, and the spices tingle on my tongue.

'Suppose I have many trapped words to spill.' She turns again and places a dented silver platter by me. There are two fat lumps of dough on it.

I raise my eyes to her face. 'Will you help me, for real? Can you—'

'Eat,' she says, cutting me off. 'The food will give you wondrous fire-in-the-belly.'

My hope fades painfully, just as one of the pipes in the wall starts to rattle and clank like a crazed thing. I scuttle backwards and my foot skids out in front of me, kicking the food platter across the floor. The noise spreads through the pipe to a small chute that enters the turret from a hole in the roof and ends in a rusty metal door.

'Ah, here he comes, at long last,' the girl says grimly. She turns towards the chute, skirts swirling. Her hem is fire-licked, like she's too close to the hearth.

'Who?' I ask, filled with dread. 'And who are *you*?'

She stares down at me, a mix of emotions that I can't read swirling behind her eyes. 'I'm Kestrel.' The way she says it fills me with a fresh burst of hope that I cling onto with all my might. I can feel the heart-strength she had to summon just to tell me her name.

The chute rumbles and clangs, gives a *thud*, then falls silent. Kestrel scowls at it, fiddling with a chain hooked to her belt, then steps towards the chute and starts wrenching her key back and forth in a keyhole set in the door.

The chute flies open and a small, fat shape gushes out, trilling *latelatelate! Latequickhelpcarryoooooooosnacks!*

The creature darts for the plate of food on the floor, but Kestrel gives it a sour look, ducks low and grabs it in cupped hands. 'Squidges don't eat pancakes!'

They do! it chatters desperately, oozing a puddle of black stuff – like ink – into Kestrel's hands.

'Oh, Ettler! Calm your silly self. Anyone would think you a fat princeling, not a sawbones' helper.' When she lets the creature go again, it stares at me, chatters *oddbeastfrightfulfeathers!* and slams itself into the wall in distress, oozing more puddles of ink. I swallow my beast-chatter, cos I don't want Kestrel knowing about it.

The beast is all kinds of oddness. It looks like a tiny

round squid, no bigger than a sea-hawk's egg, covered in shiny gold feathers. It moves through the air by wiggling and flapping, pooing ink behind it that grows an icy crust on the floor.

'Ettler, you must learn to hold your ink!' Kestrel scolds. 'You know I need it. Use an ink-pan if you want letting out.'

'What is it?' I ask. 'You called it a . . . squidge?'

She nods, eyeing the not-quite-squid. 'We've scores of the grumblesome things, working in the pantries, but this one kept stealing food—'

Not true! shrills the offended squidge, hooting anxiously at the girl. Then mischief gleams in its round black eyes, and it chortles.

'And so,' she says to me, wrinkling her nose, 'when trouble came sniffing he hid in my clothes chest. By the time I found him, all my things were covered in ink, but he was too afraid to leave my room. So I took him on, as my so-called *assistant*. What a fantastic decision that turned out to be.' She turns back to the chute and rummages inside the hatch. 'So shall we stitch that foulsome wound on your face?' she asks, voice muffled. 'You've been up to strugglings, huh?'

'I was trying to save my brother,' I tell her, curling my tongue over the edge of my teeth. 'Not that it even worked.' *It don't matter if you save Sparrow, cos you ent never gonna save him from his sickness,* snickers a wicked voice in my head.

Kestrel pulls an oiled leather bag from the chute and sits cross-legged in front of me. She roots through the bag. The squidge farts anxiously around her, dripping ink into her hair. 'Aagh, *Ettler!*'

He flaps stickily away and hides in the chute, whimpering.

'Here are the things we need,' chirps Kestrel. 'A tear-vial, for catching your tears.'

I frown, shame prickling my scalp. 'Tears are for weaklings and babs. I don't need—'

'Pish,' she says. 'Our Tribe used to wear these 'til our tears were swallowed by the air – that's when the mourning has passed.' She takes my hand and balls it into a fist, then places it against my chest. When I open my fingers there's an empty glass vial inside my hand, with a bone stopper.

She wrinkles her nose and squints at me. 'And . . . what else?' she wonders aloud. 'A spool of silk and a needle-clutcher.' She pulls a thin roll of leather from the bag, opens it and draws out a sliver of white bone. 'A needle and some—'

'Why would I let you practise your pox-ridden dabblings on me?' I blurt. My gut boils at the thought of anyone touching my face.

'That cut is too deep to be left alone.' She raises her coppery eyebrows. 'Always think you know best, huh?'

I clutch the bandage tighter and turn away from her. 'You ent touching me.'

''Twill fester.'

My forehead burns fierce, even worse than my sore throat. I know I'm already getting sick. I sigh, then nod quickly.

'Good.' She unwraps my face from the bandage I made. The cloth has stuck to the wound, so she opens her cloak to reveal a leather circle strapped to her chest, holding six daggers with leather pommels. She pulls one out and uses it to carefully slice my bandage off.

Hot, sharp pain stabs into me as the skin underneath is torn. 'Argh!' I hiss as she pulls the last of it away.

'Sorry.' She winces, and takes my chin in her hand to peer at my damaged face. 'Claws, looks like?'

'A terrodyl,' I whisper. 'Must look grim.'

'Some folks will fear to look at you. But I say away with them! What counts is on the inside, no?'

I nod. 'In heart-truth, a captain could use a frightful face.' Even as I say it, I remember how I won't be captain now, and how I don't wanna tell her anything about me.

'Captain?' she whispers in an awed voice. 'Are you

to be a sea-captain?' Curiosity shines through her.

Hawk-swift, Grandma's face appears. A voice deep inside me whispers, over and over, *you've got no home, you've got no home.* The deck flashes into my brain, clear as lightning, with Grandma bundled on the plank and Stag pointing his gun at her. Sweat coats my palms and I begin to tremble.

'I'm sorry.' Kestrel lays cool fingers on my wrist. 'Try to breathe. We will not talk about it now.'

My tears blur her face. She twists round and gives a soft whistle. Ettler pokes out of his hiding place and whizzes up and out through the hole in the wall. He quickly puffs back in again and thuds down beside us, a ball of snow gathered in his tentacles. Then he dumps the snow onto the floor and huffs back to the chute.

'For numbing,' she tells me. As she reaches for the snow, her left sleeve slips and I notice there's something different about the arm. It's the same dark grey as the glove, and it's got the sleekness of a gun. I feel my eyes widen.

She stares me down, the slush dripping through metal fingers.

'Sorry, I didn't mean—' I start, but her face splits into a grin.

'You noticed my iron-arm,' she says, gleeful as anything. She pushes up her patched, fraying sleeve to show me. The arm's made of a smooth metal, and when she wriggles her fingers, it's like some kind of magyk is letting her thoughts control them, just the same as with flesh and bone.

It's the best flaming thing I've laid eyes on. 'What's it like?'

'Ever had a dead arm?' she asks.

I nod, remembering the times in our bunk when me or Sparrow slept on our own hands. Sparrow proper hates waking up with a numb arm.

'It's like that, much of the time.' She flexes her metal wrist, watching it in wonder. 'Until I whisper to the runes that our runesmith keyed into the metal. Then it comes back to me in a wave of warmth and tingles. For a while I thought I'd never feel it again.' She takes a bottle and a swab. 'First, a saltwater cleanse.' She starts to wash my wound.

'What happened to you?' I hiss through the stinging.

'An accident,' she replies vaguely. 'So my mother travelled to the city of Nightfall to find a smith gifted enough to forge a new arm for me. That was before, though.'

'Before what?'

She watches my face, like she's quietly deciding all kinds of things about me. When she blinks, a clear membrane *slicks* up and down her eyeballs like on the eyes of a hawk. Did I imagine it? 'Before the conflict sharpened its teeth.' She dips her needle into a flame and threads it with silk, then brings it towards me. 'Before the banning of books, and study.' She drops her voice to a breath. 'Before I was forbidden to leave the mountain. Before everything changed.'

'So how long you been scrapping with these Wilderwitches?' I ask.

'Oh, many years,' she answers, eyes resting on mine. 'But there was a tense half-truce we grew used to. Then, four years ago, the tenseness exploded.'

Before I can ask why, she presses a handful of snow to my cheek and eel-quick her needle pulls through my skin. I ball my fists to keep from screaming.

She pinches the edges of my wound together with her right hand and uses the iron fingers of her left to stitch. Her sleeve is by my eyes, and I swallow back a gasp cos the stars and moons are unpicking themselves into loose strands of golden thread.

Could it be cos of her being so close to the Opal in my pocket? I pray to all the sea-gods that she don't notice anything.

Kestrel mops my bleeding face with linen and keeps stitching, poking out the tip of her tongue. 'I have fresh skirts for you, as well.'

'I ent wearing no skirts!' Despite the pain that's

making my eyes stream, a sudden laugh punches out of me.

'Stay still!' she commands. 'Those are men's breeches, and they are in tatters, and—'

'They ent *men's* breeches – they're *my* flaming breeches.' I screw my eyes tight and suck my teeth. 'Can't you patch them for me?'

She sighs. 'Very well.'

Beast-chatter greets my ears. *Men's breeches.* Ettler scuffles about inside the chute. *Witches call to me, atop the Wildersea!* he yodels. My neck prickles. That's a line from the old song – the song that makes magyk when my brother sings it. Why's this squidge chattering those words?

When the wound is stitched, daubed with ointment and dressed, the light has thinned to a greyish murk. Dawn is coming. Kestrel lifts my sleeve and starts washing the brand Stag cut into my arm. Heat spills across my cheeks, cos I didn't know she'd spied it, and a deep shame crawls through my bones when I think how I'm marked for life with the sign of the *Hunter*, slashes for the hate Stag showed my Tribe.

Kestrel fixes me with a look that stops me wrenching away from her. But when the blood and grime are cleaned away, the antlers show even stronger and I curl my tongue.

She gently rubs ointment into the brand. 'So. What's it like out there, in the great wide?' Yearning swells in her eyes.

I pull my arm away. 'What d'you mean? Don't you know?'

She shakes her head. 'Used to. Well, I knew the sky above the Iron Valley, at least.'

Hunger to rove makes my toes itch. 'The great wide is the best thing since cinnamon buns,' I whisper.

Kestrel props her chin in her hand. 'Our Protector says travel is dangerous.'

I shrug. 'Travel's how my Tribe live. It's who we *are*.'

Kestrel gazes at me with a gentle, eager fierceness. 'I think it might be who I am, too.'

Suddenly footsteps ring in the pipes. Kestrel jerks her head towards them, all the life falling from her cheeks. She hauls herself up and runs to the door, pressing her ear flat against it. 'Oh no, no, no, not now!'

The steps bang along the passageway outside, growing closer to the cell with every beat. Then a rider garbed in raindrop mail barges inside and stares at Kestrel. 'What are *you* doing in here?'

'Greetings, Pangolin Spearsister,' says Kestrel breathlessly. 'I was sent to shear the prisoner's head and I thought, whilst I was here—' Her voice trails off.

I stare at her. Is she lying?

'So why does the creature still have a headful of rat's tails?' spits Pangolin. 'Our blessed Protector will be displeased when she finds out you've been treating an outsider.'

'I'm sorry,' Kestrel says quickly. 'Please, do not tell anyone you found me here. Remember when I helped heal your wounds so you might still be chosen as a Spearwarrior?'

Pangolin watches her coldly. Then she blows out her cheeks and rolls her eyes. 'I won't tell the Protector or Lunda this time. Probably.'

'Oh, thank you, Pangolin!' Kestrel stoops to collect her things. The light dims as she tips the moonsprite out of the glass jar, into her pocket. Ettler plops down from the chute and scurries into her bag. Then her skirts *shush* against the stone as she hurries off without looking at me. My heart punches my chest *once, twice*, and she's sucked into the gloom.

Pangolin's brown eyes stare dully through her raindrop armour. 'Looks like you're alone again,' she says calmly.

When I rush at her, snarling, she brings her spear up to her chest to block me and then uses it to shove me roughly onto the floor. 'I'll be back for you tomorrow.' Then she turns and leaves.

Fright gnaws away my insides, leaving me with a

gutful of shame. Once, I was fearless – or at least I made myself believe the lie that I was brave. Now it's like my scars have cut so deep that all my hurt shows up on the outside, and I hate it.

9
The Star Door

All day and night, as I huddle amongst the goat skins, I ponder the strange sawbones girl. Why was she so frighted at being found in here; enough to bow and scrape to that wretch of a Spearsister? And why can't I shake the feeling that she might want to help us, even though she ran off and left me here?

I'm scared of dream-dancing again, so I keep pinching myself awake, but in the end I lose the battle and drift into a restless doze. *My dream-dance is short and I don't get further than the window before I jolt awake in a* frightful sweat. I pinch my thigh. 'Stay awake!'

Then, as my belly twists with emptiness, I remember the pancakes Kestrel brought. I stumble around in the half-light, clutching a goat skin around my shoulders as I search for the platter I sent skidding across the floor. Finally, near the chute, I close my fingers around a fat, greasy lump of dough. Both pancakes are drizzled with icy squidge ink, but I take a big bite of one and a wave of relief rolls through me as I swallow mouthfuls of smooth, rich stodge. I have to make myself slow down in case I'm sick again.

I finish chewing and wrap a goat skin tighter around me, rubbing my nose to keep the blood flowing. When I push my hair out of my face, it's stiff with ice.

My glance snags on a folded scrap of something wedged into a crack in the wall, level with my bleary eyeballs. I reach up and slide it out. It's a grey piece of dried fish skin. I unfold it and squint at a clutter of black marks etched onto it, but the light's too gloomy to make them out. I tuck the scrap into my pocket.

Someone grabs me by the elbow. I can't remember where I am. I'm wrenched to my feet, my arm almost tearing from its socket. The memory of all that's happened drips into my brain as Pangolin bundles me towards the door. I must've dozed off again.

'Get off me!' But I'm forced into the passageway without even being told to shut my trap.

Outside in the murk, prisoners shovel snow from the courtyard. Snow lashes my face, stinging fiercely. There's just enough dawn to see the looming outlines of frozen banks of cloud. Hail clatters against them. A pearly shimmering dances above the mountain's jags; I reckon it might be the fire spirits, veiled by the gathering fog.

I tip back my head and gift the timid spirits a *howl*, hoping to coax them brighter, but Pangolin smacks me hard in the ribs, knocking the howl from my mouth. 'Shush yourself! Show respect when the gods flicker, or you will bring sickness to us!'

I'm gonna tell her what I think about her notion of respect but then a fog-horn booms, and she pushes me to the right, towards the sweep of steps and the wooden doors that Crow disappeared through. We pass the smoking stone hut, clanking with the sound of hammers striking metal, and an armoury.

'Everyone inside,' yells the horn-blower. 'Sky-wolves have been scented in the foothills!'

I'm forced up the steps, beneath a pair of golden spears crossed over the eaves.

Inside, smoke paints the air stew-thick. I'm standing in a long-hall cut into the mountain, forming a cavern so tall that when I tip back my head I can't see the top. Clouds drift up there, made of smoke and sour breath.

Great horned stamping beasts with shaggy brown coats watch me from stalls near the doors. They stink of restless fear and their skittish nerves make me think of horses. Their fright spreads among them like fire, and latches onto me.

Hayhayhayhoofshufflehayhayhay. Whooshfear bloodstink wulffrights feardrops, safe, herd, hayhayhay, they stutter, their big brown eyes rolled back.

Pangolin ushers me past the stalls and I shudder as the beasts thrust wet snouts against me, snorting and shuffling.

Folk sit on benches along the walls, some weaving bright cloth, others sharpening weapons or rubbing fat into their boots. They keep silent, darting their eyes fearfully around.

Steam writhes from battered cauldrons set on a huge fire-hearth in the middle of the hall. Pictures of draggles, goats and warriors with spears are etched into them. We're halfway across the room when I stumble against a simmering cauldron on the edge of the hearth. The heat burns through my breeches and a greyish gloop floods across the floor. A cook in a fawn-brown shawl shoots a look of fearful disgust at me. 'Mind where it treads,' she hisses, in a low voice scraped and scratched from lack of use.

A group of thin-faced kids stare at me from the benches. I ent never felt so small and far from home as I do when their hollow eyes touch me; all painted with black stripes to their jaws. Eyes full of mistrust.

I wish I could pinch myself and wake up back on deck with Squirrel and Hammer and the others, playing a rune-game under the stars.

But the sky-kids curl their lips at me as I pass, and an old man stops picking his teeth with a quill to spit at my boots.

Then a scream rips at the air.

'Next trial!' cries a shrill voice.

I try to stand arrow-straight, even though my legs are shaking, but Pangolin shoves me roughly in the back. 'Keep moving!'

'Touch me again and the voyage won't end well for you,' I snarl, cheeks on fire. I stumble through the shifting smoke, leaving her cursing behind me.

At the end of the hall looms a raised platform of damp, glistening rock. Filthy moon-lamps hang from long chains. Spearwarriors flank a throne with clawed feet and a back carved to look like unfurled draggle wings. I step towards the platform, down a path between two rows of ancient riders who sit facing each other on high-backed wooden chairs. One by one, they turn to watch me.

When I reach the platform, I stop and stare up.

A woman is slumped in the throne with her legs hooked over one of the arms, peering round the hall through shrivelled eyes. Her headdress is a goat's head with horns so long they curve up and over to touch her shoulder blades. Red scratches are gouged down her

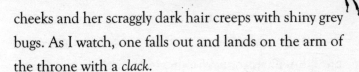

cheeks and her scraggly dark hair creeps with shiny grey bugs. As I watch, one falls out and lands on the arm of the throne with a *clack*.

I don't need to be told who she is. The sight of her shrinks my insides.

Someone darts through the smoke and a gag is wrapped over my mouth. Pain sears through me as the cloth is yanked tight over my stitches. I lash out with my fists but my hands are grabbed and bound behind my back.

At the throne's clawed feet sits a slack-skinned old woman with blue lips, using long bone needles to knit spidery lace from what looks like a pile of brown hair. To the left of the throne is a midnight-blue door decorated with yellow stars. And as the smoke drifts, another, smaller throne blurs into view on the right.

Kestrel sits on it stiffly, hands balled in her lap. Why is she up there in front of everyone?

The Protector of the Mountain jerks her face towards Kestrel, shedding more beetles. 'Daughter, what is this ugly thing before me?' Her words fall like rusty axes.

A drum booms in my marrow. Kestrel's eyes lock onto mine. Her lips are pressed tight together and her cheeks are red.

The glimmer of hope turns to ash in my mouth. I glare my hate out at her. She never would've helped me.

Kestrel stays quiet, nibbling her lips, and the Protector of the Mountain cocks her head at her, never blinking. Then she turns, slowly, to face me. 'You come before the Star Door to answer for your crimes!' she gargles, voice like a shaken bag of broken glass.

I will my heart strong, but a tear drops down my cheek.

'Don't cry,' she says with a chuckle. 'You'll be one with the wind and the rock, before you know it.'

Kestrel shifts in her throne, and the Protector of the Mountain twitches to gift her a sharp look.

I think of Crow and Sparrow. Maybe the wrecker turned into a crow and left without us. The thought pits a growling hollow in my belly, but I do want him to have gone, just to spite this lot.

A distant wolf howl judders into the hall. I flinch and glance back at the doors. The draggle-riders on the rows of chairs tremble in their goat skins. 'Younglings say they saw the Wilder-King flying with his pack, the day they netted the outsiders!' mutters one.

The *Wilder-King*?

'That drunken old witch has *no* right to call himself king!' calls the Protector of the Mountain. A frighted silence settles. She picks at her nails, eyeing me like I'm worth less than a bone button. Then from nowhere the shimmering face of the snagged spirit I saw in my dream-dance flickers behind my eyes. *My heart is awash in darkness.* The Protector is swamped in hate and fear.

Lunda and another rider barge through the smoky air, dragging someone with them. My heart stutters.

Crow's skin is grey and sweat glistens around his eyes. His rust-brown hair's shorn so close that I can see patches of his scalp, and clumps of dried blood cling to what's left of it. He's bound and gagged, same as me. When they let him go he collapses to the floor. I crouch next to him.

A violent crow-cry spews from his mouth, he starts to shake, and the cries keep coming. Why ent he changed his shape and flown out of here?

The Protector watches us. A chirping beetle falls from her tangled eyebrows and slides down her cheek. 'How should these trespassers be punished, daughter?' she rasps.

Kestrel grips the arms of her throne and stares at Crow. I squint at her – it looks like tiny bulbs of blood have sprung out across her face. She opens her mouth, but only a faint croaking comes from the back of her throat. 'I–'

'Come, now,' says the Protector. 'You while away your life watching the skies, but for once your idleness bore fruit. You spied the sea-creepers, allowing my

Spearwarriors to capture them. So speak. What is to be done with them?'

It was *Kestrel?* She's the reason they found us and shot us down? I fix my eyes on Kestrel's face and quick-sharp I reckon she knows that if my hands weren't bound I'd be the one to win a fight, though she's twice my size.

'They flew into *our* territory!' rages the Protector. Kestrel shudders. Thin trails of blood streak her cheeks. A rush of muttered curses and hollow chest-thumps swarms around the hall.

Another crow-cry bursts from Crow's lips and then he sags, weeping silent tears.

The Protector swivels her gaze onto us, thin lips stretching into a grimace. 'Stand!'

Pangolin jabs a spear into Crow's back while Lunda wrenches me to my feet by my hair.

The Protector's eyes bulge. 'You blundered into our flight path while we were leading an attack, and alerted our enemies to our presence. You cost us the life of a rider and her draggle. You almost cost us the entire party.' She says it so quietly I can feel the whole hall straining to hear. I shrink deeper into my boots.

Terror tiptoes up my spine. Crow tries to step back but Pangolin forces him still. I stare at Kestrel again, but this time I ent showing my rage. I'm trying to show my heart-strength, and tell her that I glimpsed hers.

No one here can help us. No one. But I *wish* she would, and my chest aches with it as I stare at her and she gazes back. Because I think she wants to help, but it's like her voice is trapped.

Kestrel's chest rises and falls too fast. She grips the arms of her throne so hard that it looks like the knuckles of her flesh hand are gonna break the skin.

'You have the aura of a witch about you,' bellows the Protector, making me flinch. 'Your eyes sing that you are a wicked child.'

When she stops talking, the only sounds against the brittle silence are the clack of the old woman's bone knitting needles, the snuffling of the beasts in their stalls and the bubbling cauldrons.

Why do bad-blubber full-growns always call *me* wicked?

The Protector leaps into a crouch and peers down at us. 'I find you *guilty*, of crimes against the sky!' she declares. 'The punishment?' A grin peels her face open. 'Is execution.'

Execution. It clangs around the long-hall like a dropped spear. Murmurs seethe from the benches, like the riders are gobbling up the word and tasting its bones. I think of the scream I heard and stare at the midnight-blue door. An arrowhead of fright lodges in my chest.

Fingers dig into the small of my back and I'm pushed closer to the Star Door.

Then there's a flurry of red and gold skirts as Kestrel leaps to her feet, trembling so hard she has to fold her arms around herself. 'No!' she blurts. Her voice cracks through the murk, and her hand flies to cover her mouth.

The clacking knitting needles stop dead. The hall sharpens to a tense point. The Protector stiffens. 'Did you speak, daughter?'

10
Abomination

Silence. Kestrel quivers and twitches, battling with herself. Tears drip off her chin. 'Y–' she stammers, trying to force out a word.

The Protector grinds her jaw.

Clawing pity for Kestrel twists inside me. For the first time, I can see that having a living, breathing ma ent always better than being left with hazy memories.

'Yes,' gasps Kestrel. 'I sp–' She sighs heavily and gulps a breath before trying again. 'I spoke.'

The Protector's eyes widen. Then her face sets into an iron mask. 'You are forbidden to speak unless commanded. And you risk it, for the sake of outsiders?'

Kestrel wipes her hands on her dress. Her cheeks are ablaze and her hair is wild. She snorts air out through her nose noisily and opens her mouth like she wants to say more, but can't.

The blue-lipped old woman scurries towards her and tries to pull her back onto her throne.

'No – *no*, get off me!' screams Kestrel, and all the fear in her crashes away like a falling icicle. A splodge of ink spreads across her scarlet dress – Ettler must be hiding amongst the cloth.

'Leave her alone!' I yell, but all that comes out is a thick, wet warbling.

I twist and wrench at the ropes on my wrists. Cos one girl in the sky spoke up for us, and she's filled me with heart-strength.

Slashes slice across Kestrel's cheeks. She gasps in pain, and I see that the slashes are feathers. The old woman flinches away from her.

'An abomination walks among us.' The Protector scowls. 'Those feathers tell me that you have not been drinking the potion to halt your disease. That is almost as foul a crime as trespass.'

Crow meets my eyes and then we both look back at Kestrel. Could she be a shape-changer, like him? Is that what the Protector means by *disease*?

'Please, Mother, don't hurt them!' sobs Kestrel. 'The girl was just trying to get her brother to safety, and she was injured by a terrodyl, so she can't have been thinking—' She clutches her iron-arm, pain pinching her face as she flickers in and out of shape-changing. More feathers slice through her cheeks, the air around her seems to crackle and quiver, and her eyes darken to wide black pools, ringed with yellow.

The Protector snaps her head towards Kestrel. 'Yes? And how would *you* know all this?'

'Because she snuck into the creature's cell!' calls Lunda. Pangolin must've tattled to her.

'My own flesh disgusts me!' declares the Protector. 'Remove it from my sight.'

Two guards stride forwards and drag Kestrel from the platform.

Shame on you for hurting your own kin, I think at the Protector. When she looks at me, my heart wriggles in my chest.

But while Kestrel struggles in the guards' grip, and Crow and me are shoved closer to the Star Door, my ears tune to a scratching, like claws on wood. I glance back down the long-hall, towards the doors. A wisp of fog curls through the wood and sets the beasts screaming in their stalls.

When the howls come, they shatter the moon-lamps and the moonsprites slip away through cracks in the rock.

A warrior bursts into the long-hall, beating a wooden shield with a spear. 'They're upon us!' Riders seal the doors after him.

'How did they breach the storm-barrier?' demands the Protector, gripping the arms of her throne with fingers turned white as chalk. 'I want to know how their weather-witches learned our secrets. Now!' But guards lift her to her feet and bundle her off.

'Stop the sea-creepers!' she shouts, before vanishing.

In the beat of mayhem that follows, Kestrel breaks away and bolts towards us, grabbing a dagger from the circle of six strapped to her chest. She saws our hands free as riders stream past, forgetting us in their fright.

I rip my gag away. A group of riders lunge for us, but something smashes through the doors – it's a sky-wolf, snuffling and yipping. Behind it, more wolfish wisps claw their way in.

The fog-wolves swirl around the hall, a ball of grey that whispers promises of teeth and blood.

When their fog-paws touch the ground, they settle, seem to grow heavier, like etchings plucked from a dream. The grey scrawls condense into snarling wolves of flesh and bone, and then they're here – three bristling wolves in the middle of the hall.

One prowls forwards and swipes a rider in the belly, knocking her onto her hands and knees. She scrabbles upright, reaching for her spear.

My mouth turns dry. 'Run!' I hiss, snatching at Crow's sleeve. We race away from the wolves, weaving past riders, towards the doors. Kestrel follows.

On the steps, Crow staggers and falls into the snow.

'Go without me,' he gasps, his voice a scratchy whisper.

'Not a bleeding chance!' I grab the back of his cloak and wrench him to his feet, then we wheel away across the courtyard, the snow flying at our faces and stinging our eyes.

I cast around for Kestrel. 'Where are they keeping my brother?' I shout against an iron-strong gale that pins down our arms and forces us backwards. Kestrel's reply is swallowed by the wind.

When the wind dies, I sway in the stillness. And that's when I hear it – the *crunch* of heavy paws through the snow.

'Move!' grunts Crow, so I kick forwards, pushing against the storm. Crow flickers in and out of sight, between the folds of driving snow. Kestrel is behind, I think, and I try to look for her but then I'm stumbling over something lumpy on the ground. I put out my hands as I fall – and touch the angle of a jaw and a stiff, frozen beard. I snatch my hands back. 'Gods swim close,' I mutter through chattering teeth, cos the horn-blower's lying in the blizzard, guts steaming where they've been torn out by sky-wolves.

Kestrel grabs my arm and hauls me upright. 'Come on come on come on!' Then she screams and we dart out of the way as a pack of sky-wolves – two black, one grey, broad backs speckled with snow – pace towards the fallen man. They sniff the air, breaths frosting, and release a mighty howl – it shakes through my marrow, niggles the back of my throat and rattles my ribcage – then the biggest of them dips its snout to the man's body. The other wolves shuffle and wait their turn. Then one lifts its muzzle and stares into my eyes.

It's taller than a polar dog and it reeks of old kills. Its fur stands up in a ridge along its back. It prowls closer. The lack of beast-chatter is a black hole in the air.

The sky-wolf growls and rushes at me.

Kestrel sends a dagger sailing straight into its chest. It yelps and crashes onto its side, dark wetness staining the snow beneath it. The soft fur and long snout are sucked into the skin, until a black-haired man lies still in a pool of blood and fog.

I drag Crow towards Kestrel and we slip-slide across the yard. There's a flash of gleaming wolf eyes and teeth and Crow pitches forwards, a wolf's bloodstained muzzle clamped on the end of his boot, shaking him.

He kicks back and Kestrel flings another shining dagger. The blade pierces the wolf behind the ear and it flinches away, yelping. We flee as the wolf uses its paw to try to loosen the dagger.

Kestrel grabs my sleeve and makes us duck low against the rocks. Her face is taut with terror as a troop of riders race past. My heart slams against the roof of my mouth.

Then they're gone, and Kestrel looks at us. 'Are you all right?' she asks Crow.

'Never been better, thanks to my steel toecaps,' he mutters.

Kestrel beckons us out from behind the rocks and ushers us on. Then she signals for us to slip behind the hut I saw before, with its billowing chimney. We gulp the thin soup of air, full of smoke and snow. Kestrel sweeps an armful of snow towards her, packs it into a tight ball and hurls it at the door.

'My brother,' I gasp. 'If he hears all this howling commotion he's gonna be proper frighted, I need to—'

Kestrel presses a hand over my mouth to shut me up, but before I can sink my teeth into her flesh the door inches open and a short, flushed girl with soot-smeared cheeks pokes her head out. She's holding chains of spinning raindrops between her fingers and she stares grimly at Kestrel. 'What's happened?'

Kestrel lifts her hand from my mouth and jumps into the girl's arms. They hug tightly. Then Kestrel turns back to us and waves us on. 'Get in, quick!'

Kestrel pushes us into the baking hot room and the girl slams the door closed with a snowy *thud*.

Set in a huge stone hearth is a fire that swallows all the air. Kestrel unfastens her feather cloak with shaky fingers and lets it tumble to the floor.

I look from her to the other girl – she's busy bolting the door. Then she presses her hand against the wood and it glows with hidden runes that flash and settle back into quiet waiting.

Kestrel looks so sad and frighted that I put my hand on hers. 'Heart-thanks for saving us, Kestrel. My name's Mouse, by the way. And that's Crow.'

She presses her fingers to her mouth. 'Oh sky-gods, I cannot *believe* what I've done!'

The other girl faces us. Black smears of coal, burn-marks and silver runes clutter her brown arms and hands. Her cheekbones are traced with the silver outlines of mountain ranges. As I gaze at the tattoos, Da's enchanted message with its map lines rushes into my mind. She raises her black eyebrows. 'These the sea-creepers? What are they doing here?'

'I'm no sea-creeper,' mutters Crow.

The girl clicks her tongue. 'Sea-creeper, land-lurker. Same difference, round here.'

'There's no time for squabbling.' Kestrel steps towards the other girl and clasps her hands. 'Can you spare some weapons?' she asks.

The girl stares up into Kestrel's eyes, her expression hardening. 'What *have* you done?'

Kestrel utters a small whimper of panic and drops

the girl's hands. She runs across the room and starts casting around, eyes wild. Then she wrenches open a wooden chest and roots around inside.

I follow her. 'I need to get my brother!'

'I've told you, he is asleep. He won't be afraid.'

'And if he—'

'The sawbones do not fight. Someone will be there with him. He will be kept safe.'

I know a stranger ent gonna be able to comfort Sparrow if he wakes. 'But—'

'But nothing.' The other girl stalks past us, sweat running over her lean, muscled arms. She stops in front of a linen dressmaker's model, with a half-finished raindrop headdress on. She drapes her raindrop chains around the model's neck, then wipes her hands on her brown leather apron. 'I'm Egret Runesmith,' she tells us, silver nose-ring and silver eye-paint flashing as she turns her head to squint through a narrow crack in the wall. 'And this is my forge. So if my girl says your sea-creeping brother is safe, you'll listen.'

11

The Runesmith and a Borrowed Longbow

I step closer to the raindrop armour and reach out to touch it. Though it looks as soft and blurry as water, it's hard, cold and sharp-edged. It's just like the net we were caught in. I pull my finger back. 'How do you make that?'

Egret narrows her dark eyes at me. 'Alloy of rain-gems and tears of the moon,' she says in a bored tone. 'Spelled with runes for living and for battle.'

Tears of the moon . . . I remember, when I had only six or seven Hunter's Moons, Da brought me a silver necklace from his rovings on land. *Traders call these silver drops moon-tears*, he told me.

Are they Ma's tears, fallen from the Tribeswoman in the moon? I asked.

This girl clutches battle-powers that I don't understand. I press my back against the warm stone wall, bones itching to run and get Sparrow. But it's like Kestrel reads my thoughts, cos she shakes her head, then gestures towards a low wooden bench cluttered with tools. Me and Crow sit down and glance around the forge.

Against the opposite wall is a low bed covered with white goat-hair blankets, shelves full of boxes and a table cluttered with clay mugs. The blackened walls are spattered with soaring arcs of pink, purple and yellow paint. Kestrel watches me, clears her throat. 'We paint our emotions free, so they don't rise up our throats and spill everywhere. We're not supposed to have feelings.' She laughs tightly.

'So. Are you ever going to tell me what happened?' demands Egret, eyes fixed on Kestrel.

Kestrel stares at the floor. 'I have to leave, right now, or they will kill me. And them.' She nods at me and Crow.

'Leave?' asks Egret doubtfully. 'What do you mean? You know you can't.'

'It's all changed. One word was all it took.' Kestrel sounds close to panic. 'Now there's no choice.'

'What did you do?' Egret steps closer and wipes a streak of blood from Kestrel's cheek.

'There's no time!'

Egret takes Kestrel's wrist, forcing her to meet her eyes. 'You're not going anywhere until you explain what's going on.'

'At the trial, I – spoke out, against Mother.' Kestrel raises miserable eyes to Egret and then stares round at the room.

'You *what*?'

'I know!'

Egret gives a shocked laugh and folds her arms. 'So much for biding our time. I'd no idea being with me meant so little to you.'

Crow catches my eye and frowns. I shrug.

Kestrel swats the hair out of her eyes. 'It isn't like that!' she pleads. 'I just – couldn't stay silent any longer.'

I take Crow's arm and we edge towards the door. Egret catches sight of us and barks a laugh. 'You won't get past my runes,' she says sternly. 'And if you did, the storm or the wolves or the spears would finish you.'

Kestrel chews her lip. 'I'm trying to help you,' she tells us.

'Why?' I ask.

'Yes,' says Egret, wrinkling her nose. 'I'd like to ask the same thing.'

'Because too many times I've risked healing a prisoner, and then they just *disappear* and – it was all for nothing.' She blinks fast and looks away. 'I *won't* see it happen to you. Our treatment of outsiders makes me sick!'

Look in a person's eyes, whether they're born of Sea or Sky or Land, and you'll learn there's not so much difference

between you, shimmers Bear's voice in my memory.

Slowly I realise that Crow's watching Kestrel with soft eyes.

I lift a brow. 'Hope you realise that just cos she's another shape-changer, that don't mean you straight-off know her.'

He glares, face reddening. 'Would you mind shutting your face?'

Kestrel breaks off her row with Egret and glances over at him in surprise. '*You're* a shape-changer?'

'Someone's got good ears,' he grumbles. 'Aye.'

'I've never met another before!'

'Me neither.'

'Though I'm not really one any more.' Kestrel's got her arms wrapped around her body, and she's still trembling.

'What happened?' he asks, as close to shy as I can imagine ever seeing him.

I stare at Kestrel's iron-arm and remember her talking about some accident.

'I lost a wing in a terrodyl attack. My Tribe found me in the valley, half a bird, half a girl, all a-flicker. Now it's too dangerous for me to change, and besides, it is forbidden. They stop it with a medsin, so I don't bring mother's wrath, or start changing around my iron-arm.' Her face speaks louder than any words could about how painful that is. 'But I – have not been taking it. It dulled my feelings.'

'Aye,' mutters Crow darkly. 'That must be the same filth they fed to me.' He watches Kestrel until heat spills across her cheeks and she turns away to start searching behind a wooden chest.

I follow her, pulling my hands free from my pockets, but as I do it something flies free from my cloak. The Opal! My gut clangs and I scrabble to my knees to grab the gem, but it bounces under a cabinet with a high *shill* against the stone.

I drop to my belly and peer underneath, put my hand under and fish around on the floor, but I can't reach it and I could scream. I sense Kestrel lying down next to me before she speaks. 'What did you lose?' she asks.

'Nothing,' I say quickly, straining and stretching. But the Opal lies faintly glowing against the wall under the cabinet, far out of my reach.

Kestrel pushes her arm into the gloom and her fingers sweep against the Opal, nudging it closer. I swipe for it, but she flicks it into her own palm and pulls it free, standing and dusting off her skirts. She frowns into her hand, turning the Opal over as I leap to my feet. Loose strands of hair pull free from Kestrel's braids and weave around her head in a breeze that ent there. 'What's this?' she whispers, eyes bright and curious. She sucks in her bottom lip and darts her eyes at me. 'Why is it so warm, and bright? It feels alive.'

The others crowd close to look. I force myself to breathe, but their eyes touching the Opal feels like having my cabin stolen again. Like having a layer of skin peeled away. 'Give it to me,' I say quietly, filling my eyes with iron.

Three pairs of startled eyes fix on my face. Then Kestrel steps close and holds out the Opal. I snatch it up, and my breath comes easier. I wish I'd calmed my sails, cos I don't want anyone thinking the Opal is halfway near as important as it is.

Crow stares at the Opal, arms crossed tight. He shoots me a look of betrayal, like he's hurt I never told him. I realise he might know something about the Opals, cos he spent so long working for Stag.

Egret watches me intently.

An itchy flush steals up my neck. 'It's nothing – just a keepsake from my da.'

'I can always smell a lie, especially when it stinks as much as that one.' She scowls. 'We're already risking everything for you sea-creepers. Tell me what it is, or I'll shove you out into the snow and see how you fare alone.'

I ent never gonna be able to deny the power of the thing when they can all see it for themselves, and the story she's begging for presses hard against my lips. The Opal oozes salt-sticky dampness into my palm.

When I start to tell them, it's like I'll never stop the flood of words. I tell them everything I can: Da not coming home, Bear finding the carving of our ship, and Da's secret message appearing on its sails, telling me to find the Storm-Opals.

But I don't tell them about what happened to Grandma, cos when I think about doing that my breath grows shallow and I'm frighted of getting plunged back through time again.

'Mouse,' says Kestrel, gently touching my arm.

I blink at her.

'I'd not a clue the Opal Crown legend rang with truth,' she says. She flexes her metal hand. It's easier to see in the firelight, and proper beautiful – a dusky grey with shimmering pink-gold runes under its surface. 'So, if you don't find each Opal and restore them to the crown–' Her voice trails off hopelessly.

I stare at my boots and heave a sigh. 'All Trianukka will turn to ice. So many creatures will lose their lives. And after that, who knows what?'

You can't save them either, slithers a mean voice in my head.

Egret sighs loudly, grabs a small white cake from a platter and stuffs it in her mouth. She gestures roughly at me and Crow. 'Eat,' she says through a mouthful. 'It's clear we have to get you out of here somehow. The fog will try to make you forget your own name – you need to stay strong.'

'What are they?' I ask, picking up a sticky cake. When I bite into it, a sweet burst of cream fills my mouth. The fat and sugar seems to drip straight into my veins and the relief loosens my tight breath.

'Snowy mooncakes,' enthuses Kestrel. 'She bakes them just for me. We should take some with us.'

'Oh should you now?' says Egret. Then she flinches as a sharp squeal fills the air, like giant claws scraping against ice. The mountain is smashing its enemies with more bombs.

'Take them *where?*' I ask. *If we even get past the sky-wolves, the ice-bombs and the storm-barrier.*

'There is a boy called Yapok,' says Kestrel. 'Among the Wilderwitches. I think he could hide us. He was a keeper of books.' She gives the last word the same weight as *death*, or *bombs*.

Egret smirks. 'She writes him secret love letters.'

'They are not *love* letters.' Kestrel rolls her eyes. 'He was my friend, when we were children. But now such friendships are forbidden, we can only write.' She throws her mooncake back onto the platter with a sticky splat.

Ettler wriggles free from Kestrel's cloak and follows Egret around, grumbling. 'Get out of it, you!' she snips.

He wheels away towards the bench and lands with a squelch in Crow's lap. 'Urgh!' bursts the wrecker-boy. He prods the squidge with a cautious fingertip.

Kestrel turns to Egret. 'Yapok is the only one beyond this prison who won't turn us away if we go to him. I'm sure.'

Egret moves towards the fire. 'Are you trying to convince me, or yourself?'

Kestrel takes the other girl's hands in hers. 'Please. I am tired of folk telling me how to sit, what to wear, if I may speak. I am ready to be useful. I am ready to see more of this world, wars and perils and all.'

'I thought we agreed that if we ever left the mountain we'd do it together, and we'd head for Nightfall,' hisses Egret.

Nightfall. The place where Grandma said Stag did his book-learning.

Kestrel raises her coppery brows. 'But – that was just a silly dream! We'd never really disguise ourselves as boys!'

'Wouldn't we?' snaps Egret.

Kestrel's mouth falls open. 'How could we live in a place where women aren't even allowed to tread? Wouldn't that be exchanging one prison for another?'

Egret picks up a poker, darting a furious look at Kestrel. 'You're right. I was only making fun. Forget it.' She stokes the forge-fire. Bright flurries of sparks rise up. Sweat trickles down her face and arms.

'You can't have thought—'

'It's fine, Kes. Just leave it,' says Egret. Then she bursts into a snort of laughter that she stifles with her wrist, but I reckon she's only laughing to make sure she don't cry. 'So you've made up your mind. You're going.' She speaks with a dull flatness.

Kestrel stares at her back. 'I have to.'

Egret nods. 'If they come, I will hide you.' She turns around and her eyes sweep over our faces. 'All of you.'

Kestrel crosses the room to kiss her cheek. Egret brushes Kestrel away, pain flickering over her face.

'Heart-thanks,' I tell the runesmith awkwardly.

'Not for long, mind. The inspections are much more frequent now. I'm being watched.' Egret stares at my face and my hand flies to my scar.

'Don't touch the stitches!' scolds Kestrel, so I fold my hands in my lap, biting my tongue.

Egret rolls her eyes and gifts me a small smile. I grin back and it feels like the frost in the room has started to thaw. 'What weapons are you skilled with?'

'A longbow.' Crow and me say it at the same time, then swap sidelong grins.

'Well, this is an iron-works, so I have arrowheads but only one bow, left to me by my mother when she was captured by the Wilderwitches.' She chews her cheek and looks down. 'You may borrow it, along with some bowstrings, but you will have to craft the arrows yourself.'

'Oh, no – I ent gonna take that from you.' But even as I say the words I'm filled with heart-riot gladness. It wouldn't be my own bow, but I'd be able to feel the springy yield of the sapling wood and the steadfastness of the heart-wood, be able to string it and feel the taut power to send an arrow whistling into an enemy's throat . . .

Egret smiles. 'That face confirms there is no choice.' She goes to a corner of the forge. When she turns back she clutches a tall wooden longbow and two small grey parcels. 'Here. You can each take a raindrop cowl, as well. They'll guard your necks from blades and arrows.' She hands out the cowls.

I take the bow. The wood is cool and smooth under my touch and I can just feel the deeply buried runes carved into it.

'The runes etched into the yew are focused on uncloaking the witches' ways,' explains Egret. Then she turns to Crow. 'I will lend you a sword, if you can use one?'

'I ain't bad,' he says, puffing out his chest.

Kestrel and Egret look at each other, doubtfully. I frown. Wonder if he's just blowing gas cos he won't stop staring at Kestrel?

'Good. Here.' Egret lifts a sword from a bench beside the fire. The tip scrapes the table and sends out a song-note that's sweet and deadly. '*Blood-singer*,' says Egret, eyes on Crow's face. 'Wield her well, land-creeper.'

When she hands the sword to Crow he misjudges the weight and staggers under it, clanking the tip of the blade to the floor. I wince. Egret and Kestrel put their hands on their hips and cock their heads at each other.

'It's fine, I'm fine. I've got it,' murmurs Crow, wiping sweat from his brow with the back of his hand.

'You sure you can—' I start.

He holds up a hand, a warning in his eyes. 'Ah, do you have some sort of, um, holder, for it or—'

'A sword-belt?' asks Egret briskly.

'Aye, one of them,' he says, smiling broadly and standing straighter. Kestrel comes to help him secure the belt, and he blushes deeper than sunset when she touches him.

Egret and me exchange glances and it's all I can do not to roar with laughter. I shove my hands in my pockets and tighten my lips.

Egret strides away and starts searching through a

tall cabinet. 'And you'll need goggles to stop the snow-blindness – that's a thing you need about as much as a spear in the brain.'

'We need them for my brother, too.'

'He won't be well enough to come with us,' says Kestrel, sorrow filling her eyes.

A sick feeling plunges into my belly. 'I don't flaming care,' I tell her. 'I ent leaving him behind!'

Egret nods briskly and passes me an extra raindrop cowl and a spare set of goggles.

Kestrel shakes her head, then throws her hands into the air with a sigh. 'Why should anyone listen to a sawbones, huh? What do I know.'

Suddenly, on the other side of the wall, beyond the howls of the sky-wolves and the clang of weapons and the grumbling of Hackles, there are voices.

'They can't have disappeared! Why weren't you looking?'

We freeze, looking round at each other. The voices drift closer. 'The storm hid them,' whines Pangolin.

A boot kicks the door. 'Open up, Runesmith!'

12
Hidden, Secret

'Quickly, in here!' Egret falls to her knees, peels back a coal-smeared rug and uses a chisel to lever up one of the floorboards. It's a narrow, dark space, barely big enough to squeeze into.

'They won't get past your rune-casting, will they?' asks Kestrel.

'No, but if I do not admit them they will suspect something. They will starve us out or burn this forge down.'

Kestrel nods reluctantly and lowers herself into the ground. I push Crow ahead of me. Kestrel rolls out of the way and he squeezes under the floorboards with her. Then I join them. I've just pulled my foot inside when there comes a frenzied rattling at the door.

'Open up, or we force this door and take you captive!'

'As though you could!' mutters Egret. She presses her finger to her lips, then lowers the plank of wood over our faces.

In the darkness and dust we listen as Egret strides across the room to the door, bare heels banging the floor. The door whines open and wind whistles into the forge.

'Lunda, Pangolin,' she says stiffly. 'May swift-feathers bear you glad tidings, Spearsisters. My forge is here to warm you.'

'Oh, spare us,' snaps the frosty voice of Lunda. 'Get out of our way.'

By my side, Crow breathes heavily through his nose, but Kestrel lies silent, fingers splayed against the floor above, eyes flickering back and forth as though she's trying to see through it.

Dust prickles the back of my throat and my eyes water but I force a deep breath. If I choke, they'll find us and we'll be executed before the sun sets.

Boots stamp across the floor. The boards over our faces creak and groan. I shut my eyes and will them to leave. But the boots prowl to every corner of the room above us, and there's a crash as something's thrown aside. Next to me, Kestrel jumps. I turn my face and meet her eyes – the bird membranes on them drag up and down as she blinks.

'Where are they?' shrills Lunda.

Egret says nothing.

I breathe thin, prickly breaths. My gut clenches when

there's a clang of metal and something rolls overhead. Sounds like the Spearsisters are tearing the forge to shreds.

Then a silence stretches. Dust stabs into my throat again. I clamp my mouth shut and rake a breath through my nose. But my pipes are squeezing shut. Kestrel turns her face towards me, shaking her head rapidly and stroking my arm. I brush her off.

'Pang, keep searching,' snaps Lunda. 'When we find them in here we'll—'

I begin to splutter and gulp for air, tears streaming down my cheeks.

As my cough rattles and grates, shouts ring into the night from outside, cloaking my noise.

'The sky-wolves have regrouped,' says Pangolin. 'They're making for the draggle-caves.'

'You'd better get out there,' says Egret. 'I've got to get back to work myself, or we'll run out of weapons to fight this attack.' Real fright scratches her words thin.

'This time, you have escaped me,' says Lunda. I picture her mean face; all narrowed blue eyes and neat little ears and teeth. 'But I know you've been hiding something. You should skate very carefully from here on, Runesmith. The ice is prone to cracking.'

There's a crash as the forge door slams shut, cutting dead the sound of the swirling wind and snow. I can't breathe, and I scrabble against the floorboards as a hacking cough scrapes my lungs.

'Mouse?' Crow thumps the floorboards with the edge of his fist. 'Get her out of here!'

I gasp for breath, tears streaming down my face, and bang my legs against the bottom of this dusty pit.

The boards creak as Egret levers them up. Then she grabs my wrist and hoists me out of the hole. I brace my arms against my thighs, head stuck between my legs, desperately gulping air.

'The fighting will keep them from my door for a few wing-beats,' says Egret, when my sails are calmed. 'Long enough for you to prepare yourselves more fully, while I work.' She turns to a rack of bent, bloodied spears, and sets to heating one over the fire, hammering it back into shape.

Kestrel wraps some mooncakes in a piece of cloth and tucks them into a bag at her hip. Ettler settles himself inside. 'No munching our supplies,' she warns. Then she sorts through a pile of blades, filling the gaps in the circle on her chest, and hands me a long, skinny dagger.

It's a proper one, made for a full-grown – the type Grandma always said I was too young to have. I test the point against my palm and gasp at the sharpness. Then I stick it in my belt and tug my cloak closed to keep it hidden. 'Heart-thanks!'

I'd give anything for my *own* knife, my own longbow, my own home. My own Tribe. But the kindness of this sky girl smashes a tide of heart-gladness over me.

We wait, watching Egret repair old armour and forge new weapons. She pulls her gloves off to write runes along the length of a spear, whispering under her breath. Then she plunges it back into the fire to seal the magyk.

Finally, she steps back from the fire and crosses to the door. Sweat zig-zags down her neck. She presses her ear to the wood. 'You don't have long,' she says. 'There may be a lull – Spearwarriors will come to refresh their weaponry.'

Nerves skitter in my belly as I shoulder my bow and pull on a raindrop cowl. It smooths itself over my face like a cool second skin. Crow does the same, then tightens his sword belt.

'When we get out there, stay close!' Kestrel warns. 'To reach your brother we need to sneak through the pantries.'

We move towards the door. Egret grabs Kestrel's arm. She pulls her into a fierce hug, and kisses her. Two bright spots of colour bloom in Kestrel's cheeks.

Then she slips through the door, and we follow her into the jaws of chaos.

13

Swift Feathers

The wind shrieks, stabbing pain deep into my ears. We fight our way through snowdrifts and patches of slippery slush, sticking near the edges of the fortress, in the shadow of the mountain's jags. I squint through the ice crystals glittering in the air.

Fallen sky-wolves and Spearwarriors are strewn across the courtyard. The ones still fighting are a grey-red snarl of shield-heavy paws and fang-sharp spears.

I fumble to string my borrowed longbow, then remember I ent got any arrows yet and swallow back a yell.

When the battle sways towards us we lie flat behind a boulder and breathe sticky clumps of snow into our mouths. I'm almost too tired to be frighted. Then the fight spirals away again, and Kestrel scrambles up.

'Come on!' breathes Crow in my ear. As I push myself upright my hand sinks into the steaming warmth of a sky-wolf's sliced-open belly. When I fall,

Crow drags me up by the back of my cloak.

Kestrel pushes open a low window set into the side of the mountain, and we drop into a flickering, crooked passageway. We run past great looming tapestries woven from bright thread, showing draggle-riders flying into battle. At the end of the passage Kestrel turns a ring in a door, and the shadows suck her inside.

We follow. I blink in the gloom. Crow is a tall, panting blur next to me. 'Where'd she go?'

I feel him shrug.

Something moves below us. Kestrel waves frantically, a grainy outline against a cave-dark wall. We edge forwards and tip down a wide stairwell. Kestrel waits for us to catch up.

Then we hurry to the bottom and rush through a tall archway. We enter a sprawl of huge, connected caverns, hewn into the guts of the mountain and lit by cracked, guttering moon-lamps. Kestrel pushes us flat against the damp wall as a dozen squidges – all as small and fat as Ettler – huff past, rolling a great stinking cheese across the floor. *Heavepushnolicking!* The cheese wheels past, as tall as I am, cloaking us in a sickly vapour. Crow staggers, wrapping his hands over his mouth and nose. 'Take it we've found the pantries, then,' he mutters between his fingers. 'Should be called the putrids.'

We prowl between teetering wooden shelves that

121

stretch to the distant ceiling. The breathless ranting of row after row of squidges is deafening. They chug along in lines, hauling jars, pans, boxes and tins with their chubby tentacles.

Goats' milk to the snow-chests, with the meat and butter!
Quag-eggs to the lower shelves, nest them in beds of nettles!
NO nibbling the mooncakes. No bites, not a one!
Spices middle shelves, berries in our mouths!

I cover my ears and try to suck enough thin air through my cold-numbed lips.

'All right?' Kestrel asks. She tapers off with a snatched breath of alarm as the door squeals open. 'Down!' she whispers.

I roll underneath one of the enormous shelves, praying to all the sea-gods it don't squish me. Crow dithers, then Kestrel shoves him towards another shelf and he squeezes under it. I watch Kestrel sweep underneath a shelf on the other side of the room.

I peer out as two riders stride in, garbed in iron-grey cloaks and tall leather boots. One, a boy with yellow braids tangling over his shoulders, fingers the dagger at his belt, gold spikes gleaming on his knuckles. He eyes the squidges with bored disgust. 'I could've told them she wouldn't be in here. She's long gone.'

'Gone where?' says the other, a girl with flame-red hair and a surprised-looking mouth. 'She's still the

Protector's daughter, and anyway, she knows as well as we do that beyond sky-territory there's no clean air left to breathe.'

'I hope she tips herself right off the edge of the world.' The boy reaches out and flicks a squidge, making it squeal. 'She'll do it, too, if she knows what's good for her. Better that than face what's waiting for her in the long-hall.' He moves to the shelf Kestrel is hiding under, his toecap inches from her terror-stretched eyes.

There's a bang as the girl opens a cupboard and closes it. 'The Protector's been at the sleep-struggles again, by the way,' she whispers. 'The night frights. Last night she jumped to the top of her canopy and started scratching at the ceiling! She scratches herself, she scratches the walls, she scratches *us* if we try and stop her. I don't know what to do.'

Kestrel makes a fist against the floor and presses her lips into it. She frowns, shaking her head slightly.

'Sometimes I find her *here*, stuffing her face in her sleep!'

The boy grimaces. 'Quiet!' he orders. 'Our Protector brims with mountain-strength.'

'Something is wrong, Spearbrother!' insists the girl. 'In waking hours she is exhausted. At night, she is afraid to sleep. My pa says she is not the Protector she once was. Don't you remember before, when things were different?'

There's a pause, while the boy looks at her blankly. 'This is the way it has always been.' His expression hardens. 'And if you don't shut up, Tern will be weaving lace from *your* hair.'

While they gabble on, I flatten my ear to the ground. Strange shouts and snores twist in the deep underground. The floor chills my bones. I lie still as oak.

Finally, the warriors fall into uneasy silence. They pace the length of the pantries, turn and stalk back again, then leave.

Kestrel rolls out from underneath her shelf and helps us out of our hiding places.

'C'mon,' I say, casting around. I spot a low wooden doorway on the other side of the pantries. 'Is it this way?'

No answer comes, and when I look back, Crow's watching Kestrel suspiciously.

'How could I ever leave?' she says, eyes full of heart-sadness.

I move to her side and reach for her but she backs away from me. Her mouth is drawn into a tense line. 'I can't,' she says quietly, beginning to turn away.

I grab her arm and make her look at me. 'What

about Yapok, and the great wide? You're almost there! You've almost left your ma's grip.'

'That Spearsister spoke the truth.' Her breath comes too fast. 'The Protector says that there's no clean air beyond our sky-territory, and if I ever left, I'd suffocate. She says my arm would die. She says my bones would turn to mush without the strength of the mountain to hold me up. She says—'

'When did she start spouting that bilge to you? It ent true!' I take her limp, sweating hand. 'All you've gotta do is put one foot in front of the other and not look back.'

But she's caught in some inward tide and travelling further from me with every beat. Reckon this mountain's marked her the way the sea brands a shell. 'I can't,' she whispers, glancing around like a spooked horse. 'I – I'm sorry.'

A cold fist settles in my stomach as she tells us how to find the sawbones' nest. Then she bolts, her skirts rasping along the stone floor.

'We don't need her anyway,' I say hollowly, the lie scalding my tongue.

'Never did,' says Crow, scuffing his boot against a shelf, making a squidge trill angrily at him. 'Let's find your brother and get out of here.'

We run across the room, ducking under and

weaving round huffing, puffing rows of squidges. *Heavepulllugdon'tdrop! Keepgoingheavytiredfatarmsouch!*

A stone archway yawns overhead and we tear through it, dodging shelves. Our boots slip in puddles of squidge ink. Crow blunders through what's left of a smashed moon-lamp, scrunching through shards of broken glass. We whip around corners too fast. My fingernails rip painfully on the stone when I flatten myself out of the way of a frighted squidge.

Our breaths wheeze, too loud in the silence. The walls are so thick in this part of the stronghold that the sounds of battle outside don't reach us and the world shrinks to nothing but my raggedy breath and my swooshing blood and my boots too loud on the stone. I try to remember the way Kestrel told us, but my ears are clogged with the Protector's threat. *Execution.*

Another sweep of steps. A huge, dusty tapestry of Hackles under a full moon. Our boots fall so loud. How can no one come? Then a door thuds closer and closer out of the murk.

We sneak through and loop up a spiral of rusty metal stairs on the other side. I stumble and put out my hands just in time to catch myself against the wall.

Crow grabs my sleeve and we duck next to a round, dark wooden door.

'Reckon we've found the sawbones' nest,' I whisper.

14
Stench Songs

The door creaks open when I give it a push, and we step silently inside.

The nest reeks of sickness – sour, stuffy and sweet all at once. Two rows of rusty metal beds line the room. Half the beds are filled with moaning or sleeping folk, gashes on their heads, legs wrapped in bandages, faces greyer than whale skin. One or two cry garbled words. A sawbones hurries between them.

We hover in the shadows. I look around for my brother, and finally my eyes snag on a rusty old iron bed that's set apart from the others. Sparrow's tangled in a mess of furs slickened with strands of whale-song. In his palms sit puddles of liquid purple fire. My heart stammers. Has he had more shaking fits?

Despite everything Kestrel said, he *is* awake, and sure as rotten teeth he's frighted. His filmy eyes search the room. He whimpers under his breath, twitches his head this way and that, and folds and unfolds his fingers, stretching purple webs of lightning. But he's finally looking a lot more like my little bag of bones whale-singing brother.

Sitting by his bed is a curly-headed woman with the gold eye-paint of a sawbones. She's wearing gloves and a mask, and she's using a moon-lamp for light – when I squint, I realise Thunderbolt's the moonsprite trapped inside the bottle, and she looks proper furious about it.

The woman leans forwards and scrapes globs of foamy whale-song from my brother's mouth – he wriggles and spits – then she pushes the sticky strands into a bottle. 'Don't want you choking on all this gunk,' she murmurs.

'*Guts and tails and skins and fins!*' sings Sparrow, and I grin as I recognise the start of one of his best stench-songs.

'*Mix 'em in a pot with crumpled old wings!*'

'Will you shut that sea-creeper up?' someone shouts.

'*I'll pluck out your eyes and saw off your hair, touch me again if you dare!*' Then he starts belching the tune. The sawbones jerks to her feet and pushes her chair away. Me and Crow draw deeper into the shadows.

'I can't help you if you're going to threaten me,' she says angrily, eyeing his lightning. Then she turns and ducks through a side door, muttering, 'I shouldn't have to look after outsiders!'

Me and Crow stay still, watching the other sawbones make her rounds. My toes itch to run to Sparrow but I can't risk it while she's there.

Across the room, my brother thrashes suddenly, balling up his fists and pressing them to his eyes. Lightning licks into his hair. He cries out in pain.

The sawbones straightens up and stares across at his bed. But she shudders instead of going to him, and hurries from the room through the side door, cursing.

I nod at Crow and we sneak between the rows of beds, towards Sparrow. The sick folk that're awake murmur as we pass, some asking for help, others spitting insults. One threatens to call the sawbones. I flinch, begging them to stay quiet, as we creep closer to my brother.

'Sparrow,' I whisper, resting my hand on his arm. 'I'm here. Hang on.'

His eyes flicker open, but there's just thick white film and his grimace don't ease – he's stuck in the nightmare but I reckon he's awake. His nightmares have always seemed frightful-real, but this feels different.

Crow tenses. 'What's wrong with him? Does he always sleep with his eyes open?'

I peel back my raindrop cowl and put my mouth next to Sparrow's freezing ear. 'Sparrow? Wake up! We have to get out of here, right now!'

He jumps, filmy white eyes searching the space next to my head. 'Mouse?'

'Aye. We're gonna get you out of here, but we've got to be quick!'

I snatch the moon-lamp and pull out the stopper. Thunderbolt flicks up and out, showering me with a grateful burst of jittery moon-sparks. Then she zooms over to Sparrow and skitters up the bridge of his nose, into his hair, shedding pale light over his face. Her light thins the film on his eyes and he relaxes the tiniest bit. 'Hello, Thunderbolt.' Then he squints up at me. 'Is it really you, stinker? I can see a black blob that might be your rat's-nest hair.'

'Shhh!' I look over my shoulder, but most of the other sick folk have fallen asleep or been carried off on waves of pain. I take his hands and pull him upright, biting my tongue when his lightning zaps up my wrists. His bad arm's been wrapped in thick, padded linen, so it's twice its normal size. 'I saw a face under the ice, somewhere far away, coming for me!' he husks.

'It was just a nightmare,' I tell him. 'Let it fade. And keep your voice down!'

He curls his lip. 'It was real.'

'Up you get – I don't know how long we've got. This ent the time to be stubborn.'

I lift a scratchy old goat skin from the bed and as

Sparrow climbs dizzily from the sweat-stained mattress I bundle him up in it.

Then I tear a ragged strip from the bed sheet and make a sling for his arm, like I used to watch Grandma do. I search for his boots, and find them under the bed with his stockings still stuffed inside. Crow helps him shove them on, pulling faces at the stink, while I look for anything else we might need.

I root around on the table by his bed, find more of the yellow flowers Kestrel gave me and cram them into my pockets. I pocket a small brown bottle of liquid, too, in case it's some medsin they've given Sparrow to help with his fits.

My neck prickles. I whirl around as the curly-haired sawbones steps into the room, carrying firewood. We freeze. She stares, mouth falling open. Fright boils my insides. The firewood falls out of her arms and *thunks* onto the floor.

Sparrow props himself up on an elbow and gives a little snarl. He flicks a sticky lightning web at the woman's heels, but it misses and fizzles uselessly on the floor as she turns on her heel and sprints from the room.

Her footsteps ring along the passageway. 'Help! Prisoners are loose!' she yells.

'What now?' groans Crow, watching tensely as the

eyes of sick Sky-folk blink at us from their beds.

I pull him and Sparrow towards the far wall. 'I reckon there's only one way Kestrel would've got us out of here – the draggles. We've got to find their cave.'

Downdowndown, chitters Thunderbolt, whizzing moon-sparks in my eyes and up my nose. I sneeze. *Doorwaybacktherebackthere, secret!* She flits over to a tapestry on the wall and wriggles under a loose corner of it, spreading silver streaks over the thread.

I race to the wall, lugging Sparrow with me, and jolt the tapestry aside – there's a door hidden in the wooden panelling. I grab the iron ring in the door and twist it from side to side. 'It's locked!'

Crow takes a slender feather from his pocket and wiggles it in the lock. Sparrow presses his free hand into mine. It's still warm and feels ash-gritty.

Outside the room, footsteps clang closer. My heart stalls.

Crow curses under his breath as his feather snaps in the lock.

'Hurry!' whimpers Sparrow. 'I can feel them getting closer!'

Crow fumbles for another feather. He screws up his face in concentration. But the quill snaps again. He yells through his teeth.

Suddenly the lock crunches and the door's flung

wide, just as a gaggle of Spearwarriors burst into the nest behind us. 'Stop!'

A cloaked arm sweeps us into a darkness full of the stink of damp and picked bones. Then there's a metal clunk as whoever pulled us to safety locks the door. Fists pound against it on the other side.

The figure sweeps past us and footfalls echo away through the murk. We stumble after the sound. Thunderbolt fizzles ahead of Sparrow's face, turning back every few beats to chirrup and make sure he can see enough to keep walking. My heart swells with gladness that we've got our moonsprite with us.

We walk through sloping, slippery corridors with ceilings low enough for Crow to bump his head more than once. 'Stop!' I hiss, but the figure walks faster and we're forced to hurry to keep up.

When we reach the end of a passageway, the figure pauses and turns to us. Thunderbolt's moonlight shows spiky white hair, brown skin and the black paint that strikes through the eyes to the jaw. It's Pika – the boy that dared to tease Lunda when we first landed on the mountain. He leans close. 'I heard the sawbones' war-cry. I can get you out of here.' He turns to the right and strides on.

I run and catch his arm. 'Why?'

'I'm a friend of Egret and Kestrel. Come on!' He

hurries off, head bowed.

'Will Kestrel be safe?' Crow asks quietly.

'I don't know.' Pika twists round to eyeball us. 'But you won't be if you don't get a shuffle on.'

Me and Crow swap heart-sad glances and hurry after him, herding Sparrow in front of us. He follows Thunderbolt; a scratch of light in the dark.

I grapple with the weight of the longbow that's no use until I can craft some arrows. At the end of the next passageway we reach a steep set of steps. Darkness presses to either side and I can't see if anything's lurking there. We start climbing downwards. Some steps are so high I have to jump into thin air and there's a beat before I land, jarring my ankles. When they get too steep for Sparrow, me and Crow are forced to pass him between us like a wriggling parcel. My breath is a thin wheeze.

Pika pulls a mooncake from his pocket and nibbles on it as we plunge down the break-neck stairs. Our boots make a hollow echo every time we land, cos there's a sheer drop to each side of us and nothing to swallow the sound. Then Pika drops his mooncake, and it falls for beats and beats until finally, a long way down . . . *smack*.

And somewhere very high above, there's a thud, and bellowing voices.

We climb down faster. When we reach the bottom,

a damp breeze ruffles our hair and the floor's so sticky it sucks at my boots. Whenever I move my head, a rich, clogging stench fills my nose.

'Urgh! What's that smell?' asks Crow.

'Shh!' says Pika with a quick glance up into the darkness of the stairway. He gets onto his knees and scrabbles around with his fingers, looking for something. 'Come on,' he mutters under his breath. Finally, as the footsteps above us grow louder, he finds an iron ring and hauls on it, until a wooden trapdoor yawns open in the ground. He ushers me through.

I lower myself into the space but I can't feel the ground underneath my boots. I frown up at Pika.

'Your fall will be broken,' he hisses. 'Let go!'

'What? Why should I—'

'Let go!'

I do as he says.

My belly flies into my mouth.

Greasy air rushes over my skin.

Rough walls scrape against me.

I'm falling.

Falling.

I'm falling for much too long, deep into the mountain. Then I land with a squelch. The foul stink has swelled to fill the world.

'Mouse!' comes a faint, urgent call. I roll just in

time, as the bundle that is my brother comes hurtling through the air and lands in a tower of sticky white goo. Sparrow bursts into a snotty laugh. 'Can I have another go?'

I pull him out of the way and after a few beats Pika and Crow drop out of the sky, landing with a *squelch*.

Pika looks up. 'I tried to press a sealing rune into the trapdoor as we fell, but I don't think it worked.'

My gut heaves and bubbles with sickness at the stench of the dung we're flailing in.

Then there's a shout from the trapdoor above.

'Go!' I yell.

Crow pulls Sparrow onto his back and we tear through the cavern, towards the sound of draggles. My boots slide on the slippery white stuff and I have to steady myself against the jagged cave walls. Ent long before my fingers are grazed and bleeding.

We reach the main cave and I feel my jaw grow slack.

15
Trespass

Thick orangey-brown shapes hang from the roof of the cave like hairy ropes. Draggles. Hundreds of them. *Clamp teeth, sup blood,* chatter the beasts in their sleep. *Hollow guts, slither, scurry. No hiding.*

To our right, the cave yawns open into a void of endless sky.

'Into the tack room, quick.' Pika leads us into a cluttered nook off the main cave. I stare at rows of saddles, coiled whips and stacks of boots with gleaming spurs.

Sparrow trots around, touching everything he can lay his good hand on until Pika holds him still. 'We'll find a ladder and choose a draggle,' he says, lifting a black saddle from a hook. 'I'll saddle it for you and then you'll be on your way.'

Pika leans out of the door, watching a warden guarding the cave mouth. 'Now!' he says, as her head lolls in sleep.

But we've barely taken ten paces when Lunda's

sprinting down the passageway towards us. Her lips quirk into a sneer. Behind her, Pangolin cries out. 'I'm drowning in this stuff! Wait for me!'

I grab Sparrow and we run through slippery white draggle dung, Crow on our heels. We head for a ladder that teeters skyward between the matted orange pelts of the snoozing draggles.

'Out of our way, Pika!' screams Lunda behind us.

Metal *sings* in the dank gloom. I glance behind me. Pika has drawn his sword.

I help Sparrow onto the ladder, then haul myself after him, struggling with my longbow. Crow clambers on behind us and we squeeze between the tightly packed draggles. Sparrow's climbing is painful-slow and proper awkward, cos of his sling.

Curious green eyes snap open as we pass. We're waking them up – dread traces its cold spear-point along my belly and chest. What if we spook them? They shuffle, fur pressing tighter around us. My hands brush long, fleshy snouts. Strings of drool drip off bared brown teeth, landing on our heads.

'Wait,' pants Crow. 'We'll be smothered if we try to get all the way up there. Come back. I've got a better idea.'

I look down at him. Crow roots in his cloak pocket and pulls out a vial of what looks like blood.

'What's that for?' I spit out a mouthful of rancid fur.

He looks up at me, startled. 'If I ain't got energy to change, the . . . blood lends it to me.' He looks away, jaw flickering. 'Need it more than ever after that potion they made me drink.'

'How do I know you ent just gonna fly off and leave us here?' I hiss stupidly, before I can stop myself. The sounds of the battle between Pika and Lunda are muffled by the stinking press of fur.

He shoots me a frustrated look. 'Would you *stop* pushing me away? Anyway, now ain't the time!' Then he smears stripes of blood from the vial onto his cheeks, and pushes his hands against the air – they fade in and out of sight with every beat of my heart, like he's pushed through a gap into another world.

I can see the edges of him pulling and squeezing and blurring, his face lengthening and his arms shortening, glossy black feathers sprouting all over him, clothes shrinking into the enchantment, becoming wings and scaly legs. His sword becomes a silver feather, bright against all the black. But it all happens in a beat – a fold – between this world and some other. Time slows.

A shudder ripples through me. He wheels past our faces, up to the roof of the cave. I pull Sparrow back down the ladder, willing the draggles to stay asleep. We huddle among hanging vines of filthy orange fur.

Then a draggle pulls free from the flock and flexes

her wings. Crow must've untied her. She swoops down and stands at the cave mouth. *Day hunt? Hunt?* she asks, chatter quivering with puzzlement.

The warden's disappeared. She must've gone to raise the alarm.

A dark shape zooms towards me and Crow's emerging bigger and closer from the murk, quicker than I'd expected. He gestures with a wing that's still changing back to an arm draped in his stained black cloak. Slowly the black feathers shrink into his skin and his face broadens, the yellow beak sucking back and back like a tide, until the boy stands in front of us. 'Quick!' he croaks, voice still half a bird's caw.

But behind us, the other draggles begin to unfurl their wings with a *slick* and a *click*. They start squabbling and shrieking, and I cover my ears, sickened by the rolling stink of the place and the blood-hungry beast-chatter.

'Over there!' yells Pangolin.

Pika stumbles towards us, a trickle of blood weaving past his ear. 'Go! I can't hold them off!'

I grab his sleeve. 'Come with us!'

But he turns away from me, bringing up his sword to block Pangolin. 'Go!'

I heave Sparrow onto the draggle's back and Crow and me leap on behind him. Lunda grabs my ankle but

I kick her away.

Flyflyfly draggle-beast! I scream. *Hunt!* And then the wind's burning my cheeks as the draggle swoops from the mouth of the cave. The cold is like an ice-axe in my chest. I pull my raindrop cowl up and over my face.

The draggle wheels away from the cave underneath Hackles. Far below, the black streak of the Iron Valley waits to catch our bones. I can sniff another storm brewing.

Foodwherefindyellinsectspritehunthunthunt! shouts the draggle.

The mountains gather close, each one jagged, dark, cracked; a cluster of cut-throat peaks, touched by last light. They are a grey slap. A drumbeat shock to my marrow. Suddenly I know why Kestrel couldn't leave their grip. Heart-fright for her and Pika storms my bones and I curse that wretched Protector and her Spearwarriors.

Above us, terrodyls circle, and fright shoots through me. They've flown away from the cave. What if Stag's still controlling them?

My sky-sickness writhes in my gut like an eel. *Thaw-Wielder!* I bellow to the sky. *Where are you?*

Pooled around the mountain's feet lie inky bogs that creep and crawl with shifting mist; I catch a glimpse when the cloud thins. The draggle bucks, beast-chatter

141

terrified into a gaggle of nonsense. Crow yells, struggling to keep his feet tucked onto her back.

Hold steady, draggle-beast!

But she's panicking, tipping off balance, flying too fast then too slow, trying to throw us off. We zoom lower, the bogs rushing up beneath us.

'Let go!' shouts Crow, and he flings himself off the draggle's back into the black bog. My foot is caught in a tangle of fur and I'm dragged along, head upside down. Sparrow's terrified face appears over the side of the draggle, staring towards me. 'Get back here!' he demands.

What Black-Hair do NOW? shrills Thunderbolt, buzzing outraged moon-sparks into the air.

Then I wrench myself free and slip into the edge of the bog, *cracking* through a layer of ice. A heartbeat later and I'd have been smashed on the rocks. The draggle rights herself and flits around overhead, with Sparrow still hunkered on her back, clutching a fistful of orange fur and screaming like a mad thing, Thunderbolt riding in his hair.

Squidges scull around, gobbling frozen bog myrtle and moaning about the cold.

Hurtteethfreezebrainowowowowow!

'Over here!' calls Crow from my right, but he's hidden in fog.

I try to swim towards his voice but the inky gloop is

sticky as tar, sucking me down. Crow grabs my hand and tries to drag me towards him. We're alone, struggling in the bog, our clothes and hair dragging, under the looming spines of Hackles. Inky shapes writhe and twist, pulling us down.

Then I sense movement and jerk my head up. Two purple circles glow towards us through the fog. Crow's hand tenses in mine. He must've seen it too. Behind the fire straggles a cloaked figure, shoving against the wind. Balls of purple fire sit in the figure's palms.

'Sparrow!' I yell. 'Help us!' But there's no answer, and in the depths of the bog, skinny fingers wrap around my ankle.

Then there's a new noise. The steady beat of strong wings. An orange shape thrums towards us through the gloom.

Kestrel stands tall on a draggle's back, twirling daggers in her fingers. She utters a war-cry and sends the blades whistling through the air, straight into the bog.

Something screams, and the painful grip on my ankle eases. I swim through the ink for the bank. Crow follows. The figure in the mist pauses, watching, a red cloak billowing around its thin frame.

Kestrel swoops low, leading Sparrow's draggle as well as her own. I leap into the air, grasp fistfuls of orange fur and haul myself onto Sparrow's draggle. Crow wrenches himself out of the bog and onto the same draggle as Kestrel. His cheeks burn red as he's forced to hold onto her waist to stay put.

I kick a slimy tendril from my boot as we're lifted up and away into the sky. In front of me, Sparrow sobs into the draggle's furry neck.

'Never stray near the bogs when the fog comes!' gasps Kestrel.

I nod dumbly, thoughts still on that figure in the fog. Whoever it was, they had the red cloak of a mystik and purple lightning like Sparrow's.

Suddenly a graceful bolt of striped feathers swoops through the snow-filled sky. *Thaw!* Hope burns in my chest.

Battlehugewingcreakybatthingleavetwolegsalone! she screeches furiously.

Thaw! It's all right, she's saving us!

She's too spooked by the draggles to come close, but she glides alongside us, wings strong and powerful, eyes wide and bright in the dusk.

Kestrel cries a command to the draggles and then we're lifting up and away from the bog, heading north towards the Wildersea.

Below us, the shadows of two giant draggles and one sea-hawk are black and huge enough to blanket herds of grazing reindeer in darkness.

'Let's go and find Yapok!' calls Kestrel.

But all I can think about is the figure battling towards us across the mountain. Could it have been one of Stag's mystiks? Has he sent them to hunt me?

It can't be – how could he know I was trapped in that sealed-off place?

I hunch on the draggle's back, willing it to fly faster, and check my pockets for the Opal and Da's carving of the *Huntress*. They're both there, but something else is, too.

I pull out the rolled scrap of skin I prised from the wall of my prison cell. The grey surface is cool to touch, smooth, and flecked with patches of light pink. It's dried fish skin – I ent sure what kind of fish but I reckon it's freshwater, not salt. I turn it over in my hands. On the underside is a scrawled mess of runes, but they're torn through like the skin was quickly ripped. Who hid this in the wall, and what does it mean?

Suddenly Kestrel shouts and pulls on the reins, her draggle dodging a frozen cloud. Our draggle dodges, too, but I almost lose my balance. 'Careful!' squeals Sparrow.

I stuff the fish skin back into my pocket and let out a tight, shaky breath. We escaped the Protector of the Mountain. I gift a chestful of heart-thanks to all the sea-gods that I never left Sparrow behind in the clutches of that old babbler. And Kestrel found the heart-strength to leave the mountain. I glance across the sky at her and grin. She's crouched low on her draggle, head twitching sharply to left and right as she keeps watch, messy braids streaming behind her and thumping Crow in the face.

Maybe now we can get back on track, and search for the Sky-Opal.

Hope glows in my chest as we streak north-east through the sky.

PART 2

Hidden Places

16
Bedraggled

Steaming pools of blue-grey water glint on the foothills of the mountain below. Riding a draggle is proper different from riding a terrodyl. The draggle's body pings up and down in the air, her wings grasping the wind and flinging it down past our ears, then hurling it back up again. It takes all my strength to grip her furry back.

A velvet-blue night thickens around us. We follow a star that Kestrel watches fiercely. When we lose sight of it she tuts and scolds, searching and weaving until it shows again, a bright chip of light in the dark.

In between bulks of frozen cloud, faint green-pink fire spirits emerge. The colours gleam deep inside the sky, like the flecks deep within the Opal. As I watch them, the spirits curl to make the shape of Rattlebones. In my bones she's begging me again. *Help us!*

Sparrow sings, the blue notes of his song drifting past our faces and bumping against rocks so we don't crash into them. It reminds me of how the whales guided the *Huntress* to keep us safe. 'Thank you, Sparrow!' calls Kestrel. 'You are so helpful!'

He shrugs awkwardly and keeps singing lines from battle songs.

'How is the pain?' she asks.

'A bit better!' he sings. Reckon even if the pain was bad he'd still sing, though. Nothing stops him spilling notes.

'If it worsens, tell me,' she says, keeping her gaze fixed on the star.

'What happened back there, with them nightmares? You had the shakes again?' I ask Sparrow.

He don't answer at first, so I pinch him under his ribs and he jabs back at me with his good elbow. 'I ent been shaking, don't think, but the nightmares are even worserer than ever. I've seen faces stuck right under the ice. Horrid scaly tails. Eye sockets, all dark. Burning houses and burning boats – that one's the most real.'

'It ent—'

'It *is* real, I *know* it's real! Why don't you ever believe me? I keep seeing monsters prowling in the corners and it ent just when I'm sleepy, but sometimes when I'm wide awake.'

'That's just cos they took Thunderbolt away,' I tell him. I watch the back of his yellow head, how all the hair's bunched into filthy tangles, and wish I could've kept him much, much safer than this.

'Why can't we go home?' he whines at me. 'I hate it up in the sky.'

'We just can't. Not yet.'

'Ent Grandma looking for us, though? You're gonna be in big trouble!'

I shut my eyes and weep silent tears that turn to ice on my cheeks. When he asks again I pretend to be asleep.

Thaw-Wielder's plucked the heart-strength to get near the draggles, now. She nests herself on Kestrel's head, moon-bathing. When she twitches to look at me, her eyes are wide and shining with wildness.

We fly through the night, until I'm sore and starved.

Kestrel makes us change course to dodge hunting packs of terrodyls. 'And if draggle-riders do follow, I don't want to lead them straight to Yapok. A wiggling route is better.' She grips her draggle with her toes, rummages in her bag and passes each of us a snowy mooncake. I wolf mine down, then have to watch Sparrow eat his in bites so tiny I want to scream.

The air turns to filthy gloop as we pass over the billowing funnels of Nightfall, the great Land Tribe city of smog where scholars go for book-learning. Even all the way up here I can hear the cogs and wheels and engines clanking. I think back to what Egret and Kestrel said about it. What's the good of a learning place that not everyone is allowed to go to? Scorn burns my chest. Stag must've brought them stupid land-lurking ideas with him when he said women shouldn't be captains.

'We can rest here,' says Kestrel. 'The draggles need to hunt.'

The draggles drop us off on a huge chimney on the outermost edge of Nightfall. Below us spreads the thick green silence of a vast forest. The beasts circle away from us to hunt among the evergreens. Thaw goes with them, the night gulping her fast. When the moon gets blotted out by black smoke, it feels like anything could be out there, skin-close, and we'd never know.

Kestrel fishes about in her bag, then flings a rippling square of black cloth over us. When it settles over our shoulders, my muscles begin to warm. Crow pulls it further over him and I glare, snatching some of it back. Sparrow snuggles into my armpit. We lean against the stone funnel. Under the quiet moon, my eyes grow heavy. The funnel belches out thick yellow smog.

Later, I'm pulled out of a doze by murmuring voices. 'You and Egret,' whispers Crow. 'Are you?'

'What?' says Kestrel.

'You know.'

'Do I?' she snaps. Then she snickers. 'You can't even

say it.'

I open my eyes and pull a gruesome face. 'What you two babbling on about?'

Crow winces. 'You wouldn't understand.'

'Ha! So much rudeness in one child,' Kestrel tells him.

A slap of shame splays across Crow's face, and he turns away.

Kestrel unscrews a bottle, and the sweet steam of spiced goat's milk touches my nose. When she tries to pass a cup to Crow, he keeps his arms folded and pretends sleep, so me, her and Sparrow drink the milk and try to untangle our thoughts. She tells us how Egret helped her see sense about leaving, cos she'd never have survived the night if she'd stayed. How Egret's gonna be safe for now, cos the draggle-riders need her rune-magyk. How what *I* said about her ma spouting lies helped her get the courage to leave the mountain. When she says that, I know it ent just the goat's milk warming me.

I try biting my tongue but the words spill out all the same. 'You'll never be allowed back, will you?'

'I don't want to go back to that place, sea-sister. Except to get Egret and Pika.'

'But it's your home, ent it?' says Sparrow. His voice catches on the word *home*, and it makes my chest ache.

'Not any more.' She rubs the ice from her brows. 'What if home's not a place, but with people?'

I nod, thinking of Bear and how he found our Tribe when his own was destroyed.

Soon sleep makes Sparrow lean heavily against me. Crow sits with his legs crossed at the ankle, snoring.

'What d'you reckon will happen when we get to this Yapok boy?' I whisper.

Kestrel links her arm through mine and leans her cheek on my hair. 'Honestly, I cannot say. He was apprenticed to care for books when he was your brother's age, a few years before they were banned. When they were burned, he helped try to save them. He put himself in so much danger. I only hope we find him safe. He hasn't replied to my latest letters.'

'When did you last get word from him?'

She hesitates. 'Five full moons ago.'

'*Five?*'

'Please, after all that's happened, no doubts,' she begs.

I let out my breath, and nod. 'How do you know where to find him?'

'His letters always came to me by berg owl, and the owls followed the same star-path we're following now. He always said the owls preferred to roost amongst his quiet, away from the other Wilderwitches. So if we follow them, maybe they'll lead us to him.'

Her words prickle me with wonder. 'How do you know him?'

'When I had eleven moons the war worsened and my mother cut off all outside contact. The Sky-Tribes were severed. I had a group of Wilderwitch friends, who I used to see at Sky-Tribe Meets and feast days, and I lost them all. But Yapok kept writing. He refused to give me up.' As she speaks, she feeds pieces of mooncake to Ettler, who quivers inside her cloak. And I know without her saying it that the old friendships, the lost ones, are like scars that never healed, and me being around has picked open the scabs, and she likes the pain a little bit.

I breathe the smell of night. 'Is flying like you remembered?' I whisper finally, as Crow snores.

She nods quickly. 'It is wondrous. But . . . nothing is quite like flying alone, in my bird-shape. I envy your Crow for that.'

My Crow. Hah. 'What happened?'

'After my father was hunted by a terrodyl, Mother became over protective. She had a clip fitted to my arm, to try to stop me shape-changing. But I changed even though it was painful, and I flew even though the clip made me clumsy. When a terrodyl came, I was too hindered by the clip to fly away from it.' Suddenly she looks straight into my face, and I flinch at the rawness there, as though her own skin has been peeled off, layer by layer. 'No one except Egret understood my wish to travel beyond-the-mountain.' More feathers have broken through and little bulbs of blood roll down her cheeks. 'Until I met you.'

We let our bones rest, the smoke-tinged night brushing our faces. 'I love this night-silence,' Kestrel murmurs sleepily.

I try to imagine proper silence, but it's so hard. Cos even now there's beast-chatter drifting up from the forest far below and wafting from Ettler and peeping from Thunderbolt's moondreams.

'You're lucky,' whispers Kestrel suddenly, making me jump.

She leans forwards and it's like half of her wants to hit me, and the other wants to scoop me into a hug. 'If I had a chance to be a captain – to be a real leader, make real changes . . . I'd take it in both fists and I wouldn't let go,' she tells me, eyes burning into mine. A flash of anger burns inside me. Cos I won't be captain now, I *can't* be. But then she gifts me a bright, hopeful grin, and my anger fades. 'You can call me Kes, if you'd like.'

'All right. Kes.' The name tastes strange and clipped short on my tongue.

Then we sit, not knowing what else to say. I wait a beat, trying to untangle my thoughts. But her breathing lengthens as she drops into sleep.

In my dream I'm trudging through treacherous ice, following the paw-prints of a polar fox. I'm screaming for Da. The paw prints are speckled with drops of bright blood. Beneath the ice, the eyes of whales watch me and the hands of merwraiths beat and claw, trying to escape. If they die, he dies, throbs a voice.

I bolt awake, eyes damp with tears and chest sore with missing Da. Feels like I only slept for a few beats but the funnel has stopped belching and the smog has thinned. From far below comes a strange *click click click* that moves in and out of hearing. On one side of me, Kestrel breathes softly, hair tangled in her eyes. On my other side, Sparrow whimpers. Next to him, Crow's wrapped a scarf around his face and he's still snoring.

My heart settles as a gap chinks open in the clouds. A beam of pale light pokes out – a silvery strand like Grandma's hair caught in the wind. The fire spirits have started their dance, and they're seeking me out. Their pictures make me think of Sparrow's nightmares and my dream – eyes trapped beneath the ice.

I watch, chest aching, as the fire spirits tumble, closer to me than I've ever seen them, cos this is the first time I've been in the sky with them when they want to play.

The pale pinks and shimmering greens swirl to make the shapes of Ma and Da's namesake animals:

a snowshoe hare, kicking her spirit legs into the sky as she chases a polar fox into the tops of the distant trees.

I touch my dragonfly brooch for heart-strength. 'Ma,' I murmur, watching the hare and fox disappear. 'Where *is* Da? When can we have him back?'

I search the fire spirits for more signs but sudden doubt rattles through me. What if Stag's right, what if the spirits *are* just a clutter of lights in the sky? I remember the night I shot that terrodyl, when I searched the sky for signs of Da, and Sparrow said he weren't up there. I still ent no closer to knowing when I'll see him again. If he was here, he'd make me feel heart-glad with just a story and a belly-laugh.

He'd remind me about getting ready to gift my arrows to danger, too, so I push my thoughts away and reach into my pocket for a handful of the feathers shed by Thaw. When my hawk whizzes back to me, shaking the frost from her feathers, I ask her to gather some twigs from the forest. Then I dig out the arrowheads Egret gave me. When Thaw comes back, I use my dagger to whittle the wood into the right shape for an arrow-shaft, then set to fixing the arrowhead and the fletching using a thin length of sinew that I've sawn from the too-long ends of Bear's amber amulet. I work until I'm clutching a fistful of roughly made arrows.

I lift my hand to return the dagger to my belt, and jar Kestrel, waking her. I'm about to say sorry when the draggles wheel back to us and Kestrel stands and stretches up onto the balls of her feet, yawning.

'Ready?' she asks me, all aglow with thoughts of flying again, so I lean across and nudge Crow. His eyes flick open straight away, but Sparrow's his normal stubborn self and it takes all three of us and Thaw's wing-tips on his face to get him to wake up.

We ride on, the draggles dodging hail showers and chasing moon-bows. We're flying towards the sky-wolves that Kestrel's Tribe spend their days running from or trying to blow apart.

Maybe that's why I feel her joy at flying melt away, leaving tight, tense fear.

But inside *me*, there's something else. There's a hunger – a feeling of being pulled towards something wild, the memory of howling and the sky-wolves answering. I feel like I'm flying into a skyscape made of battle-howls and my blood zings with it.

We pass over a jagged shoreline of black sand and finally the Wildersea yawns below us. My heart aches all the way into my throat. Heart-sadness for our terrodyl wriggles through me again.

Sea-smoke rises from cracks in the ice far below. What if there are already whales getting trapped underneath? I sneak a hand into my pocket and grip the Opal. *I swear I'll get you back to your kin, and your rightful home*, I think at it. *Just please stop making the sea freeze solid 'til then!* But I know the Opal can't change a thing. It's nature's kin, and nature's been split into three parts that can't live without each other.

We fly deeper into the northern sea, past the sea-paths my ship once sailed. My heart jolts against my chest when through the shifting fog I glimpse a hulking fleet of ships far below. 'Look!' I call, pointing. 'The *Huntress* could be down there!'

Sparrow cranes his neck, then sighs irritably. 'Even with Thunderbolt I can't see that far! Is our ship there?'

A pang of horror at his ruined sight stirs in my chest. 'I don't know.'

A low rumble ripples through the air. The sky darkens like a bruise and spits ice. Then lightning splits it apart, and the draggles startle. 'We're flying into a storm!' yells Kes.

I make Sparrow lie as flat as he can along the draggle's back and put his hood up. Then I hold tight onto him and chatter to the draggle. *You can do this, brave thing. You're strong and bold. Fly steady, follow cave-mate!*

We're whipped and whirled and the thunder's like a drum beating hard enough to explode my chest. I flatten myself along Sparrow's back and press my hands over his ears to protect his hearing.

When we break through the storm, we've reached the depths of the Iceberg Forest and a frozen hush settles around us. Wonder seeps into my bones. The skinny sea-paths we sailed weren't even a hint of the wild tangle waiting deeper inside the Wildersea. The icebergs' flanks are wind-licked, so they look like they're wearing cloaks of blue-white fur. Old power rolls off them.

These icebergs clutch for the sky with sharp claws. One has a fringe of icicles like the baleen of a whale. Another has fins and gills and a jutting edge shaped like a whale's tail, unless that's just my home making me see pictures of the sea in the ice.

Close to the forest's heart we pause in front of a criss-crossing web of glowing pathways. They're round silver-grey tubes that spark between the icebergs, connecting them.

'What are they?' I gasp, spear-tip cold diving down my throat.

'Did you hear something?' says a woman's voice. I startle and look around – one of the tubes to our right is quivering with the echo of the words.

I meet Crow's eyes. He's sucked in his lower lip and we stare at each other, hardly daring to breathe.

'Where did that voice come from?' I whisper to

Kes, but she presses a finger to her lips and guides the draggles lower.

Sparrow sings softly under his breath, and Thunderbolt flicks his shimmering strands of song with her wings. I pinch him quiet. But then I see it – the swirl of grey bodies beneath the icy sea far below. Rattlebones said the whales listened to my message and fled the far north – what if Sparrow's whale-song brings them closer to danger again? My Tribe always pray for the sea-gods to swim close. But now I wish they'd swim far, far away.

I dig my fingers into thick draggle-fur. 'Kes,' I whisper. 'Where do the Wilderwitches live? Ent we gonna fly on?'

'Shhh,' she murmurs, staring at the top of a nearby iceberg that looks like a stooped old man, hunched high over the sea. She's sweating the stink of fear. How does she know her friend's still alive? And why would she look for him in this icescape?

Then a flurry of blue feathers streaks past, making our draggles whimper and veer to the right. There's a tiny parp of ink as Ettler, hidden in Kestrel's bag, gets frighted by the movement. The berg owls whirr out of sight, before I can ask for help.

'Sour dratted milk!' Kestrel curses, startling me. Her voice is muffled by a *crack* and *splinter* as a streak of cloud freezes and shatters down over our heads. I

raise my arm to shield my head. *Thaw!* I lift my hood and my hawk swoops in underneath the folds of cloth, shaking icicles from her wings and croaking her heart-worry into my ear.

Kestrel watches one of the silver-grey pulsing tubes. 'That way, I think?' She nudges her draggle closer and stares into it. Our draggle follows. Kes reaches out a finger and jerks it back again. 'Ugh! It's like – touching something that should be secret. A dream, or – a bone.' She shivers.

When I touch the tube, it reminds me of a strand of whale-song – like cold, sticky silk. The tube twists away towards an opening in the top of the iceberg, carrying a bundle of blue feathers inside it. Kes puts her face near the tube. 'Yapok?' she asks. The silvery pathway throbs where her voice touches it and pulses along, like an eel swallowing a crab. She presses her hands over her mouth as *YapokYapokYapok* is carried through the sky, and into the top of the iceberg. She lifts her shocked eyes to us and then there's a wrenching *crunch*.

I spin around in the saddle. In the very top of the iceberg, shrouded by wisps of cloud, a hidden window whines open, showering us with icicles.

A boy with a squashed-looking face and wooden goggles pokes his head out. 'Shut up!' he whispers anxiously.

Shock whips through me and a thousand questions thud in my throat. What's a boy doing *inside* an iceberg? I remember sailing through the Iceberg Forest, the night I shot that polar dog, and my bones-deep feeling that the icebergs held secrets. But I'd thought the only things living here were berg owls.

The draggles swoosh closer to the berg, up into the cloud. The air's even thinner than it was at Hackles, and my head whirls. 'Yapok?' hisses Kestrel. 'It's me!'

'I don't know any *me*. What do you want with Yapok?'

Kestrel peels back her raindrop armour.

The boy lifts his goggles, revealing red-rimmed blue eyes. He rests them in his shock of spiky brown hair. His nose is bent, his skin is blotched and his brows look like they're brawling for space. He squints. '*Kestrel?*'

17
Yapok's Iceberg

The bright lantern-eyes of berg owls peer at us from cracks in the ice. 'We coming in, or what?' I call.

'Keep your voices down,' pleads Kestrel. 'And hurry up, Yapok, let us in!'

The boy glances over his shoulder and back at us. 'I can't.'

'But we've come so far.' Kestrel sounds close to tears.

I fix my eyes on the boy. 'You ent got a clue what she's been through to get here! I could tell you the story, or let my dagger tell it. Your choice.'

Kes gives a startled laugh and Crow grins over at me. Yapok's narrowed eyes flick to my face and away again. 'Be quick! And get rid of those creatures.' Then he ducks out of sight, his hair brushing snow off the top of the window. But he leaves it cracked open.

Kestrel grapples with our draggles, trying to get us close enough to climb inside. 'You go ahead,' she tells us. 'I'll send the draggles to roost and then join you.'

Crow's the closest so he takes Sparrow from me and posts him through, then wriggles headfirst through the narrow opening, turning and twisting to get his shoulders in. Then his sun-bleached boots disappear inside, and there's a thud and a yelp and a shout.

I push my longbow ahead of me and force my body over the thick edge of ice. The cold whispers against my lips.

Then I'm tumbling forwards into a huge ice-cave. I land on a squashy old chair with stuffing spilling out. I peel back my raindrop cowl and warm my eyelashes between my fingers, to melt the ice that's trying to seal my eyes shut.

There are burrows tunnelled into the walls and owls huddle inside, watching.

Sleeppeepsnoozesnugglefeedwormswormsfishesiccccciclesss. They fluff their feathers and stretch their necks up and down.

Thaw pokes her head out of my cloak and watches them suspiciously. *Istheysaidworms? Fishes?*

I stroke her head. *We'll find some for you soon.* I struggle to my feet, but then I'm flailing like a mad thing, cos the floor's solid ice.

A blanket-filled hammock is strung between the walls. Cloaks and tunics are hung from hooks and a

166

battered black kettle sits in a small hearth.

Kestrel lands behind me and puts her healer's bag down on the floor. Ettler pokes his squidgy, feathered head out of the bag and then topples out of it onto the ice, screaming about the cold and farting ink everywhere. 'So this is where you live!' Kestrel's eyes sweep the cave.

Yapok glides towards us on creaky leather boots with skating blades fixed to the soles. 'You brought strangers.' Behind his words lurks a question he don't need to ask. *How could you?*

Kestrel stares at him, nibbling her lip. Then she seizes him in a hug. 'I've dreamed of this since we were first separated!' she says. Hisses seep from the folds of Yapok's white cloak.

He stands back from Kes, red in the face, and opens his cloak to let out a bundle of berg owls that flap away, squeaking angrily. Then he hurries back to the window we crawled through and uses a long wooden pole to swing it closed. He spins to stare at us. 'Who are you, and why are you here? Did anyone follow you?'

'This is Mouse, and Crow, and Sparrow,' says Kestrel, gesturing to each of us in turn. 'My mother was going to execute them for nothing more than straying into her territory. I spoke up for them and lost my home. You're our only friend beyond Hackles – we have nowhere else to go. No one has followed us.' She ducks as a bolt of blue light shoots from the wall, skimming the top of her head – a berg owl. Another one pops its rumpled face out of a hole in the wall, takes off and swoops overhead, its frosty blue feathers showering us with slivers of ice. 'Will you help us?' asks Crow.

Yapok flares his nostrils, watching the window we came from. 'I will hide you, because you're Kestrel's friends – hiding things is what I'm best at.' He plunks pairs of worn leather skates at our feet. 'Hopefully one or two might fit. Pull them on over your own boots, and then come with me.'

'Thank you, Yapok!' Kestrel's shoulders sag. 'Thank you so much!'

I reach down to pick up a skate – it's shaped from age-softened walrus skin and a rusty blade is fixed to the sole. A memory trickles through me. 'Da once took me to a midwinter Tribe-Meet,' I tell them. 'I remember folks rushing round and round on these things, but when I tried it I fell, scraped my head open and never wanted to try it again.'

Crow's watching me with such bubbling mirth that I feel my cheeks grow warm. 'So what you're *saying* is, there's something you ain't too good at?'

'Clam your pipes, land-lurker,' I spit.

'Well, you won't get far around here without skates,'

says Yapok, rubbing at a patch of flaky skin on his hand.

Sparrow giggles. 'She won't get better – she's the worst at skating!'

I scowl. 'You weren't even born when I tried!'

'So what?' he huffs. 'Grandma told me all about it – just ask her!'

Hollow guilt rattles through me again. Heart hammering, I stoop to pull on the skates. Once I've laced the boots I stand, wobbling like mad. Kestrel does the same, and I help Sparrow with his. Then Yapok leads us towards the hearth. Kestrel tows Sparrow along on his skates.

Yapok gets us crowded in a circle around the kettle and makes us hold hands. Me and Crow pull faces at each other. Then Yapok slides his fingers behind the mantelpiece and there's a loud click. 'Hold tight!'

We're whipped round in a circle and flung into the space behind the hearth.

I blink the dizziness from my eyes, and my breath catches in my chest as I tip my head back and stare. We're standing in a cavern deep inside the iceberg, with round glass lanterns hanging from the ceiling. Wisps of whale-song swim inside them, sparking blue light over icicles longer than daggers. All around the walls tower shelves packed with books, their spines a mix of colours, some gleaming with gold lettering. Tables and shelves are stocked with scrolls in bottles. Dark pathways are cut deeper into the iceberg, and when I crane my neck I see that they're filled with even more bookshelves.

'There are so many books!' I exclaim. Then I hold my breath, listening hard. When I said the word books, it's like faint voices started to mutter and growl.

'Are there?' whispers Sparrow. 'With stories and everything? Can you read them to me?'

Yapok plucks at his hair. '*No one* touches the books!' He shakes stray owls from his cloak. They wheel away towards another of the silver-grey tubes we saw outside the iceberg, flickering on the ceiling. When the owls draw close they're sucked inside and pulsed through a hole in the ice.

Slowly, we peel ourselves away from each other and move into the cave. I hold onto the wall to stay upright on my skates, and Kes keeps hold of Sparrow's good hand, whispering things to him that make him giggle.

Hung between the lanterns is a hammock, and nested in the hammock is a husk of an old man. His long silver hair spills over the edges of the hammock and trails over the floor. His chest flutters and his lungs crackle as he rasps long, irregular breaths. His eye sockets are ancient hollows and his clothes are scattered with owl pellets.

'He's a human cobweb,' whispers Crow.

'He's a wisp,' I murmur.

Yapok blows out his cheeks. 'He is the Skybrarian, and will be treated with due respect!' he scolds.

The old Skybrarian mutters and turns over in his sleep, and Yapok freezes. He presses a finger to his lips. 'The Skybrarian is sleeping,' he whispers. 'You have to be quiet.'

Kes stares around her, eyes brightening. Somewhere close by, drums beat and a book inches towards the edge of its shelf. Yapok rushes to catch it and push it back.

'So the books *were* saved!' marvels Kestrel, turning in circles.

'What is this place?' asks Crow.

'A hidden Skybrary – the only one in Wildersea,' Yapok whispers. 'No one knows about it, except the Skybrarian and me. It's every Sky-Tribe manuscript he saved before the burning. He brought them to this iceberg and hid them, then dug deeper into the cave to make a home to live in and protect the books. I am his apprentice. I hide in plain sight, among the other Wilderwitches. But I try not to draw even a speck of attention to myself!'

'Yapok, I am so sorry,' says Kestrel. 'But I didn't know. You stopped answering my letters.'

He nods slowly, then sighs. 'I've been busy.'

'Can you help me learn to skate?' I ask Crow.

Crow grins, eyes flooding with golden light. 'Aye!' Then he's off, gliding fast with an ease that makes my jaw grow slack. 'Race yer!' he cries. 'C'mon, it's easy. One foot in front of the other, build up a rhythm.'

'Please, be careful!' calls Yapok. 'And keep quiet, even in here. We don't want to make any sky-wolves' ears twitch. They may be nearby!'

Crow turns to skate backwards, sticking his hands in his pockets and winking at me as he passes.

My feet move forwards and my body flails backwards and my arms start to paddle frantically. 'This ent possible!'

Crow almost cracks a rib laughing. 'Use your belly muscles and your arms for balance,' he tells me. 'Stick near the walls—'

'Not my shelves!' interrupts Yapok.

Crow ignores him. 'And that way you can grab on if you start to wobble.'

'Don't worry, I flaming will!' In spite of everything, skating is – *fun*, and even thinking that word shocks me.

We skate round and round the edges of the cave. I can't stop laughing, even when I fall onto my hands and have to scramble up again, but every time we loop back and pass Kestrel and Yapok their voices have grown more strained.

Kes's voice is scratched by heart-sadness. 'How can we stop the war when no one's known the Sky-Tribes exist for a hundred years? We need to forge connections with other Tribes.'

Yapok lifts his eyebrows but before he can talk Kestrel keeps going. 'The hearth-fires have lain cold too long. The Sky-Tribes must unite with each other, and then with the world.' There's a pureness to her *unite*, like she's struck a small bell.

When the boy only studies a patch of flaky skin on his palm, she sighs. 'You seem different with me, Yapok. It's like you hardly remember our friendship.'

Suddenly I'm pitching sideways into a shelf leaning and groaning under the weight of thick manuscripts. An owl darts from its burrow, chattering angrily around a beak stuffed with little black ice-worms.

'No!' Yapok lunges after me, grabbing at my cloak.

A book slips to the floor and Yapok gasps. 'Nonononono, didn't I say not to touch anything?' The cover turns bumpy, like a rash spreading across skin. Then it froths and hisses and spits. When I pick it up, the book sucks at my fingertips and I jerk back with a startled yell.

Yapok shoves me out of the way. He plucks at the air above the book like he's playing the strings of a harp, and a snarling creature is revealed, gripping the crinkled pages. Sweat breaks out across Yapok's brow. Then he sneezes and the creature melts back into the cover, leaving an angry, sizzling blotch in the middle. 'Most books have secrets hidden amongst their runes, and my monsters guard them,' pants Yapok. 'The monsters need to be subdued before the books can be disturbed, otherwise the pages will be damaged. So *please* take care.' He glares at me.

Crow swishes to my side, stops with a shower of ice and nudges me in the ribs. 'Loony,' he mouths, eyeing Yapok. Then he slumps into a squashy chair, sticks his legs out over one of its arms and belches, startling an owl.

Ooooooohh meanpricklingboy! it scolds.

I press my fist to my mouth to stopper a belly-laugh.

Yapok stows the book back on the shelf. He yanks off his goggles and throws them onto a chair. I can see the fright shining in his eyes. He jabs the tip of his skate into the wall, getting redder and redder in the face but still not saying anything. Then he erupts.

'Right – would you all please study the rules.' He points to the back of the room, where a list is tacked above a table piled with books with broken spines. *Rules for Skybrarians.* 'There are no visitors' rules, because, ah, we have never had any, so I'd thank you to be directed to the Skybrarian's rules.'

Keep the Skybrary secret
Remember, the books are sensitive
No running, jumping, or shouting
No folding pages or bending spines
No unnecessary talking
No tea near the books
No writing in the books
No tampering
Wear gloves
If in doubt, consult the owls

'No tampering with what?' Kes asks.

'Anything!' replies Yapok.

Seeing the list pinned up like that makes me think of how Grandma scribbled notes and stuck them in her medsin-lab. 'You got somewhere for him to rest?' I ask Yapok, jerking my thumb at Sparrow. I want to get him away from the others and tell him what I have to tell him before the guilt and horror tear me to pieces.

'Ugh, people,' Yapok grumbles. 'With all their people-needs.'

I stare at him.

'I ent got *people-needs*,' says Sparrow, flushing angry blotches.

'Oh, really? You seen the state of you?' I ask.

'The spindly child can have a hammock if he must,'

says Yapok with a heavy sigh. 'There is a sleeping loft.'

'I don't wanna go up there!' complains Sparrow.

'I need to talk to you, alone.'

'Why?' He wrinkles his nose.

'Sea-Tribe stuff. None of this lot would understand.' That shuts him up. I can feel Kes's eyes on me, but I don't look at her as I bundle Sparrow away. I realise how scrawny he is and how filthy all of us must be.

We step into a rickety iron cage, and Yapok winds a crank to hoist us to the upper level of the Skybrary.

When we reach the top we're in a circular sleeping loft closed in by the uppermost rows of bookshelves. Sparrow clambers into a hammock and burrows into the blankets, suddenly beaming like he's heart-glad he came up here after all. And I'm about to smash his heart-gladness to splinters.

When I sit next to him I reach for his hand under the blankets and grip it. 'Sparrow—'

'Ugh, what you doing – get off!' he whinges, trying to prise my fingers away.

'Gods, all right then. Thought you might want some comfort or – forget it, I ent your flaming ma.' I roll my eyes as soon as the words are out, cos once again I'm remembering the fight we had in our cabin.

'No, you ent.'

Thunderbolt watches me from the top of his head.

Keeptrykeeptry, Yellow-Hair frighted.

I know, I tell her. I suck in my bottom lip and hide my face in my hands, the sweating and sickness starting again.

'Sparrow,' I start. His sour breath hits me in the face. My eyes ache and my throat's raw.

'Spit it out!' he warbles. A dark wisp of whale-song curls from his lips. It's lost the brightness it had at sea and a prickle of homesickness spikes my throat.

I pinch the whale-song out of the air and stretch it between my fingers. 'There's something you need to know.'

He peers at the space next to me, digging his little finger into his ear to scoop out a plug of ear wax. 'What?'

Horror creeps through my blood and curls my tongue tight behind my teeth. 'You've missed a lot of stuff since—' My words crash into the room. I swallow against the rock in my gullet. My voice trails away. Since what? Since Crow smuggled him off our ship, doing Stag's dirty work? Since I betrayed him by saying I hated him for Ma dying giving birth to him?

Then the words spill out in a sea-tumble.

'Sparrow, when they took you, I was asleep. I'd almost drowned.'

'You almost *drowned*? But Grandma says you can't

177

drown cos of being born in the caul.'

'I know, I'm saying I *didn't*, ent I? A merwraith found me before I could put the not-drowning to the test.'

'Ooooh, really?' He bounces in the hammock, hawk-keenness lighting up his face.

My voice is barely a breath. Somewhere below I can hear the others chattering. 'And when I woke up that wretched blather-blubber, Stag, was in our cabin.' My throat closes and I cough it open and keep going. 'But you weren't there and I got such a fear creeping over me.' Tears splosh onto my stitches, and the salt stings. 'And Grandma weren't there neither.'

'She was out looking for me, stupid! You don't have to *cry* about it.'

I shake my head. 'I flaming do have to cry about it, slackwit.' I'd give anything not to have to say the next bit. Cos then it wouldn't be true, and I'd finally wake up, in our cabin, with Grandma bossing me to tar the ropes. But it is true, and he needs to know.

I lean closer, propping my chin on his damp forehead, my tears spilling into his hair, my lips struggling to form words around the loss of her, that thing hulks like a shadowy monster inside me. 'Stag took over our ship, calling himself *captain*.' I spit the word. 'And then he killed her. He killed Grandma.' My sobs echo off the walls and I can't breathe, I'm being crushed under this weight. 'I couldn't get to her. I couldn't help her.'

Purple fire begins to crackle in Sparrow's good hand. There's a beat, a sudden hush, the space that waits for his song to fill it widening around us. The song that can make a map. But instead of singing, he fills his stunned-fish silence with a sudden, echoing sob that makes me flinch. Then he kneels up, lifts his good arm and starts hurling lightning around the ice-cave.

He blasts a small round hole in the wall. The ice crashes out and the wind whips through, stinging my eyes. A tendril of lightning weaves through and joins to the lightning in his palms. 'Sparrow! Stop!'

There's a squeal of frenzied cranking as the metal cage sways into the room and Kestrel and Crow burst out.

Then Yapok flies up the slope as fast as his skates can carry him, puffing and wheezing and batting owls out of his way. 'Stop!' he cries. 'Someone in the next iceberg might hear!'

A spot of glowing light burns through the pocket of my cloak and lands in the hammock, fizzling – the Opal is being pulled towards my brother by a vine of lightning. Sparrow smashes a whole shelf full of glass bottles and blasts a lamp into a thousand slivers. I try to pick the Opal up and snatch back my hand with a yelp. Then I grab a piece of bedding and wrap the gem in it before it can burn a hole in the floor. Yapok stares at the glowing bundle of cloth, and I can't make out his expression.

Sparrow burns a table into a pile of ashen splinters. Everyone's running for cover, crawling on hands and knees to hide.

Finally I wrestle my brother's arm down by his side. His fingers are charred and his sobs are hot and endless.

'We'll run wild along our deck again,' I whisper. 'Promise.'

But he just pulls away from me and turns to face the wall.

18
Tea and Books and Butterballs

I leave Sparrow sleeping and make my way back down to the lower floor. The cold reaches up through my boots to the top of my head. I stare around, and startle when I see the old Skybrarian sitting up in his hammock, sipping a steaming brew through crinkled lips. 'People, heh? Bless my stars!'

'You woke him up.' Yapok's proper moody now, glaring at me like Sparrow's lightning was *my* fault.

'I don't mind, boy! Not a jot. I thought it would come to this, eventually. Trouble's brewing hotter than a kettle of wish-tea.'

'Trouble?' I ask, curious to hear what trouble he's heard of, stuck in here.

'Yes, child. There are murmurs that the giants are waking up,' he says. 'There are storms unlike any I have known in my long life. And what a vicious early winter!

I've an inkling it won't want to thaw.'

A shiver brushes my skin. *Giants?* If Grandma was here, I'd ask her why she never said so many of the stories were flaming *true*.

'What about that village that got sucked right into the rock, when one of the mountains cracked? All the Witches were talking about it,' says Yapok nervously.

Kestrel skates out from between two bookshelves. 'Yapok,' she says. 'Could we look through the books?'

'No,' he says, gliding off to collect an armful of bottles and books from a nearby table. 'Sorry.'

Her eyes follow him as he whizzes around the Skybrary. 'Why not?'

'Because I have enough work to do,' he says, sneezing again and wiping his nose on his grubby sleeve. 'And because I've already broken enough rules, bringing you here.'

'Rules are for breaking,' rasps the old man from his hammock. 'Especially at your age.'

'But—'

'Apprentice, I insist that you show these curious young minds around our home.' He props himself up on one crackly elbow and peers at us. 'I believe you'll find something to suit every taste. My own favourite shelf is our lovely collection of wish-tea-fuelled poetry. I also have a whole case devoted to the construction of the first ghostways . . . you've seen those, I suppose?'

'The silver tunnels that carry voices?' asks Crow.

'Yes, yes. And owls. Those are the ones.' His ancient blue eyes flutter around the ice-cave. 'Yapok, dear, would you show them? After all, knowledge must be passed on, if it is to survive.' He settles back into his hammock and begins to snooze.

Kestrel claps her hands and grins until her cheeks squash her eyes.

Yapok watches the Skybrarian. 'I am trying to look after him as best I can,' he whispers. 'And preserve the collection. And all the while, the wild weather is trying to destroy our iceberg.' Then he looks around at all of us, his mouth setting into a grim line. 'But who am I to disagree with the Skybrarian?'

We follow him away from the central cave, down one of the paths between the shelves. Our skates crunch the bones and teeth hidden inside the owl pellets littering the floor. I wobble along slowly, frighted I'll fall and wrench a shelf down on top of me.

The books are sheltered by taut awnings made of animal skin, to catch the icicle-melt. Some of the spines show names written in runes I understand, but other titles are written in letters I've never seen before – other Tribe-tongues. Maybe even ancient lost ones. Excitement flutters inside me, and Kestrel stops to touch every other spine, exclaiming in wonder.

'So over here is Natural History,' calls Yapok, and when I ask what he means he tells us they're books about birds and animals and fish, trees and plants and rocks.

'On this side we have world monarchies of Sea, Sky and Land—'

'Kings and Queens!' whispers Kes.

'And then we find Star Travel, Owl Breeds, Owl-care . . .' Yapok's voice dwindles as he careens off down another path. 'Ice-sculpting, different types of ice and their names, Hunting, Ice-worms, Poetry and a few volumes on draggle-riding!' he calls back to us. Then his skates slish to a stop and he rushes back to us, pale face looming out of the murk. 'I forgot to say, *don't* startle the monsters. They're used to me, but they won't like strangers. They're guards, after all.' He cocks his head and we all pause, listening to a steady, wet breathing that's coming from the bookshelves.

Soon exhaustion's crept over me, and I can hardly stand in my skates. But when I lean too heavily against a shelf, Yapok squawks at me until I straighten.

We keep moving, and Yapok points out more and more books. 'Gods, Philosophy, Shape-changing, Mystik-cism, Legend . . . we have one or two on giant-lore but most are with the land-lurkers at Nightfall.'

My eyes boggle in my head. I never knew so many thoughts had been scrawled. And maybe we can use some of them to help us get the next Opal.

Then a faint voice wheedles through the path behind us. 'Mouse?'

'Sparrow's awake,' I tell the others. 'I'd best go back and check on him.'

My brother's call throbs into the air again and suddenly one of the ghostway paths sucks it up and hurls it around the ceiling. *MouseMouseMouseMouseMouse!*

'Aagh, come on!' says Yapok in dismay, eyeing the ghostway. 'We have to get him to quieten down!'

As we turn around, I notice Kestrel stuffing a few small books into her cloak. When she sees me watching, she grins.

We reach the main chamber and see Sparrow peering down from the loft, chattering to the Skybrarian, who's listening keenly. Thaw's perched on the old man's knee. 'Yes, yes,' he tells Sparrow. 'My goodness! Little wonder you're forced to get cross with people, if no one ever understands you!'

'Aye,' agrees Sparrow, nodding.

I roll my eyes. Then Yapok cranks me up to the loft in the metal cage, and I help Sparrow down to the first level. He still looks pale and shaken from what I told him. Tears have made tracks through the grime on his face, and his hair's sticking on end. Sparks crackle through him, from his hair to his feet, and carve craters in the floor underneath him.

Kestrel takes the books from her cloak and spreads them out on a fur on the floor. She brings a gold-tooled leather tome to her nose and inhales the scent of the age-browned pages. 'This used to be one of my favourites,' she whispers, eyes still closed like she's trying to get back to some other time. 'I never thought I'd see another book as long as I lived!'

'Is that so?' asks the old man. 'Well, I am extra glad to have rescued it, then.' He sinks back into the pillows and gives a long, thin snore, his papery eyelids fluttering closed.

Yapok flushes, but before he can speak Kes lifts a hand. 'I saw this and wondered if we could read it to Sparrow?'

I stumble closer, putting out my hands, and drop to the floor next to the books. '*Whale Travels*,' I read out. The book is a deep blue, speckled with coarse white spirals, like barnacles. Forgetting about the monster guard, I pinch the edge of the cover to open the book but a slimy green tail lashes out, stinging me across the knuckles. I jerk back, sucking my fist.

'No!' Yapok turns to a cupboard and stoops to rummage inside. Then he stands, pulling on a pair of white gloves. 'That is a very old volume,' he tells Kes, disapproval dripping from his words. He picks it up like it's made of crystal, and blows a layer of dust from it. Then he puts his face very close to the cover and whispers odd, garbled words. He snaps his fingers and a small green beast with a spiny tail slips from the book and puffs into a stinking cloud of green vapour.

Crow winks at me. 'Now *that* was witch-work!'

Yapok gifts him a sharp look and passes the book to Kestrel. When she opens it, whale-song yawns out, lighting her face blue. 'Can you do these, too?' she begs, opening her cloak to produce two other books she nabbed from the shelves. Yapok sighs, but when the Skybrarian gazes at him over the edge of his hammock he does as she asks. Soon she's sprawled on the fur with Sparrow, reading whale stories to him. His hair settles down as his lightning calms.

Yapok brews a kettleful of tea and passes around steaming goblets of it – it's dark purple and sweet-smelling.

When I sip it, startlement widens my eyes. The tea tastes just like Pip's cinnamon buns. I gulp it down, wiping my mouth with the back of my hand. The bones-deep chill is banished, leaving me aglow with warmth. 'What is this stuff?'

Yapok grimaces. 'Wish-tea. Tastes of whatever you

wish for. Waste of time if you ask me, using magyk to brew that, but the dear old Skybrarian insists on it.'

'But I didn't wish for anything!'

He scowls. 'You might not *think* you did, but inside, everyone wishes for something.'

I grin at him and close my eyes, gulping the tea. One heartbeat I think of oranges, and my tongue fizzles with sweet, sharp juice. The next beat I picture a jar of honey and after that Pip's best squid tentacle stew. But my favourite is when I wish for the taste of nutmeg and the feeling of being in our old bunk, snuggled beneath the open porthole, watching the stars. The tea's flavour shifts as fast as the fire spirits, and I can almost imagine I'm home.

'What's yours?' I ask Kestrel.

'Dried starfishes!' interrupts Sparrow, happily.

Yapok clears his throat. 'That's not a thing you're allowed to ask a person,' he says sternly, making Crow laugh his tea out through his nose.

Kes winks at me. 'Flight,' she whispers in my ear. 'Mine tastes of flying free.'

Crow takes another sip of his, eyes closed. 'Mulled apple juice.' Yapok gives a muffled squawk of annoyance.

Sparrow falls asleep on the floor. Kestrel's still reading when I climb into a hammock and shut my eyes.

*

Something cold prods my neck. I blink my sleep away and roll onto my side – my eyes meet a row of toes and the sole of a small, grubby foot. Then I stare down the hammock. Sparrow's fast asleep at the other end, singing out his dreams. Thunderbolt floats around his head, riding a strand of whale-song. *Tangle Hair sleeps, Black Hair wakes, Thunderbolt flies!*

I grin. They must've crept in with me during the night.

I can taste blood, and when I run my tongue across my lips they're split open from the cold. I bundle my arms around myself as the iceberg sends up a booming *crack*.

Thaw-Wielder bursts from a hollow in the wall and lands on my hip, setting the hammock to swaying madly. She leans forwards and breathes fishily into my face. *Morning, Thaw-beast*, I mumble.

She belches in answer, and the stink tells me she's snuck out through one of the burrows to hunt for Wildersea herrings. *Good for you, Thaw.* She chortles in my ear.

'Are you awake?' asks Kestrel. I force my eyelids open and watch her slip-slide towards my hammock in her stockings, carrying a wooden bowl. 'Look at these treats I found! I'm sure Yapok won't mind us helping

189

ourselves. They're fat-dipped nutmeg butterballs! Have you tried them before? They're the finest breakfast!'

When I open my mouth to gift my heart-thanks she stuffs one of the snacks inside and my world explodes into rich, spicy sludge.

Then she tucks herself back into her hammock and feeds Ettler a crumb of butterball. He trills joyfully. *Yumyumyumumbrrbellypop!*

I watch Kes's hand dart quickly to the bowl. She stuffs a whole butterball into her mouth and wipes her fingers on her dress. When she sees me watching, she flushes. 'Sorry,' she says around her mouthful. 'I'm not used to there being enough.'

Soon Crow and Yapok are awake and Kes passes the bowl to them. As everyone eats, I keep thinking about how Yapok said the wild weather was destroying this iceberg. It creaks and groans around us and every now and then icicles shower down from the ceiling. Now we've escaped from Hackles I need to be on my way to find the next Storm-Opal.

'There's no time for any of this,' I tell them, my fingertips itching with the urge to rove. I sit up and stretch my aching arms above my head.

'Mouse,' says Kes gently. 'We needed to get to a safe place, and you needed to rest.'

'Well, now I've rested.' I swing out of the hammock,

making Sparrow grumble, pull on my skates and face Yapok. 'Heart-thanks for the food, but can I have a few beats alone with my crew?'

'Mouse!' scolds Kestrel.

I shrug. 'What? There ent no flaming nicer way to put it.'

'It's fine,' says Yapok. He stoops to fiddle with one of his skate-blades – I notice his hands are covered in raw-looking burn marks and older scars. Before I can ask how he got the marks, he's swishing away across the ice.

Once he's gone, my breath comes easier. We settle on some furs on the floor, and I look at the faces of my crew. 'I need to get Da's magyk map to find the Opals. At Hackles, I had a dream-dance to my ship.' I meet Kes's eyes and look away, cos I didn't admit my night-flying to her before.

'Go on,' she whispers keenly. The Skybrarian gives a sudden loud snore.

'What if I could get there again? And somehow bring the message back with me?'

'You'd need a binding,' says Crow firmly.

'And can you touch waking-world objects, when you're night-flying?' asks Kes.

I chew the inside of my cheek. 'No,' I admit. 'At least I don't reckon so.'

Sparrow wakes up and starts whimpering, so Kes hurries to get her healer's bag from under a table and roots around in it for his medsins. 'Let me see that arm,' she tells him. 'Ah, look at that! It's set nicely. We'll get the elbow moving gently once the pain eases.' She comes back to us and settles herself on the furs.

Crow squishes another butterball between his fingers. 'How about I shape-change and go and get your message back for you?'

Unexpected venom leaches into my throat. 'Oh, aye. It'll be just like old times.'

'What do you mean?' asks Kes, looking startled.

I flush, wishing I'd kept my mouth shut.

Crow gifts me a sour look. 'Go on,' he challenges. 'Tell her.' When I hesitate, he curses and rounds on Kestrel. 'I was a rotten *spy* aboard her ship, and she'll never let me forget it, which is fair enough.' He flicks the hair from his eyes. He spits his words like poisoned arrows. 'But what she don't know is what set me on that path. I was raised to keep my crow-shape secret – folks don't like anyone different, my mother always said. One day, a wanderer came to her for healings. A man with a fat belly and an even fatter purse. A fool could see that he weren't paying my ma anywhere near enough silver in exchange for lodgings and medsin.' He clears his throat. 'We barely had enough to eat. Long and the short of it is the old crook caught me taking what we was owed. I used my shape-changing to escape him and he told the whole village, and the next ones over, about me becoming a crow.' There's a hot crackle in the air, like lightning. I know something worse is about to spill from his lips but it's too late to stop it, now.

Crow looks at me, eyes like iron. 'So you want to know why I ended up where I did? Why I had to use my crow-shape for spying?'

'No,' says Kestrel, laying a hand on his arm. 'It doesn't matter now, does it, Mouse?'

But Crow shakes her off. 'That wanderer killed my ma for *my* stealing.'

I drop my eyes to my hands. Crow's breathing too fast, and there's naught I can say, or do, there's just fierce heart-sadness stretching the air like a bowstring.

I risk a look at his face and tears are shining on his cheeks. When we lock eyes he rubs the wetness away roughly with his knuckles. Kestrel presses her fingers to her mouth.

'What happened after that?' I whisper, so quiet I almost don't hear myself.

'The village wanted to cast me out after they found out about me. But my father came back from gods-know-where and—' He stops, swallows, keeps going. 'I thought I'd be safe. But he sold me to the wreckers at Orphan's Hearth. When I was sent to smuggle your brother it was meant as a test – to make sure I had enough rot in my heart to be one of them. After that, my nerve failed. Wish it had sooner.' He puffs out a long, weary breath. 'I'm sorry for what I've done – can't you see that?'

I let out my breath, crushed under the weight of everything he told me. I can hardly imagine growing up with that much guilt hanging over me. 'Aye. I gift you my forgiveness,' I say, like I once heard Grandma tell an enemy. Cos forgiveness ent just a gift to someone else. It's what frees you from your own poisoned hook.

He grins, in that way of his that spills burned light into his eyes.

I return his grin something fierce. 'If you're serious about getting my message back, I'm still dream-dancing and going with you.' I swallow, feeling a crackle of the fear stirring. I ent tried dream-dancing since that lost spirit tried to steal my body.

'Will you be able to follow me?'

'I'll try.'

'Will I be able to see you?'

'I don't know! I've never tried to dream-dance somewhere with a shape-changer before, all right?'

Crow jams his hands in his pockets and whistles through his teeth. 'How will I know this message if I find it?'

Telling them makes me feel like I'm stripping away a layer of my own skin, but I do it anyway, shutting my eyes to whisper Da's words.

'*Keep this hidden, Little-Bones. I cannot return, there is grave danger. Seek the scattered Storm-Opals of Sea, Sky and Land, before an enemy finds them and uses them to wield dark power. Take them to the golden crown before all Trianukka turns to ice, trapping the whales beneath a frozen sea. Remember the old song? The song will make a map. Keep your brother close by your side, and know you're never alone. I will find you when I can. Da.*'

Crow puffs out his cheeks and blows out all the air in a rush. 'Cripes. He ain't asking much, is he?' I scowl, and he raises his palms in apology.

'You spoke of a binding, before?' prompts Kestrel.

He opens his mouth, but the voice that greets our ears ent the wrecker boy's.

'I believe you'll find a useful volume under Star Travel,' crackles the Skybrarian. I freeze, and the hairs along my spine prickle. How long has he been awake? Could his ancient lugholes have caught my whisperings about the Opals?

The old Skybrarian cranks himself up on an elbow

195

and stares across at us with moon-pale eyes. 'Don't gawp, girl. Sky-gods know I didn't save these books just for them to sit here, caged by a set of *rules*. So do you know where the section is to be found?'

'Aye, Skybrarian,' says Crow.

'Find it quickly,' he warns. 'My apprentice – the real Skybrarian, now – won't like it. Bring it back to me.'

'Heart-thanks!' I tell him.

'Heart-thanks,' he mutters to himself as he burrows down among his blankets. 'My ears have gulped that somewhere before. It's like a phrase from a dream.' As we skate away, I feel the old man's eyes boring into the back of my neck, like owls in the ice. How much did he hear?

'Girl!' he hisses suddenly, as Kes and Crow swish out of sight. I hurry back to the hammock and crane my neck to stare past the strands of silvery hair trailing over its edge.

'I have another volume which might prove useful to you. You'll find it under Legend. Many moons have risen since I heard utterings of the Storm-Opals. Or – no, no. I beg your pardon. Did I not in fact hear something much more recently?'

My gut twists.

'Mouse?' Kestrel's voice floats back along the path. 'Are you coming?'

'What did you hear recently?'

'Go,' whispers the old man, as he sinks back down among his pillows.

'Skybrarian? Did you hear it from me, a few beats ago, or someone else?'

But the old crumbler's already started to doze, his snores joining Sparrow's. As I move towards the pathway between the bookshelves, a stifled sneeze throbs through the ghostway path into the room. 'Yapok?' I ask. But silence answers me.

19

Owl-weather

'Mouse?' floats the call again. Icicles scrape the top of my head as I flail to catch up with my friends. Blue owls *ping* past my face. But at a crossroads between the shelves, I break towards the section Yapok showed us, shutting my ears to Kestrel's call.

I weave down path after path, heart thrashing as I stare up at the crowded shelves and try to remember where we saw Legend. I stumble on my skates. The paths grow darker and I wish I'd brought Thunderbolt. There's a pale glow coming from the berg owls and one or two dusty whale-song lamps, though, and that's enough for me to see the books' spines if I squint.

I pull out book after book. Some gargle and growl. Others spew clouds of brown dust that make me cough. Through the dust I glimpse stories with faded pictures of strange animals. I can't believe the Sky-Tribes keep their stories on paper – at least a tusk or a bone can't be ripped or ruined if it's dropped in water. But I like the rich smell of the old parchment. My feet are hot and sore. I rest against a shelf and peer inside an owl burrow in the ice between two shelves. A pair of yellow eyes stares back.

Who? chatters the owl at me. *Whoyouwhoyouwhoyou?*

Mouse, I answer.

The owl utters a raucous chortle and lifts its foot in some kind of salute.

Heart-thanks, I tell it. *Do you know if there's a book here about gems like this?*

As I bring the Opal from my pocket, there's a deafening flurry. Owls stream from their burrows over my head and circle around me, making Thaw spit and hiss something rotten – she must've followed me.

Wisdomwisdomwisdom, chant the owls. *WisssssDOM.* One dives for the Opal and I cower, covering it with my cloak. *Just to peek*, it chatters mournfully. *Stone for all things, lifelifelife.*

Stone for life? I say *It feels alive, that's for sure. Do you lot know your way around these books? Do you know if there are old, old stories here, legends?*

A hoarse shout goes up from somewhere to my left.

'I think I found something!' Kestrel calls faintly.

Soon a great tangled knot of owls have gathered, all hooting and making a commotion around a heavy-looking leather book they've plucked almost off a shelf.

I dart forwards and catch the book before it splays onto the ice. The front is so covered in dust, and the light's so dim, I can't make out the runes. I wipe away the thick dust and tilt the cover towards a nearby whale-song lamp, but it's too dim. I stretch up and flick the glass to make the strand of song thud about, jangling enough to shed a pool of light.

When the runes emerge from the murk, it's like a hundred pins have been stuck in my skin.

The Legend of the Storm-Opal Crown.

I skate back into the main cave.

'*There* she is!' Crow lays a book on a table and scowls at me. 'You do know you could probably get lost in there for days, don't you?'

'Ignore him and help me with this,' says Kestrel.

She's trying to open a book with a midnight blue, star-speckled cover and white runes spelling *Tales of Night Flight.* But it's starting to ooze fizzling liquid that makes her snatch her hand back. An angry red rash spreads across her palm.

'Skybrarian?' I ask. 'Can you help us with the book-monster?'

He splutters awake. 'Yes, yes. Without question. Now, two of you help me down while the other fetches that whale book I heard you reading last night.'

'Help you down?' repeats Crow in disbelief.

'Yes, boy, yes. I'm not dead yet, am I?

While Kestrel gets the book, Crow and me stand under the Skybrarian's hammock and catch him between us as he tumbles free, hair dragging along the ice behind him. Owl pellets fall from his long nightgown onto the ice.

'Do be quick and find me a chair,' he says urgently. 'My bones are book-dust.'

I push an armchair towards the table and we prop the Skybrarian up in it, draping a fur over his knees. 'That's better. Now. Would you open that book, please? Any page.'

Kestrel shoots me a baffled look and opens the whale travels book.

The old man nods. 'That'll do. Now stand back, and whatever you do, don't move!' As Kes moves back, concern etched across her face, the Skybrarian grasps *Tales of Night Flight* and wrenches open the cover with sudden strength, revealing a small scaled beast dripping more fizzling black slime. The old man yells, flinging the creature by the tip of its tail towards Kes. She shrieks. The creature splats into the pages of her book.

'Close it! Oh for the gods' sake, be quick!'

Kestrel slams the book shut and it twitches for a few beats, then stills. She puts it down with shaky hands. 'Skybrarian, I – thought you would use magyk!'

'Magyk?' His eyebrows quirk upwards into his silvery hair, and he smiles at her. 'Not everyone is as young as you, you know! Try remembering all the spells when you're my age and then ask me to use magyk. No, sometimes all one needs is brute force.' He breaks off into a rattly cough, and Kestrel reddens.

'Skybrarian, can I see that book?' I ask.

He jolts, spinning around to goggle at me. 'Why, yes!'

As he begins to snooze in his chair, I take the book and open it at a page showing an old woman flying above a village at night. An image flickers in my mind – the spirit snagged like a cobweb on the mountain. The one that tried to slip into my body. I breathe to try and slow my thudding heart. I still feel wrenched by the memory, and every time I blink I see the spirit's anguish, stamped behind my eyes.

'*Night-beings can sometimes take possession of a person's body,*' reads Crow over my shoulder, '*particularly if that person is a dream-walker. To prevent this the dream-walker must paint runes of binding around themselves. Helpful rune groupings are described below.*'

'Can you paint the symbols around me before we go to find Da's message?'

'Aye, though you ain't to pass judgement on my penmanship.'

'As if I would, pearl-brain.'

He glances at the book under my arm and taps its cover. 'What's that you've got there?'

I fix my eyes on the slumbering old man. 'A book of legend.'

As I say it, the Skybrarian's pale eyes flick open in their baskets of wrinkled skin. 'I did ask for a book, didn't I? Now what was it . . .'

I glance around me. Even though I heard that sneeze before, I ent seen feather nor tail of Yapok, so he must still be gifting me time with my crew. 'It's *The Legend of the Storm-Opal Crown*,' I whisper.

Kestrel gasps. Sparrow sits up in his hammock, rubbing his eyes. 'That's my favourite one!'

'Is it, dear?' The old man beams. He does the same trick again, to get the monster guarding the book to leap into another unguarded one that's waiting for its spine to be mended. Then he opens the book of the legend, presses a single glass lens to his eye and starts to read, glancing up at us now and then. '*The Storm Opals were cut from one larger piece, when the great Tribe system was being built. They were each instilled with a sliver of the elements: a foam of sea, a fragment of sky and a fracture of earth.*'

I pluck at my sleeves impatiently. *Aye!* I know all this.

'*So, the people of Trianukka felt that each Opal contained a piece of themselves.*' He looks up at us. 'The little sliver of life instilled within each jewel would affect its behaviour, don't you think?'

I remember the Sea-Opal growing wet and sticky in my palm.

He clears his throat loudly and keeps reading. '*In the old times—*'

'When you were more younger?' blurts Sparrow.

'No, dear, much longer ago than that, if you can imagine such a thing. *It was agreed that there should be a king or queen to represent each of Sea, Sky and Land.*'

'So the world used to be more fair and equal?' says Kestrel keenly, as my mind begins to wheel. The story in the bone-etching at home only told of one king of Trianukka.

My mind dances and wheels like a sea-hawk, but the Skybrarian reads again from the book. '*A ceremony was held on the mountain. Each Opal was placed in the crown, at dawn, by a representative of each Tribe branch and guarded there by a giant. For thousands of years, the Kings of Sea, Sky and Land kept the three Storm-Opals in the golden crown and the tribes were at peace. They were united as long as the Opals were together and safe in the Storm-Opal Crown. However, over time, power struggles took over and one person wanted to rule over all of the world.*'

For *thousands* of years? I thought the last King was planning the ceremony only one hundred moons and suns ago! But this book's saying the Opals were already in place, and for so many suns and moons . . .

'Skybrarian, what if we needed to find that crown? Would there be anything in this book to help?' I ask.

'Patience, child.' His throat bubbles as he clears it. *'Over the course of many years, the legend of the Storm-Opal Crown grew gnarled and twisted as the truth behind it was forgotten. A theory is that one king spread a falsehood, accusing a Sea-Tribe captain of stealing the crown and hiding it in the belly of a whale.'*

My heart clangs against my ribs. So that part of the story might just be a rotten lie? Rattlebones never took the crown! My face heats up so fast that my stitches throb. All the troubles that swarmed the sea, leaked from one man's lying mouth?

'What is it, Mouse?' asks Kes.

'It was a lie?' I croak.

The Skybrarian blinks slowly at me. 'Vexing, isn't it? Yes, the Sea-Tribes were very hard hit by the consequences of that myth, spread by one greedy king. Captain Rattlebones fought hard for the Sea-Tribes to survive it, but sadly her efforts were not enough. The lie took on a life of its own.'

And why didn't I think to ask her about it? I let the old man's words slosh around my brain.

'Rattlebones was a just soul,' muses the Skybrarian.

'Always willing to discuss a matter at length, over a pot of wish-tea.'

'Did you *know* her?'

His pale eyes meet mine, but before he can reply an angry hiss stabs my ears. 'You got the Skybrarian out of bed?'

I turn to see Yapok gliding towards us. 'And you're not to touch books without gloves. You know the rules!'

'Boy, I elected to rise, you needn't kick up such a stink. I am a little overtired now, though.' The ancient book-rescuer twines his hair round his neck like a scarf.

'Skybrarian, what you said before, about—'

Yapok barges past me to help the Skybrarian to his feet. 'Didn't you hear? He said he's overtired. Can't you leave him be?' He helps the old man back into his hammock while I glare at his back.

'Who made those marks on you, Yapok?' asks Kestrel, when he's finished. She takes his hands, peering closely at the angry burns. When she pushes back his sleeve, she gasps at the sight of the burns spreading up his arm.

'Oh, it doesn't matter,' he says, blushing so hard it looks painful.

'Who hurt you?' Kestrel looks suddenly at the Skybrarian. 'It can't have been – him?'

'No!' snaps Yapok. 'Of course it wasn't him!'

'Then who?' Kes folds her arms.

'No one, just – someone who found us by accident, all right!'

A sick feeling starts to swill in my belly.

'When?' demands Crow.

'Who?' asks Kes at the same time.

Yapok's face glows bright red. 'The day before you all blew in. A traveller came, looking for the Skybrarian. I said I hadn't a clue what he was talking about. But he kept sniffing around. Said he wanted help deciphering something. In the end I said I'd try to help, just to get rid of him.' He drops his voice. 'But I *don't* want the Skybrarian to know that trouble came knocking.'

'Why did he burn you?' asks Kestrel.

Yapok frowns. 'He worked me to the bones, trying to break a spell. When he saw I couldn't do it . . .' He glances down and frowns at the mess of twisted burn scars on his hand, but when he sees us watching he pulls his hand up into his cloak sleeve and grits his teeth.

'Did something else happen?' Kes asks, rubbing the slope of her nose. 'You have not told us everything, I am certain of it.' She tries to wrap an arm around his shoulder but he steps out of reach, hitching his shoulders up round his neck.

I stare at the boy. A deep, sharp coldness steals from the base of my spine to the roots of my tangles. 'What did the traveller look like?' I ask. My own words have dimmed, like I'm underwater.

The others look at me in surprise. Yapok clears his throat. 'I can't remember.'

'You don't remember someone that did that to you?' Cos I do, I want to scream. He marked me, too. Stag's been here. My insides twist like a wrung cloth. I turn to Crow, pull him to one side and hiss in his ear. 'We have to get to the *Huntress*, now! Stag might find a way to crack the map at any moment.'

Yapok blinks at us. 'What are you planning? I don't want mixing up in your troubles! If you're up to no good I want you doing it somewhere away from here.'

'Yapok,' says Kestrel. 'Don't push us away.'

I glare at him. 'It's all right Kes. We'll go through to the first cave.' I wobble over to the hearth and Kes, Crow and Sparrow come with me. When we're all standing around the kettle in the middle of the hearth, I search for the switch Yapok pressed and we're thrown round and round until we're on the other side of the iceberg.

20

Crow and the Dream-dancer

I spread a thick fur over the ice and lie down, touching Ma's dragonfly brooch for heart-strength and squeezing Bear's amber amulet tight in my fingers. Sparrow curls up in an armchair and Thunderbolt watches from the top of his head.

Crow kneels beside me and holds *Tales of Night Flight* open in one hand. With the other, he takes my dagger and scratches runes for warding and protection into the ice around my body.

'This is your binding?' asks Kes.

'Aye,' says Crow, passing my dagger back to me.

Kes kneels by me. 'Are you scared?'

I suck in my cheek. Once I'd have said *no* without waiting a beat. But now I know that I've *always* been frighted, I just tried to keep it hidden, and I tried to be the bravest anyway. I don't mind showing her my truth, so I force it through my teeth. 'I'm frighted more than I reckoned possible.'

'You're strong though,' she says. There's a light of awe in her eyes, a thing that once I'd have given anything to see.

'Heart-thanks.'

'Ready?' asks Crow.

I nod. Kestrel goes to the window we first tumbled through and props it open just wide enough for a crow to fit through.

Thaw circles over me, keeping a fierce watch.

Crow leaps into the air, like black ink spilled into water, becoming a crow as he jumps. He pulls Thaw's tail feathers in his beak, cawing cheekily as she rounds on him, and then darts through the window.

I close my eyes, feeling out for the world between waking and sleeping. I remember making the carving for Da, not long before he disappeared, and how heart-glad I was when he unwrapped it, cos of the huge grin he gave me. When I think that Stag's robbed the sails that Da added to my carving, fury pushes my spirit against the edges of my skin. I let my spirit *leap up, shedding my body like a cloak.*

I soar through the window and then I'm racing alongside owls that pulse between the icebergs. One swerves into my path and I put out my spirit-hands to stop myself blending through its feathers and thieving its body.

My face feels puffy and blotched from the flying. A swift black shape streaks ahead of me – Crow. But what if he can't see me? I catch him up. He gives a startled thwawk and a glint in his crow-eyes tells me he knows me. It's like we're both in the world between waking and sleeping, together.

A woman leans out of a window in the top of an iceberg, painting one of the ghostways with a gloopy liquid. Inside each strand, the tiny blue owls shoot along, barely needing to flap their wings. Scrolls are clutched in their beaks.

I hold a picture in my mind of the Huntress. Where is my ship? If my fears about Stag are true, my ship might be close by. Like last time, I feel for the invisible cord connecting us and let homesickness guide me.

Above the western Wildersea, we're jostled by a fierce wind thick with snow. Then we catch the right current and we're soaring, gliding, riding the wind like a wave.

We are one with the stars. A girl's dream-spirit and a boy in crow's garb. We're part of the wild, wide sky. Crow's eyes glow gold, like fire spirits from a dream-world.

On the eastern edges of the Wildersea, a fleet of ships lined with guns is thrown roughly by huge waves.

I lose sight of them when a cyclone full of fish, stretching high from the sea to the clouds, whirrs towards us. We dodge, then tear away from jagged spears of lightning.

Then the view clears again and I see her – the Huntress.

I fly up her flanks, past the oarsmen's benches. When I see a weary brown face slumped over an oar, and wrists wrapped in chains, I reach out and stroke Bear's cheek with a fingertip. The tenseness leaves his face, and he smiles.

Crows lands in the rigging and resettles his feathers. I coil my spirit-arms through the ropes and float next to him, watching the deck. There ent a soul awake 'cept one or two half-frozen oarsmen.

A lightning storm has come close and brought a smell of burning. Snowflakes fall more thickly and when I catch a few on my spirit-tongue they taste scorched.

I turn to look at Crow and he takes to the air, thrumming his wide black wings powerfully against the storm winds. We glide close to the aft-deck hatch and land there, looking around to make sure. Crow's got no choice but to change back into his boy-shape, cos we need to open the hatch to get below decks.

His neck lengthens and his skull broadens, scalp-feathers stretching into human hair. His wings blend into a flapping cloak and arms shoot through the fabric, clutching the wooden hatch for support. His yellow claws thicken and darken into breeches and the claws lengthen, grow stubby, until he's wearing his old salt-stained boots. When his mouth is back where it should be, he splutters and gasps, spitting out snow. He hauls open the hatch and hurries inside. I squeeze through after him, into the below-decks gloom.

We steal through the shadows. Crow steps as silent as a

212

thief down the steps to the captain's cabin. No lamps are lit. Once or twice he looks round. 'Ruddy hope you're with me,' he whispers softly.

I pray with every inch of me that Stag didn't bring the runes of Da's message to life, and that the old song is only magyk when Sparrow sings it. Cos Stag might have slaves aboard the Huntress that could have taught him the old song.

Like Vole. Did she turn her cloak? I've never known how Grandma's prentice really felt about me. Most times, she acted like I was naught but a pox-ridden pest, caught in her curls.

But would she really betray us by helping Stag? She never made no secret of her love for Sparrow. Anyone would reckon he farts rainbows, the way she carried on about him.

Inside Stag's thieved cabin looms a huge white chair. When I touch it, I shudder. It's carved from whale bones.

I drift through the cabin, searching. Crow stumbles behind me. 'Where are you, ghost-girl?' he hisses. The air is heavy with Stag's sour breath. Crow scrabbles amongst Stag's things, and I float around, sweeping my gaze over everything, but there's no sign of Da's message anywhere. Then Crow sweeps a hand under the map table, pulling out clumps of dust.

Footsteps thud on the stairs. Panic simmers in my gut.

'Hell's teeth, that storm!' comes Stag's voice, followed up with a great rattling cough.

Crow ducks behind the huge clothes chest. I reach across the dream-realm and use all my force to try to touch his arm

213

and let him feel it. He jumps slightly, spinning to face me. Then calmness fills his eyes and he nods. He knows I'm with him. Wonderment fills me – this is the strangest dream-dance of my life, and the most powerful.

Stag enters the cabin with Axe-Thrower, the Fangtooth, prowling in his wake. She pulls something from inside her cloak and I yearn to snatch it straight out of her fingers. It's the message. 'This is useless,' she hisses around her fangs. She throws it down on the table. 'It means nothing beyond what we have already read.'

Stag throws himself onto his whale-throne and scratches his face irritably, fingernails rasping against his silver-flecked beard. Even through the smoke and the dream-dance I can smell his metallic sharpness and his soapy cedar scent, as though it's seeping out from beneath his skin.

A massive wave hits the ship, showering against the porthole, and Stag leans over and throws up into a bucket by the side of his gruesome chair. Then he sits up, panting and wiping his mouth. He stares at Axe-Thrower, fiddling with a ring on his little finger – Grandma's merwraith-shaped poison ring. Rage bubbles inside me. 'The Tribesfolk must know something about how to work this vile sorcery.' He spits the words through his teeth like they're poison.

Axe-Thrower looks down at her boots. 'They deny all knowledge.' She steps closer to the clothes chest. Crow tenses like a bowstring. 'Vole refuses to speak, and continues to *starve herself.'*

So Vole is loyal! Guilt prickles me, together with fear.

Stag grabs the Fangtooth's wrist and drags her closer to him. 'I have taught you all the ways I know to make people obey. Remind me why I ever thought your Tribe would prove useful to me?' he snarls.

'I am your first mate! I am the reason you can keep all these pathetics in order!'

'You are nothing to me unless you do your duty.' He rolls his eyes up the length of her, coldly. 'I need the old song to reveal the secret of this message. So you will force the song from someone's mouth–' His voice rises in fury, then he takes a deep breath and smiles. 'Otherwise, you will be sent to the breaking yards along with this ship and her crew.'

Fright sets my insides on fire. I feel my spirit flickering, fighting, wanting to flee.

Axe-Thrower pauses, fingers on the message.

'On reflection, I'll do it myself,' says Stag. 'Leave the note with me, and get out.'

But Axe-Thrower sniffs the air. 'Captain – something is here–'

'I said get out!' he roars, and it's the first and last time I'll ever be grateful to that grim-blubber, cos he's just saved Crow from being sniffed out by a Fangtooth.

Suddenly I can feel feathers from far away, stroking my face. Thaw? Then fingers gripping my arm and shaking me.

'Mouse, wake up!'

We have to hurry! What if Sparrow's in trouble?

Waves hurl the ship suddenly to the right and Stag's whale-throne is heaved towards the wall. He stands, clutches at the wall, cursing bitterly under his breath. Then he strides from the cabin, cos even a murdering wretch has to be a captain when that's the life he's asked for.

As soon as he's gone, Crow snatches Da's message from the table. He puts it in his mouth as he runs up the stairs, legs beginning to shorten, nose growing long and sharp. I swim through the air after him. I reach the deck and freeze. Crow's a bird again, soaring away from the ship, but Stag's standing there watching him with a frown. Did he recognise Crow?

When Stag lifts a gun to his shoulder to take aim at my friend, an image of Grandma punches into my mind and my spirit roars like a beast. I arrow through the space between sleeping and waking, willing my fingernails long and sharp as Thaw's, and then I'm dragging claws across Stag's face. He reels back, dropping the gun, and Crow zooms away into the leaden sky, dodging lightning bolts. The message is clamped tightly in his beak.

Blood washes down Stag's cheek as though from nowhere, and he clutches his face. 'Light lamps!'

I spring into the air, as guns crack the sky.

I follow the sleek black flicker of Crow's wings, leading us back towards the Iceberg Forest, as the fire spirits flicker over the icescape. A lightning storm flashes bright, beyond the forest. The Opal sparks its reply, sending tiny shocks through my pocket that I can feel even in my dream-dance.

Blue tangles of whale-song brush my cheek. Higher and higher we fly, into fog and cloud.

Every few beats, near and far, the icebergs creak out sad groans. Sometimes their voices are lost in the crashing of the sea at their feet. Other times the wind carries wolf howls.

Suddenly a lightning bolt slashes into one of the bergs, carving off a great slab of gritty ice. The slab smashes into the iceberg lower down and someone screams. Then there's a huge thunk-crash-sshhhhh as it plunges into the sea.

Above a rocking bridge between two icebergs, three tribesfolk lean out of a window in the ice, throwing ropes around the top of another berg to try to keep it from being wrenched in two by the storm. But then another bolt of lightning pierces the frozen clouds, and the sky erupts in sharp, glittering shards and the stench of burning. The peak of the iceberg peels in two and the ropes are ripped from the tribesfolks' hands, pulling one out of the window. He screams as he's thrown into the air and gulped by the darkness.

Soon we're flying over Yapok's wonky iceberg. Crow swoops through the window and I follow.

A black-haired girl is curled, asleep, on a fur. Glowing runes are scratched into the ice around her. A blind boy shakes the girl's arm. 'Wake up! Thaw is vexed at you!'

*When I op*en my eyes, I'm back in the Skybrary.

Sparrow crouches next to me. 'You took ages to wake up!' Thunderbolt clings to a strand of his hair and he peers through her light into my eyes. Thaw sits on his shoulder.

'Yes,' agrees Kestrel, Ettler's round black eyes gleam inside her cloak. 'My mother used to tell me about night-flying. She sometimes flew too long, too.'

'Your ma's a dream-dancer?' I breathe.

She nods. 'She flies most nights – I mean, she used to. I wouldn't know, now. It seemed to me that she grew to prefer the dream-world. You must be careful.'

'I can handle it.' But I struggle to sit – it's like only half of me's come back. Spots tumble before my eyes.

My sea-hawk splutters out a herring bone and swoops onto my head, talons digging into my scalp. She's almost heavy enough to push me over, like she's grown again overnight. *Thaw! You ent a nestling no more!*

I see Kes looking from me to Thaw with wide eyes and I realise she ent heard my beast-chatter before. She smiles. 'So many wonders!'

Crow spits out Da's message, along with a mouthful of ice-worms. I have to pick up the message cos his fingers are still half bent into talons. Thaw's hunched on my head and won't budge even when I try to brush her off.

I unroll the crinkled message. It looks like just a ragged, dirty strip of old sailcloth. Triumph floods my chest. That's all Stag could get the message to be – but my brother can make it into a magyk map.

Drums start to boom nearby, shaking icicles to the floor.

Sparrow tenses, digging his nails into Kestrel's arm until she yelps.

'It's starting again,' she whispers.

'What?' asks Crow nervously. Sweat gleams on his forehead and he sways on his feet. The shape-change must've drained him.

'Yapok told me about it. It's a debauch,' she replies. 'A Wilderwitch feast.' The music grows louder, making the iceberg throb.

'Maybe we should read this somewhere safer, if Witches are on the prowl,' I suggest, pocketing Da's message. The others nod.

We make our way back to the hearth and stand in a circle around the battered black kettle. But when I reach to find the switch to transport us into the Skybrary, nothing happens. The wall behind the hearth is smooth and cold, and I can't find anything to press. Crow and Kestrel try, but don't have any luck either. Then we stare at each other helplessly.

'He must've locked it for a while, to venture deeper

219

among the books,' says Kestrel uncertainly.

Crows eyes darken, and he curls his lip.

'We'll be all right in here,' I tell them, stepping off the hearth. 'Let's just get the map working and leave Yapok to it.'

But then a voice breaks into the cave and rattles off the walls.

'Told you I heard a commotion,' a woman croons, outside the window.

'*I* told *you* I sniffed a draggle, but you said I was too drunk to be believed!' drawls a man's voice.

Bad-blubbers, warbles Thaw as two wild-haired strangers climb into the iceberg and grin toothily at us. Their teeth are too long and pointed. They belong to wolves.

21
Debauchery

'How did you find the heart of our forest?' barks the woman. She's all straggling purple hair and bulging green eyes.

'I was sent by the Protector of the Mountain,' says Kestrel fiercely.

My heart plops into my belly. Is she using this for a chance to bargain with them?

The other stranger is a skinny man with a fat middle, grey skin and a scar down his left cheek. He stares round at us without blinking, then starts to laugh. 'You must be even dafter than you look, admitting that right to our whiskers! Come on with you, then. Come to greet the King!'

My heart thumps against my ribs. None of us move. Then the man grabs Crow's arm. He twists, yelling, Kestrel shouts, and I race towards them and start kicking the man with my skate blade. 'Let go of him!'

The woman weaves closer to us, yipping, and the

man yelps back to her. Fur has sprouted on his cheeks. 'Wouldn't fight if I were you,' says the woman. Her mouth and nose have lengthened into a snout. Sparrow starts to cry. I bare my teeth.

They bundle us outside, onto the roof of the iceberg. I grab Sparrow's hand and he makes a fuss, but when I try to calm him he cries harder. Then we're angling our skates down the slope and my heart's in my mouth as I teeter and plunge downwards. There's a shelf of ice halfway down the berg and even with Kestrel's help I smack into it, jarring my ankles and wrists. Then we pick our way down to a bridge between the icebergs, carved from a gleaming ribbon of ice.

Suddenly we're hurled into a world of creaking leather skates and clouds of jewel-bright dragonflies. Wilderwitches skate at high speed across the bridges connecting the icebergs, calling to each other. I join the stream of skaters. Now I'm closer I can see that most of them are changed part-way to wolf and fright knocks against my ribs. They sniff the air, watching us keenly.

A fierce wind presses bony fingers into my mouth and eyes. The orcas sing far below, their voices bouncing strangely off the sides of the giant bergs.

We reach the other side of the bridge and go through a jagged doorway in the side of another iceberg. Inside is a vast hall of ice, set up as a market. The din of trading is deafening. We're shoved past throngs of Wilderwitches selling food, garb and skate blades, and through another jagged doorway in the other side.

We emerge deeper inside the forest, beneath a flickering canopy of silver ghostways. Soon there's naught but white blizzard; a blurred world of sky and cloud. I blink and spit, wipe my face, wishing for snow-goggles.

There ent hardly any other folks around by the time we reach the next great iceberg. It's crisscrossed with deep cracks like old skin. There are imprints in the ice of faces and runes. I shudder as a strange twilight crawls over my skin like an eclipse.

Smaller icebergs groan as they're carved apart into the sea far below. Ice and waves smash against each other so loud I can't hear my breath, and I can only feel my heartbeat in my neck.

'Get a move on!' shouts the woman. She pushes us inside the ancient berg.

As the stars blink out I stand still, listening to the blood in my ears and the sea in the distance. Light drifts in from a hole in the roof, swirling in colours of amber, green and blue. The fire spirits? Owls are burrowed into the cave walls, watching us. There's a crunch and a huge clump of ice smashes near my feet.

I press my fingers against the rough, icy wall to slow

myself as we wind deeper and deeper down a wide spiral into the heart of the iceberg. At the bottom, the close, thick walls make me sweat in my furs and suck away all the sound, leaving our voices heavy and dead. Are we under the sea? I remember Grandma's teaching about icebergs; how the biggest chunk of them lies underwater.

We're led along a tunnel cut through the bottom of the berg. 'Weapons!' barks the scarred man. The woman searches us, and throws our daggers onto the ice. Then we're pushed into a sprawling ice-cave.

Three thrones stand against the back wall, piled with slumped, drunken Wilderwitches. Behind them hangs a tapestry of flying sky-wolves. On either side are tapestries, too. On the right is a picture of mountains and to the left, a shark leaping from the sea to take a bite from the moon. Sea, Sky and Land.

Wilderwitches wrestle, belch and guffaw. Full-growns watch witch-kids hurl bread loaves at each other's heads. They goad them on, cheering.

Wolf muzzles twitch to stare as we're prodded forwards. Some are a ghoulish mixture, like they've forgotten how to change back.

At the head of a huge oak table slumps a bored-looking man with long tangles of purple hair. His doughy skin is riddled with deep crags. He combs the

grey fur on his cheeks with claw-like fingernails. Dead
black butterflies with golden spots adorn his knuckles.

'Wilder-King,' calls one of the guards, and the man
gazes towards the speaker idly. 'We bring captives.'

The woman sitting by the King's side claps her
hands in delight. She wears a necklace of blue feathers
and long, pointed orca teeth. Her face is mostly human,
except for a twitching pair of grey-brown ears that poke
through her fall of dark hair.

The King gives a dagger-tip stare, and sniffs deeply.
With a sick pang I realise his nose is lengthening into
a black muzzle. 'I detect stinks of bowstrings, tar and
tallow,' creaks his old crackled voice. Owls rustle and
hoot. 'And stenches of sweat and salt, mud, and sun-
baked seaweed. Where have they crept from?'

Ahead of me, I see Kestrel shudder. I chew my lips,
sucking off the salt of my snot.

'The long girl says she's been sent by the Protector of
the Mountain, sire.'

I swallow. All along the table, Wilderwitches flick
their ears back and sink their heads low. They growl
and hiss, and tear at their tangled ropes of hair.

The King's lips peel back in a grimace. His eyes shine
as they fix on my friend, like she's an ingot of gold.

Kestrel flinches and wraps her arms around her
middle.

'Let the captives feast with us,' declares the King.

The guards push us towards the far end of the table. We duck under flying chunks of bread. A loaf hits a man and his owl-feather crown falls to the floor with a snap of quills. A witch skates past wearing a silver platter full of steaming goblets balanced on her head.

The King rises and skates over to us. He reaches down and grips Kestrel's hands roughly in his. I want to kick him away from her, cos I can smell her stink of fear. 'I know you, girl. Now you have fledged, and fate has delivered you to my forest. Here is the birth of an iceberg,' he rasps, pressing her hand over his heart.

It's a friendly greeting, uttered in a murderous tone.

'And here is the birth of a mountain,' whispers Kestrel tightly, bringing his fist to her heart.

'May swift-feathers bear your Sky-Tribe glad tidings,' they say together, the King's voice steely, Kestrel's fluttering in fright.

Across the cave, the wolf-eared woman begins to growl, spit dangling from her gums. 'She is a draggle-rider,' she crackles, voice half beast, half human. 'I will not suffer her in my presence!'

The King freezes. 'You may be my newest queen,' he mutters calmly. 'But you shall make no demands of me.' Then his hand delves into his cloak and with a flash of silver he flicks a throwing arrow at the wall behind her.

It grazes her ear. She yelps, pressing her hand to her head. Blood puddles between her fingers. A great noise of sniffing fills the iceberg as snouts lengthen, questing the air for blood. The queen pushes back her chair and hurries from the cave, skirts crackling with ice.

'Fill your cauldrons well, and feast!' roars the King, fixing us with his cold stare until we obey, sitting down stiffly in high-backed wooden chairs. Sparrow whimpers, Kes's hands tremble and Crow twitches his glare from side to side, muttering under his breath.

The Wilderwitches are gobbling so much food I feel my eyes bulge. There are baked owls' eggs sitting in cream, and pickled herrings, and mooncakes decorated with patterns of feathers. Piles of squid-ink noodles shiver on platters and rolled pancakes seep grease. Wolves dip their muzzles into bowls of gold stars that float in pink goo.

I put my head close to the table. 'Reckon we'd better go along with this for now.'

My friends hesitate, but I take pancakes for me and Sparrow and put one in his hand. He tears into it greedily. Crow helps himself to noodles, looking dazed.

But Kes's face is taut with heart-worry, and I feel sick. It's like we've been invited to feast at our own sea-burials. How am I gonna get us out of here?

The King's eyes linger on Kestrel's face. 'Is something

wrong with my feast?' he asks, softly.

'No,' she says quickly. 'It's just—'

Crow kicks her under the table. 'It's perfect.'

'It's just what?' asks the King, wet nose twitching. 'I am all ears.'

She glares at Crow. 'My belly's writhing with the terrible things I've heard, Wilder-King. Folk are suffering, all across the sea, sky and land.'

The King's eyes brighten like blue fire. Wolf-teeth lurk in his gums. 'I wish I could do something to help, I really do. But as you see, I have my paws full being a king to my own kind. Besides . . .' He shifts on his cushion and turns towards a guard, holding out his goblet for more wine. Then he whips back around, purple liquid sloshing over his bejewelled fingers. 'You won't be here for long, so your belly needn't *writhe* so.' He grins.

Sparrow's been stuffing his face with as much sickly grub as I can help him lay his good hand on. But now he looks up, chin wobbling. 'Why?'

'Quiet!' howls the Wilder-King, sending owls rustling for cover in pits on the ceiling. 'You will speak when spoken to. You will feast yourselves sick if I command it. And you will tell me your Protector's war-plans, or be dashed on the ice.'

Kestrel swallows loudly. 'We don't know her plans. And we seek – we *need* – unity.'

The King's ears flicker. 'Lies. Your Protector does not seek unity.' He leans across the table and takes another witch's flagon of ale from their hand, tipping it back to drain it down his throat. Then he belches.

'But the young do!' says Kes. 'We do not fight her fight. We wish to talk peace.'

The King hunches over his wine cup, shuddering. It takes me a breath to realise he's laughing. 'Wilderwitches never use words when they can wield weapons. And the wishes of puny younglings are of no insignificance. Now tell me – when is she next planning to attack?'

'I don't know,' says Kes miserably. 'She never tells me anything.'

The King slams his fist onto the table. His pupils swell into wide black pools. He pulls a throwing arrow from the depths of his cloak and twirls it between furred fingers. 'It doesn't matter if you speak now, or not. The ending will be the same.'

His threat sends a crackle down my spine, and I'm sick of the feeling of fright.

Kestrel stares into her lap, tears on her cheeks.

'Don't take your sails down just yet,' I whisper in her ear, while the King glugs another flagon. 'Look how sozzled they're getting.'

She answers through the corner of her mouth. 'So?'

'So we need to keep the King talking and drinking

until I can sneak us a way out of here.' The King sniffs suddenly in my direction and his ears twitch. I tighten my breath. My mouth grows sharkskin-scratchy. The King's lips draw back. Through the fur on his cheeks, thick whiskers begin to sprout.

'I know what to do,' huffs Sparrow, as he clambers to his feet and grips the edge of the table for balance. He tips back his head and starts to sing at the top of his lungs.

'I'll sing you a tale of a bunch of stupid tails, wagging and stenching like feet!'

The King shakes his head roughly and his whiskers sink back into his cheeks. He slams his fist onto the table, making berry-wine slosh over the edge of his flagon. I'm about to tug Sparrow back into his seat when the King's muzzle splits into a bloodstained grin. 'A singer has graced us! Sing, boy! Sing as though your life depended on it.' He hiccups and slaps his thigh with laughing so hard.

Then I see again how much Sparrow has been through and how he don't need me the same way he used to. Cos the King's words don't faze him. He just grins and keeps singing, faster and louder, and the King drains another flagon, slapping the table for more even as he swallows.

'You're a great lumpy wolf with a big rolling belly,

And foul dripping teeth all covered with jelly!

Oh you belch and you stink and your gut's heaped and smelly,

Oh, gift me a silver for your goblets of puke!'

The wolves lift their heads and join in, some still able to make human words, others just howling. '*Gift me a silver for your goblets of puke!'* they slur.

'World's gone topsy,' murmurs Crow.

The King slumps to one side. He props his head in his hands and peers gleefully at Sparrow, through dizzily swimming eyes.

Wilderwitches shriek with laughter, duck flying handfuls of food and clutch their heaving bellies. One wipes her muzzle with the tail of the wolf sitting next to her. Then they snap and growl at each other, muzzles wrinkling.

Crow pushes his chair back an inch, gripping it hard. 'Now what?' he husks.

Kestrel murmurs softly under the cloak of Sparrow's singing. 'We have to get out of here before he's swallowed the next flagon. But we need the draggles, and I don't know where they're roosting . . .' Dismay gobbles the rest of her words.

'One thing at a time,' says Crow, eyeing the King and then glancing at the door. 'How will we distract them?'

'A brawl,' I whisper. 'If they turn on each other, they won't notice us – and we have to keep Sparrow singing until the very last beat.'

'A brawl's *no* problem,' says Crow. He bends close to a drunken old Wilderwitch to the left of him and whispers something to her. Then he whispers to another wine-addled witch across from him. I watch, amazed, as they each gabble in the ears of the witches next to them, and Crow's whisper spreads around the room like a starved flame.

The King glugs another cup of wine and his head crashes down into his platter. Then he jerks upright, guffawing, arms sprouting thick grey fur.

As the first punches are thrown, the King dives into the fight, roaring. We creep towards the door. Sparrow keeps singing. The strands of whale-song quiver around the room, skimming the tops of the Wilderwitches' heads. It's different from how I've ever seen it before, though. It's like my brother's putting his will into the song, threading it with crackling power. It feels like time pulls and thickens as we move closer to the door. The Wilderwitches' pride and the whale-song gift us a pocket of air to fly away inside.

'Don't you wanna hear the words I spread?' asks Crow as we move.

'Not now!' says Kes.

'I *said* that the one to our left said the one to our right had threadbare ears and a rotten pelt. Then I told the one on our left that the other one said they were gonna skin them and sell the pelt to a draggle-rider.' He chuckles.

'Shhh!' I warn. 'Sparrow, keep singing!'

Sparrow's voice lifts higher and louder, and under my breath I start a low beast-chatter, reaching for the draggles. *Don't know where you are, cave-beasts, but we need you!*

The air rings with the clash of daggers, claws and teeth as the Wilderwitches descend into a good and proper brawl.

We're almost at the door when a witch leaps up, knocking platters and tankards to the floor. 'Where'd you think you're going?'

Sparrow's song stutters and fades. Blue gloop glistens on his chin.

'Go!' I hiss, eyeing the King.

We tear out of the ice-cave.

22

The Wild Tastes like Old Blood

The passage through the ice is gloomy and thick with drifting fog. 'Hide!' whispers Kestrel, pulling Sparrow down to the edge of the path and throwing her cloak around them both.

Crow and me do the same, and the Wilderwitch that spied us tears past, claws clicking against the ice. I catch sight of her as she disappears into the murk – her face was still human, so with heart-luck she won't scent us out. We lurk for a beat, to make sure no one else has seen us. In my bones I picture the draggle cave and remember the stink and press of all the fur and the chatterings of the draggles. I remember when I controlled a terrodyl to protect Ma's dragonfly brooch and try to send the wildness in my chest spinning out across the sea to the caves at Hackles.

'Raindrop cowls on!' says Kestrel. We pull on the

cool, rubbery skins of armour forged by Egret. Then we tear back the way we came, but pause on a smaller, quieter bridge of ice instead of making for the Skybrary.

'We can't lead them to Yapok,' says Kes.

'What about my longbow and *blood-singer*?' I hiss, picturing our weapons lying on the iceberg's floor.

Suddenly the snowy sky thud-flashes into a blanket of lightning. A tendril of lightning snakes away from the sky and quests towards Sparrow. It settles on him like a shivering ridge of fur. Thunderbolt whimpers under the hood of his fox-fur cloak, puffing out a trail of moon-sparks. We duck behind a pillar of ice.

'I'll fetch the weapons,' Kes scans the sky. 'Can you call the draggles, Mouse?'

'It's too dangerous!' warns Crow.

'Just watch over them until I'm back,' calls Kes, skating away.

I realise there's a roar in my ears that ent just my own blood – it's my life-blood, the sea, thrashing far below the Iceberg Forest, her voice thick with ice.

Draggle-beasts, I call, feeling out again with the wild thread of my beast-chatter. *Fly to us! Where are you?*

A rotten taste floods my mouth, and pictures of the draggles hunting flicker through my mind like fire spirits.

'They're alive,' I tell the others, my voice a growl as it

changes back from beast-chatter. I feel for them again. 'They're storm-frighted, but they're coming back for us!'

Crow nods, eyes widened by fear. Fright trickles through me as the beats pass and Kes don't come back. I shut my eyes and focus on the beast-chatter grunting it under my breath. Finally, the draggles thud through the fog and flicker towards the bridge. 'Mouse, you wonder!' says Kestrel, appearing from behind us, lugging our weapons.

'Thank the gods,' I spit. 'You were ages!'

Kestrel dumps the weapons and leaps to catch the draggles' long fur, then lets Crow scuttle onto one of their backs, and passes a vine of fur to me. I hold the draggle steady while Sparrow climbs on, and then leap on after him. Kestrel passes my borrowed longbow up to me and I lift it onto my shoulder. Crow fastens his sword belt and Kestrel climbs onto the draggle with him. 'We rove,' I cry, gripping tightly with my knees as the draggles swoop into the sky.

'So did you see that owl-boy?' asks Crow.

'No,' replies Kes sadly.

Sparrow wraps an arm around my waist as I quickly string Egret's bow and nock an arrow. I scan the ice bridges below.

Why ent they coming after us?

'We did it!' yells Crow.

Then a shower of black rain bursts over us. When a drop of it touches the draggle, it fizzes into her skin with a hiss and she panics, trying to throw us off. *Frightfurfleefleeteethpangbloodgetaway!*

Steady, I chatter, trying to hold her still with my thoughts even though I'm panicking too. The memory of shooting that terrodyl down on our ship, what feels like an age ago, flashes in my brain. *'Someone send for Pipistrelle!'* Grandma shouted. *'We need his cauldrons to catch that filthy slime, so it don't eat the Huntress whole!'*

'Fire!' cries a distant voice. Then more black blood hails down on us and the draggles beat the air, screeching to get away. The runes on Egret's longbow sigh and hiss as the blood burns into them. But they don't get eaten away – instead they grow warm and glow against the dark wood.

'What is this stuff?' cries Kestrel, clutching her wrist in pain as a drop of it burns a pit in her skin.

'It's terrodyl blood,' I shout, making sure Sparrow's covered up and praying they stop catapulting the blood at us. I try to summon the heart-strength to send a thread of wildness from my throat to the draggle. *I will keep you safe. Just fly, as fast as your wings will carry you!*

A ripple of fright pulses through the draggle's body. She bucks again, trying to throw us off.

Steady! Fly steady, now. Faster!

I feel the draggle's muscles relax under me, and its fur loses its electric crackle of fear. Controlling it with beast-chatter fills me with a sick feeling in my bones. I know I'm putting another creature in danger again, to keep us safe.

I search the forest for the catapult and spy it near the King's Iceberg – a wooden structure on a set of great wheels. As a Wilderwitch fills a bucket with more terrodyl blood, ready to hurl after us, I take careful aim at his upper arm, so I don't hit any big blood vessels. I breathe, then loose my arrow. He wails a broken howl, and drops the bucket. Half-clotted black gunge oozes out, eating the ice.

Finally I sag into the saddle, loosening my sweaty grip on the longbow. Thaw flaps along by my side. Then Kestrel's draggle glides to join us and we're coursing away from the forest, dodging the ghostways in case they suck us in.

A trickle of heart-sadness for the old Skybrarian spreads through me. At least he stayed hidden – maybe that's why Yapok shut us out. But I wonder what will happen to the books in the end, if no one knows they're there. Won't they just be dead words, after Yapok's gone?

We fly until a hollow pit unfolds in my gut and my belly grumbles. We need to stop to work out where

we're going but I'm too frighted the Wilderwitches will catch us, so I won't agree to land.

Finally, we let the draggles swoop to rest on a flat iceberg far to the west of the forest, but too close to the Frozen Wastes for my heart-liking. If a Fangtooth longboat finds us here I ent gonna have the strength to fight them. We huddle together for warmth, and rest while Thaw catches herrings. Kestrel unties Sparrow's sling and helps him exercise his elbow. Then she bundles the sling into her bag. 'Shall we try going without that for a while?'

'Aye!' A grin bursts over Sparrow's face.

I unroll Da's message. As the draggles vanish into the sea-mist to catch fish with Thaw, the others crowd round to stare at the yellowed cloth. It's the size of a full-grown's hand and smudged, singed and spotted. 'Da wrote this to tell me what I need to do to keep the whales – and Trianukka – safe from Stag and the creeping ice.'

'So how does it work?' asks Kestrel, voice nipped with intrigue.

My teeth chatter. 'It's a map. Least, it turns to one, when my brother sings.'

Sparrow's doubtful voice drifts from the thick folds of his fur hood. 'Hm. I don't think it does! Ent it just some grimy scrap?'

'Shut it, Slackwit.' I've pinned all my struggling hopes on this map of my da's. It has to work.

The cloth is half blackened and some of the runes are written askew. I rub my finger across the sailcloth and then flinch as a handful of runes drop off the bottom of the message and plink onto the iceberg.

23
Dead Runes

Keep hid canot return, danger scattered Storpals Sky Land, fore enemy ield dark power. Take golcrown fore all anukka ice, trap whales frozen sea. The song make a map. Ke your brer never alone.

thisdenInthereisgraveseekthemOofSeaandbeanfindsthemandusesthemtowthemtothedenbeTriturnstopingthebeneataremembertheoldsong?willepothclosebyyoursideknowyou'reDa

'Gods!' I sweep the fallen letters into my palm. They're as light and fine as dragonfly wings. Half Da's message has fallen away. 'What do you reckon did that to 'em?' I ask Kes.

'Your father may have wanted to guard his words against the wrong sort?' she replies uncertainly. 'Maybe someone was trying to break the enchantment.'

My blood leaps as I remember what Yapok said about someone trying to get him to break a spell. 'Was it that owl-boy? What if he killed these runes?'

'We have no way of knowing that,' says Kestrel.

'But what if the map don't work like it did before?' I babble desperately. 'Maybe we should go back. Maybe Yapok can breathe life back into the runes. Might be something in one of his books, or—'

Kes shakes her head. 'Egret taught me that when a rune is dead, its hidden meaning dies, too. It curls back into the spirit world. And we can't go back now. We must press on with this fight of ours.'

Ours. A bolt of bright light fills my chest and I have to look away from her green eyes. I'm more heart-glad than she could know that the fight ent just mine.

I turn to Sparrow, huddled between Crow and Kestrel. 'Let's try waking up this map, shall we? Can you gift us some of the old song?'

'Don't you know it by now?' grumbles my brother.

'You're the one with the whale-song!' I spit, my bright mood dying as fast as it was lit.

'Aye,' he says, wrinkling his nose. '*You* can't sing a stitch.'

'You'd never guess you two was related, would yer?' remarks Crow.

When Sparrow grudgingly unseals his mouth to sing the notes are tinged grey by the sourness of his breath.

Do you remember
When the sea
Lay, still, in wait for me.

Don't you remember?

Watch and see, they tread the paths, swim the seas.

Thaw wings her way back from her hunt, a streak of striped feathers tucked behind a cloud of steaming beast-breath. She drops herrings onto the iceberg with a thump, and then zooms around helping me catch Sparrow's whale-notes. She flings them onto Da's message with a wet popping *spluck*. Smoke coils into the air. I blow on it quickly, cos it smells like the map is burning.

When the blue strands touch the sail they melt into it, jerking the remaining runes to life, until Da's message has disappeared and the lines of a hand-drawn map flicker into being.

'Ahh!' whispers Kestrel.

But this time, the drawings are faded, blotched and blurry. 'That wretch,' I say bitterly. 'It didn't used to be like this!'

'But that's incredible,' breathes Kes. 'Sparrow, what a gift you have!'

My brother grins smugly in my direction.

Crow whispers his wonderment under his breath.

But I bury my face in my hands, cos the map ent a patch on what it was before. Last time I saw parts of the sea and land, but now it's not showing any waves though I *can* see the Sea-Opal. It's a green orb flickering in and out of sight to the west of the northern sea, right where we're huddled on an iceberg. At the Iceberg Forest, an amber orb glows on the sailcloth, guttering out and then popping back alight with a fresh puff of smoke. The Land-Opal? When it blinks back into life it zooms off to the western corner, that ent showing anything but smudges and stains – and then it whooshes around for a beat and pops into nothing again. I'm frighted the whole thing's gonna shrivel to ash in my hands. I can't see any sign of the Sky-Opal.

'So this map is trying to show us the Opals. But what will show us the golden crown?' asks Kes.

'I'm not sure,' I tell her, the few clues I've picked up about the crown swishing behind my eyes. If I get to meet Rattlebones again, I'll ask her what she knows about it.

'Maybe it appears once you've found all three Opals?' suggests Crow.

They fly wild through the skies,
Fathoms deep and mountains high.
They are three . . .

'Ouch!' Sparrow stops singing and blows on the fingers of his good hand. The purple lightning's burned his palms, stirred to life by the magyk. The map fades away. Fright nips at me. What if the magyk is too strong for him? Singing always used to gift him strength, not hurts.

'You can try some more later,' I reassure him, but he sets his chin, eyes turning steely under their film of blindness.

'No, I wanna do more now.' His high voice rises again, making Thunderbolt dance around like her wings are crackling with energy. The map stirs again.

Sea, land and sky,
On the sea
One travels wide.
Might he claim this sea,
Claim it for his own?
Witches call to me, atop the Wildersea,
The hearth-stones treasure their memory.

The last line makes a pulsing blue orb bloom over a settlement in the mountains. Arrows thread along a mountain path towards it. Is it the Sky-Opal? The map burns brighter than I've ever seen it, dazzling our eyes in the gloom, then dims suddenly and seeps smoke. Thaw chatters her unease, so I stroke her feathers gently 'til she settles.

The blue orb on the map shines north-west of Stonepoint. I squint at it. Faint, spidery labels appear, but they're smudged. 'Something's written here. Begins with an H?'

Kestrel reaches across our circle to me. 'Can I see?'

I nod and she takes the cloth, studies it, then clears

her throat. 'There is a village in the east – Hearthstone – where the hearth-healers dwell. They are peaceful mountain-folk, said to be descended from a mix of Sky and Land Tribes.'

I lean over her shoulder to look at the map again. 'Hearthstone? Ent that mentioned in the song, too-soon?'

Sparrow nods. '*The hearthstones treasure their memory,*' he sings quietly. Then he yawns, puffing the song out quicker. His notes trace blue spirals in the night. But now I can tell his song is full of hurt, about Grandma, cos little prickles stick out on the gloopy strands.

The song touches the map and the runes make arrows that scoot towards the sketched outlines of a cluster of homes nestled close to drawings of hills. Smoke puffs from their chimneys – the sketch moving before our eyes – and their windows are shaped like stars.

'Oh my,' murmurs Kes.

'That's where we need to go,' I whisper. As soon as I say it, the Sea-Opal warms and tingles in my pocket.

I think about that skittering amber orb and pray the map ent too damaged to help us find the Land-Opal, too.

Sparrow starts to sing again, but his voice catches and he splutters out a sob. His song has grown jagged, into strange fragments of blue and silver. I reach for his hand as Thaw catches them and puffs them onto the sailcloth.

West of Hearthstone, the snippets of song skip along, painting out a hidden picture of a stretch of steaming water, crowded with houses on stilts. A man with long hair waving like seaweed moves around the houses in a canoe. His skin and hair writhe with tiny yellow dots. Grey scales ripple under the water and the surface of the map shifts into something like . . . fish skin.

I reach into my pocket and slip out the piece of fish skin I found at Hackles, squishing it gently between my fingers.

'What is that place?' asks Kestrel.

I lift my eyes to her wide ones. 'The Icy Marshes – a Sea-Tribe place that always welcomed Grandma. We were docked there when I fled my ship.' I hope Stag left the Marsh-folk alone after the whale took me away. Would the map show me if trouble had befallen a place?

Crow touches the map with a fingertip, frowning. 'Why's it showing us that?'

I shrug. 'I don't know. Maybe there are folks there that can help us?'

Crow pulls a small grey square out of his pocket. All the hairs on the back of my neck prickle. It's a piece of fish skin, dappled in pink, just like the one I found. 'Where'd you get that?'

'I found it under the table in Stag's cabin, when we were looking for the message. Almost left it there on the floor, but I thought it were odd so I kept it. Clean forgot about it 'til now. What about yours?'

I hold the two next to each other. They're both ragged, like they've been quickly torn from a bigger piece. 'I found this at Hackles.' Why do I feel like we're on a path that I never chose, finding clues that ent the ones I'm asking for? 'D'you know what kind of skin this is? Is it freshwater?'

'Aye, it looks like pike skin,' says Crow, running his finger along the dried scrap in my hand. 'And there are marks scored on the underside.'

I look where he points. Little fish and toads have been etched there, and when I put the two pieces together, jaggedly scrawled runes are joined to make two words.

'*Pike*,' reads Crow, frowning. 'What does it mean?'

'I don't know.' I think of the Icy Marshes again.

'I don't wanna go to the Marshes,' says Sparrow suddenly, wiping a sticky smear of whale-song off his bottom lip.

'We ent, don't fret yourself,' I tell him. 'Why though?'

He gives the air next to my head a sullen look. 'There's something bad. I seen it in nightmares. I hate the stink of toads, 'specially when they're on fire.'

I rub his arm. 'The nightmares are gonna stop, y'know. And I don't know why you're gassing about flaming toads.'

He pulls away and wraps his arms around himself. 'You never listen to me.'

Thaw pings another glob of Sparrow's song from her beak onto the sailcloth, and a choppy sea is strewn across the map. A dark fleet of ships scrawls into life, and under the roughly drawn water, something moves. I hold the cloth closer to my face – tails are flicking there, in the drawing. Merwraiths?

Suddenly, the muffled call of a whale drifts through the ice. 'Oh, no!'

'What?' asks Kestrel, panic licking across her face.

'The whales – they answer Sparrow's song. They're connected. If he sings too much they're gonna swim towards him and they'll get trapped under this ice. We need to go.'

Kes nods. 'I've dreamed of learning with the hearth-healers since I was a small girl. I sketched their village and pinned it to my wall. We need to look for a star-shaped settlement high in the foothills, and wild horses with coats the colour of the hills.'

'Heart-thanks,' I tell her, though in my bones I'm shuddering at her mention of horses.

Before we leave Sparrow slurps a dropper filled with

the medsin that the sawbones made for him. Wonder spreads through my chest. What if it really will stop him shaking? That's why the Tribes need unity – cos somewhere there might be folks dying of sicknesses that others can treat.

From our draggle's back, Sparrow sings and stray whale-song floats up. But some is snagging beneath the ice, making a bloom of blue below the sea.

I watch as the whales flee south, away from the spreading ice, their breath-plumes fogging in the night. It makes me feel too un-hidden. What if Stag can see what the whales are doing and uses them to track us?

Then Sparrow sings again. I hold the map in one hand and Thaw snatches up the strands of whale-song and flings them onto the map. But this time, when he reaches what I thought was the end of the song, the words are different.

. . . You'll find it at the point high in the air,
Where life breathes strong and fierce,
And gold light graces where the sun does pierce.

I turn to Sparrow, sucking in my lip. 'Wait – there's more of the old song?'

He nods sleepily.

'You can't have thought the song finished at "high in the air" – that's stupid!' Then he tips his head back to gift more song to the sky.

Do you remember?
When the sky
Yawned wide to swallow me.
Don't you remember?
Breathe and be,
Green lights flicker bright above me.
The iron mountain
Clamps her jaws . . .

'Ugh,' Sparrow grumbles. 'I forgot again.'

'Sparrow, don't fret. That's a flaming good start.' The new words of the song have painted the map in splashes of gold and silver. Colours of the night sky.

When we stop again to rest I keep first watch so the others can nap. The snow stings my cheeks. I've fallen into a half doze when a bright bolt of blue sizzles past my face. I flail awake, cursing myself for keeping such a poor nightwatch, but there's nothing there – just the ice, and the crash of the sea below, and the sound of the draggles hunting. I must've imagined it. I wake Crow after a few hours and take my turn to sleep until the sun staggers up from the sea. As we're mounting our draggles, I spot a few stray berg owl feathers on the ice near where we slept.

We fly on. We're further east than I'd thought. In the distance, beyond frozen rivers and marshes, runs the black scar of the Iron Valley. Beyond it, just south of the Bay of Thunder, glints a column of ice. I wrinkle my nose and point. 'What's that?'

Crow leans forwards. 'Reckon that's your sea-god's breath,' he says.

'But – it looks frozen!'

'Even the geysers are freezing solid,' he murmurs.

Gods. Time's already running out. If the rivers are freezing solid, and the geysers, then how long will it be before the same thing happens to the sea? I remember when we sailed to the Bony Isle aboard *Devil's Hag*. The sea was crusted with a thick layer of ice.

The whales need us. My Tribe needs us.

We speed on, three pairs of wings wheeling blurred arcs through the dawn air.

24
Black Rain

I see them as soon as we drop into the hungry shadows of the Iron Valley, on the horizon – hunting packs of terrodyls circling near the frozen geyser at Whale-Jaw Rock. Smoke coils into the sky. The valley is littered with animal bones and tumbled boulders that look like giants' armour. 'I think we're headed the right way,' says Kestrel, when the wind drops. 'I've spotted a herd or two of horses that look as though they've sprung from the hills themselves.'

Gods. Don't let the skittish land-beasts tread anywhere near me!

We fly until the mountains have shrunk and the pulsing lighthouse beam of Stonepoint flickers to the east. My draggle quails at the sight of the terrodyls, and I've got no strength left to keep her steady. 'They won't fly closer,' Kes shouts. So I beg the draggles to drop us off gently.

Careful, flutter-beasts! No smashing our bones!

Gofleegofleequickquickscurryfly!

When we land we're still wearing our skates, so we untie them from our boots and leave them in the valley. Then we walk. My skin is snow-stung. Across the tops of the mountains, hot springs gush and terrodyl breath puffs, clouds of white smoke dotted between rock and evergreens.

Crow pinches me beneath the ribs and I clout his arm and we run, yelling, laughing, slipping, Sparrow begging us to wait up and Kestrel lost in her thoughts.

Running with Crow lets out all my trapped frights and grievings, for a heartbeat, so it's just me and him and running so hard I get an ache in my side. Finally we stop, grinning at each other, waiting for the others to catch up. Thaw circles overhead, keeping lookout.

Watch out for a star-shape of two-leg dwellings, I pant up to her.

Starstarstar! Eyessharpnofrettings!

The moon carves up and up through the dusk, pooling waxy light on the snow-blanketed foothills ahead of us.

Star! calls Thaw. *Two-legs star!*

She thuds onto my shoulder, almost knocking me into the snow. Then she peers into my face with keen yellow eyes and gives a loud, stinky, excited trill. *Two legs' stewing place of staying still – nest place!*

Heart-thanks, my Thaw girl! I look round at the others' cold-numbed faces. 'Thaw says the village is close. Hands on weapons, eyes sharp, spines arrow-straight.'

We pass a troop of hollow-eyed mountain dwellers in silver rain-cloaks, herding a half-score of skinny horses. I shrink back from them, gagging on the stink of horse-fright. They sing sad songs for the horses they've lost, and their wailing echoes around the rocks.

Then we turn a corner, cut along the edge of a snow-swollen hill and join a dirt track to a village huddled against a jagged overhang of rock. The village hugs the foothills and it's set out in the shape of a five-pointed star, with huts leading away from a central hall. The wind breathes a stink of smoke, snow, bread and spices into my face.

When we reach the dwellings, only one or two have a flickering flame in their star-shaped windows. Others are dark and shuttered. But some are molten heaps of ash and shattered glass and smouldering wood, doused in thick, hissing black goo – more terrodyl blood. The sound of metal striking metal fills my ears, and when I look for the source, I see groups of women wrapped in shawls, hacking at the frozen ground with spades.

At the centre of the village stands a hall with a thatched roof and a bell tower. Its doors are open. A storm-vane in the shape of two clasped hands moves when the wind shivers through the village. Eagle-cries pierce the silence. My boots slip in the snow-ooze underfoot.

A white, waist-high stone rises from the ground in front of the hall. Runes are chiselled into its side. '*The great plague of Hearthstone.*'

Kestrel runs her fingers around the stone basin in the top. 'They say that many moons past, the hearth-healers took in plague victims when no one else would,' she says. 'They cared for them in their hall.'

Sparrow tries to fight me off but I make him hold my hand as we step inside. I crane back my neck to watch the bell tower as we pass beneath the eaves. Kes and Crow stay close behind.

Inside the hall a few market stalls are guarded by traders with tight jaws. There are bubbling vats of stew, full of teeth and bones and ribbony innards. Tattered boots are stacked in rows next to sky-maps of the stars, and there are moon-lamps overcrowded with weak, blotchy moonsprites. We wade through the slush – and everyone in the place stops what they're doing, falls silent and stares at us.

'Your pocket!' whispers Crow in my ear.

I glance down at my pocket and my skin startles when I see the bright green glow coming from it. I shove my hand into my pocket and wrap the Opal in my fingers, to hide the shine. The Opal is growing slick and salt-sticky again.

'Do you have any bread for sale?' asks Kestrel.

'Ground's freezing shut,' barks a grizzled woman with stripes of grey in her black hair. 'Even the earth must be starving, for she won't surrender the steam to bake our bread. Now hurry your bones, before someone boils them for stock.'

'We ain't causing no harm,' says Crow, pulling himself up to his full height.

The old woman laughs, brittle and heart-sad. 'No, lad. But plenty might wish harm to you.' She turns away, but I can see the shakes of sorrow wracking her body. When she turns back again, her face holds lines as hard and deep as the valley. 'Get out of it!' she cries.

We move on quick-sharp, but I look back at her as we go.

'Where's everyone else?' murmurs Crow. 'This ain't much of a market day!'

An old trader hears him. 'The younger folk have been off gathering in the horses,' he says, between swigs from a flask. 'But lots of 'em have already perished of cold. They sent a bird with the news.' He wipes his mouth roughly.

The weight of my burden presses harder on my shoulders as I picture the dead horses strewn across the hills. I drift towards his stall, which is crowded with whips made of goats' hooves, clockwork toys and worn old pipes.

'Is this where the hearth-healers live?' I ask.

The man's mouth opens to reply, but instead of words, a drumbeat fills my ears. I frown, but the drum beats again and I realise it's coming from outside. The trader's face crumples in panic as he jostles us out and locks the doors.

I curse under my breath. My heart plunges into my gut. If no one will help us, have we come this far for nothing?

The drumbeat throbs off the rocks, making snow crash to the ground. Kestrel shifts nervously. 'I think we need to move, now,' she urges.

Just then, a horse-drawn wagon crunches through the snow into the village, whipped by men with straggling hair and iron eyes.

We dive between two dark houses and hunker down. Slush eats up my legs. I blow into Sparrow's hands to warm them as the snow falls thicker, settling its sombre hush on everything.

The wagon passes by, a few feet from our faces. If one of the men turns his head we're doomed. But beats pass, and they keep moving, and I let an inch of breath leave my lungs. Hanging from hooks along the length of the wagon are strange, glassy-eyed dolls. Grim creations, with lax mouths and stiff fingers. But as they move closer, my gut squirms and bile licks into the back of my throat.

The dolls are suspended in long, narrow jars of water. Their eyes are pale, fogged seastones. Fish-roe laces up their arms, the colour of pearls.

No. They can't be. I tell myself that despite what I saw in my dream-dance. Despite what I already know in my heart.

Thaw shudders on top of my head. I feel her peering out from under my hood, her claws digging into my scalp. *Bad-blubber*, she hoots softly.

Aye, I gurgle back to her.

Crow must've felt my muscles tense, cos he grips my forearm. 'Don't do anything stupid,' he breathes. 'Stay where you are.'

I glare at him and swallow, trying to steady my skittering heart. 'But . . . they've got wraiths. Merwraiths.'

'There is nothing you can do,' whispers Kes in my ear.

But what if one of them is Rattlebones? Or – I swallow painfully. What if Grandma managed to turn to wraith, only to be captured? 'Stay here!' I hiss to Sparrow. I snatch my arm away from Crow and scurry out into the open. I run after the cart, slush spattering into my face from the wheels.

Two of the traders from the hall walk down the steps to meet the cart. I freeze in the shadows behind it, heart stammering. 'Just passing through, are you?' demands a woman bundled in a blubbery wrapping of sealskin.

I slip round the side of the cart and stare up at the faces of the wraiths.

'You have no sway in this town any more, hearth-woman,' replies a man with gruesome, yellowed fingernails. 'Show these dredgers respect.'

'We don't want your sort here,' says the woman, ignoring him.

I don't know the wraiths, and guilty relief floods my belly.

'Stag rules here, now. What you want is of no interest to him.' The cart-driver lashes her face with his whip. She stumbles back with a strangled scream and the cart moves on.

I dig my fingers into the snow as panic bubbles in my chest. Stag's taken over this village?

Suddenly, a shadow falls, like someone's thrown a cloak across the land, blotting out the sky. My belly twists. Then a shape sweeps down, and the stalls are smashed to splinters by violent wings, and folk are screaming, scattering, dodging flying things.

A pack of screeching, cackling terrodyls career around the village. Their tawny wings slice through everything in their path. I can sense their blood sparking for the fun of destruction. *Smashscattertearrippluckseverbashsmashcrash!*

The others hurry to my side. Kestrel peers fearfully at the sky. 'I've never seen them behave like this before!' A soft weeping pipes from her bag. Poor Ettler must be frighted witless.

'They're being controlled,' I tell her, flinching as a beast-wail tears the night in two.

Crow tries to pull us away but I tear my arm from his grip. 'Wait – we need to hunt for the Opal!'

'Run, you halfwits!' bellows the old woman who tried to see us off. She takes my elbow and propels me along.

A terrodyl whistles overhead and a dwelling explodes into flying planks of wood, jags of glass, bundles of straw and mud. Then the creature zooms back into the air, stirring a gale that almost knocks me over.

My friends start to run, but I cast around for somewhere to hide. Cos we came here with a purpose – we've got to find the Sky-Opal.

'Mouse, come on!' yells Crow.

Mountain-folk and what's left of their wild herd

streak past us, making for low ground. But one of the terrodyls gives a sudden grunt, loud and low as thunder, and a healer screams as his horse is plucked from the ground and carried away. Other terrodyls swipe the dwellings from the hills. Mud, straw and timber storm through the air.

I tilt my chin skywards, remembering how Stag controlled the beasts to search for the Storm-Opal Crown, aboard my ship. He did it again to try and stop me getting to Castle Whalesbane to save Sparrow. Is that what's happening now? What if he's sent them to tear the place apart, searching for the Sky-Opal? I nibble my lips. And could *I* do it again, to counter him?

More terrodyls beat through the snow-fog, making for the village. *Go*, I will them, trying to throw my beast-chatter around the village in a circle of protection. I grip Bear's amber amulet and chatter again. *Turn back, you ent coming in here.*

Kestrel and Crow each take one of my hands and try to pull me away but I drop heavily to my knees, keeping my eyes on the sky.

One of the creatures thrashes its head like it's trying to get rid of my voice. I try again. *Turn back!* I push my chatter forwards like an arrow, and the terrodyl hovers in the air, then wheels around and throbs away. My heart riots. But more terrodyls beat the air towards the village, and I ball my hands into fists. I need to try and control more than one of them at once.

A cloaked man stalks into the midst of the destruction, carrying a gun. The wind throws his hood back.

My head spins as heavy dread drops into my bones.

Even out in the open, Stag takes up all the space. He sucks all the life and light out of the world. 'Search the moot-hall for their leader!' he barks, voice flaying the night raw.

Everything stops. That voice. It's like a blade slashing behind my eyes.

I can't move. I can't breathe. Fright wriggles through my blood. I keep Sparrow close by my side. The sight of Stag and the memories of what he did to Grandma, and Battle-Shrieker, and the whales, make my legs shake and my heart knock hollowly in my throat.

The dredgers barge into the hall. Screams ebb from inside. But a door opens in one of the squat huts across the dirt track, and a gentle-faced woman steps out.

'Stop your search!' she calls. 'I am chief hearth-healer.' She's garbed in a fur-trimmed shawl, and her dress is stitched with the emblem of the hearth-healers; a pair of brooms crossed above a fire.

'My spy informs me you possess a precious jewel that

that does not belong to you,' Stag booms. 'You will surrender it now.'

'Please, stop the black rain!' calls the woman, eyes hollow. 'We wish no harm to anyone.'

'If you stand in my way, there will be consequences,' Stag says simply. He lifts the gun – I struggle to breathe as the memories crowd my chest – and then he uses his beast-chatter to command a terrodyl closer.

The woman holds her head high, but her voice wavers. 'Please!' In the dim light from the lanterns burning outside the moot-hall, I can see the snowflakes settling on her eyebrows.

Another healer rushes to the woman's side and tries to pull her away.

But Stag twitches the gun towards the second healer. She turns to run but slips in the slush, the gun cracks, bones-deep, and she falls onto her side. The chief hearth-healer drops into a crouch by the dead woman's side, finding the wound and pressing swathes of her dress to it to try to stem the bleeding. But the woman's eyes have already dimmed to blank shiny pools.

'Will that loosen your tongue?' Stag drawls to the chief. 'Or do you require further persuasion?'

The chief climbs shakily to her feet and stares him right in the eyes, her mouth a grim line. She stays silent.

Stag points his gun at the sky, beast-chattering low

in his throat.

He's gonna summon the terrodyl close enough to shoot it down and crush the hearth-healers' hall. *Turn back, beast!* I chatter. I find the thread of wildness connecting me to the world of creatures and push into it. *Don't come any closer!* The terrodyl hovers in the sky, pulled between mine and Stag's beast-chatter, thrashing its head wildly in confusion.

It's so much harder this time. My heart flutters like a sickly bird, making me snatch for breath, and sweat weaves down my back. Stag's power is much too strong for me, and I hate, hate, *hate* it, but it's true.

Stag jerks his gun towards me. Then he lowers it slowly to the ground.

25
Quiet Warriors

For a heartbeat, Stag loses control of the terrodyl and I focus all my heart-strength on trying to send the beast away from the village, even though I know there are scores more of them and Stag can control as many as he wants.

I feel his eyes on my face and flick my gaze towards him, still beast-chattering.

Get out of here, go! You ent coming in here, turn back! Go!

In the corner of my eye there's a swirl of red and gold skirts as Kestrel stands close by my side.

The terrodyl starts to turn in the air but then Stag's beast-chatter reaches up and out and pulls it back towards the bell tower again.

Do not defy me!

Stag's staring hard at my scar. 'Very impressive. Not quite good enough, though.'

I step back, letting my connection to the terrodyl slip away. How's he talking to both the terrodyl and me at the same time?

Stag grimaces, his eyes dark pits in his long, gaunt face. 'That's right. Do not meddle – too many girls like to make trouble, and it is tiresome.' He shoots a quick look at Sparrow, nestled by my side, and I want to roar and howl and gloat that I did find my brother, even though he said I never would, I *did*.

The terrodyl jerks back to life, pulsing closer to the moot-hall. *Keep going*, chatters Stag urgently. Then he focuses on the hearth-healer again. 'Where is it?' he murmurs, almost calmly, as he opens his gun and tips powder into it.

Sparrow whimpers. I string my longbow with shaky fingers and search my pocket for the clutch of stumpy arrows I made.

The chief's lips don't move. But her eyes lock onto mine. Then they quickly dart upwards, lingering on the bell tower for barely a beat. Her eyes are back on Stag before he's finished fiddling about with the gun. My blood screams that she's sending me a signal.

'If you refuse to tell me where it is, the creature will be shot down, killing all your sick and injured,' he says in a bored tone. He hacks out a cough and spits a glob of frothing blood onto the hard ground.

A breath I've been holding onto seethes from my chest. Have we come that close to finding it, only for *him* to get there first?

The woman keeps her head high and her eyes on Stag's. The defiance lighting up her face gifts me heart-strength. I ent watching Stag use that gun a second time.

I gabble again in beast-chatter, fright panging in my gums. *Stop, fly home, seek nest-brothers!* I tell it, remembering the terrodyl we flew on, the one that got shot down by draggle-riders cos I lured it from its nest. I might be able to save this one. But Stag curses and steps towards me. I flinch and jerk away from him, slipping over and crashing to the ground, dropping my bow.

'Mouse?' asks Sparrow, reaching into the air and feeling for my hand. His white eyes go crossed when he tries to focus on Thunderbolt, buzzing in front of his face.

'Don't fret, just – stay put,' I call up to him.

Stag smirks, and I want to rip it from his face – but I know there wouldn't be anything human underneath.

'Told you I'd find my brother,' I spit.

He laughs. 'Do you wish for me to tell you what a fine job you've done of keeping this doomed cripple temporarily safe and well?' He presses his boot beneath my chin, forcing me to look up.

Our eyes meet and I'm locked in that old world of

squirming guts and feeling too small and not being able to get to Grandma. I growl.

'Stay away from her!' shouts Kestrel. A dagger slips through the air, thrown by an iron-strong arm. It grazes the side of Stag's face, snipping a cut in his ear. He jerks back from me, blood trickling down the side of his neck. Fury blazes in his eyes.

'Kes!' I shout, pushing off from the frozen ground. She stands strong, legs planted wide. She's got two more daggers in her hands. I grab Sparrow and Crow pulls us closer to him and Kes. The four of us stand, facing Stag, breathless. Thaw-Wielder circles around our heads, bristling. Sparrow balls jagged lightning between his palms and the smell of it tickles into my nose.

Before Stag can raise his gun, a yell rings out, echoing off the rocks. 'Stag! Sir, I was wrong! They don't know where it is, I – I was wrong.' The voice is familiar, but I can't place it.

I look around, bafflement plucking at me.

Yapok stumbles out from behind a boulder and shuffles to Stag's side, panting for breath. His hair stands on end and his white cloak is streaked with draggle-dung.

Stag sighs, hand clamped to his ear as the blood from Kes's dagger drips down onto his tunic. 'I know full well that it's here, and it's thanks to you that I've been led to the right place. You've done well, Yapok. Take your reward and leave these four for me to deal with.'

Iron bitterness fills my chest and my mouth tastes dry and acid.

Kestrel takes a step closer to Yapok. She opens her mouth, as though she's going to scold him. But then she draws back her iron-arm and hits him in the jaw. There's a dull *crunch*. As he falls backwards, Kes's shaky hands fly to her mouth. Then she looks at the edge of her iron-hand and wipes off a smudge of blood. Her face crumples and she grips her sides like she's trying to hold her spirit in. Yapok lies at her feet, clutching his face.

Stag reaches inside his cloak, pulls out a brown sack and throws it onto Yapok's belly. Thick gold ingots spill into the snow.

Kestrel gives Yapok a look so full of disgust and pity that a howling cry rips from his throat. 'I don't want your gold!' Then he doubles over and spits out a tooth.

'Take it, don't take it,' says Stag with a shrug. 'But you will tell me where the Opal is.' He grabs Kestrel and presses the gun to her side. Yapok shouts, struggling to his knees.

'Let go of her!' I yell.

Crow touches my elbow. 'I'll distract him,' he

whispers in my ear. 'You find the Opal.'

Crow rushes at him, leaping high and blending swiftly into his crow-shape. He barrels into Stag's face. Stag tries to turn the gun on him but drops it. It explodes in a cloud of dust and fire. Someone screams. I grab Sparrow's hand and we run, not waiting to look back, heading for the bell tower. Inside, I pray to all the sea-gods my friends will stay safe.

We burst into the moot-hall, to the spot where the Opal started to glow. The door swings on its hinges and the place is deserted now the threat of black rain has spread amongst the villagers. We find a stairway and race up and up and up, Sparrow singing to navigate his way like a whale, and keep from bumping into the walls. I just have to hope I didn't imagine the hearth-healer's signal.

Right at the very top of the tower is a dark attic room with a huge bell in the centre. There's a low iron bed, maybe so the bell-ringer can nap. At its foot is a wooden garb chest.

I step across the creaky wooden floor. The darkness presses on my eyeballs. A soft blue glow seeps through the cracks in the chest as I step closer. I sink to my knees. Snow whips through the broken window and stings my eyes. I root through the worn, patched clothes in the chest, a sob rising through me as my fingers touch cool, smooth stone.

I lift out a blue jewel. My breath catches, cos under the gem's surface shimmer threads of pink, black and gold. They twist and twine like streaks of ink. The Sky-Opal.

'Mouse?' whimpers Sparrow, from somewhere to my left, in the gloom.

'What?'

Then there's a soft, wet choking sound. The breath gushes from my lungs. My head swivels to search the dark and a match is struck against the wall, showing my brother with a pair of big, hairy hands wrapped around his throat. Sparrow's fingers crackle with lightning, but Stag don't seem to feel the pain, even though a stink of burning meat sneaks through the room.

'Very well done, Mouse,' comes the voice of my nightmares. 'But I think I'll be taking that now.'

Sparrow's eyes are wide and starting to bulge. He rasps for breath. The glow of the Opal lets me see how his skin is darkening to a blotched red-purple. Fright etches itself onto his skin, carving deep. A blob of blood rolls down Stag's arm and plops onto the floor as Sparrow's lightning cuts into his hands. But they don't move from my brother's throat.

I don't even feel myself move. But suddenly Stag's hands are off Sparrow and I'm dropping the Sky-Opal into them. I pull my brother roughly away from him in the same movement.

His thin breath scratches and then he's coughing and spluttering in my arms and I don't ever want to let him go again, not for a single beat, not ever. 'I'm so sorry I stopped thinking about you, even for a heartbeat,' I whisper into his hair.

Dimly I hear boot-steps leaving the room. The door slams and a key scrunches in the lock. Then the steps clunk fearlessly down the stairs. Life must be proper easy for loons what don't have to be quiet or stay hidden all the time.

Sparrow wipes his streaming eyes and puts his hand on my cheek. 'Sorry I got caught. Sorry about that stone we need to save the world.'

I'm bawling, then. Great, sloppy, hot tears that roll down my face and drip off my nose into his hair. For a while I can't move, and Sparrow makes me rest until my heart stops skipping and the storm in my veins settles.

I wrap my hand in some old garb from the chest and break the last shards of glass away from the window. Then we tie together odds and ends of bedding and make a rope to lower ourselves out and to the ground. As soon as my feet touch the mud Crow's streaking towards us, changing back into a boy even before he lands.

'Gods, could you have taken any longer?' he croaks, talons thudding into the ground as he grabs my shoulders. 'I chased Stag off but then he turned the terrodyls on me and got away. I was heading to the tower when he strutted out, looking mighty chuffed with himself.'

'He took the Sky-Opal,' I tell him, casting around fearfully. My failing sits on my shoulders, pushing me into the ground. 'Then he locked us in the tower.'

Kestrel and Yapok run out from behind a burning hovel. 'What's *owl-boy* still doing here?' asks Crow, striding towards Yapok.

Kestrel gets between them. 'It wasn't his fault.'

Yapok stares around at us, face cracked with guilt and shame. I try to blink away the rage clouding my eyes. 'How'd you work that one out?'

She grips Yapok's hand and strokes the scars. 'Tell them, Yapok. Tell them what you told me.'

He opens his mouth but before he can speak, a maddened roar echoes around the hills.

'MOUSE!'

I'm already scrabbling away, running as fast as I can, shouting for the others to hurry. I find my longbow and arrow lying in the snow and snatch them up.

'*Wait!*' commands Stag.

Yapok steps away, into the shadow of the moot-hall.

I can feel the way the Opal in my pocket burns brighter cos the Sky-Opal is so close. They are kin. 'He's feeling the pull of the Sea-Opal,' I gasp. 'He's gonna realise we've got it!'

Stag bounds out of the darkness, fury splayed across his face. He's flanked by filth-streaked, dead-eyed dredgers.

I fumble an arrow to my longbow, but before I can loose it, Yapok flings himself at Stag's back, his hands erupting into wolf-paws that punch Stag roughly to the ground. His gun flies from his hands. Realisation swirls through my bones – Yapok's as much a Wilderwitch as the Wilder-King. He's part wolf, too.

The Sky-Opal flies into the air and thuds into the snow. Stag lies still, stunned for a beat. Then he's fighting to his feet, but Thaw bursts into the air and swoops at his head, great strong wings and talons striking him from all sides. He drops to his knees, hands and face torn. While he's down, Yapok grabs the Sky-Opal and throws it to me.

I pocket it, grab Sparrow and run past the houses of the village. Crow, Kestrel and Yapok tear after us. *Thaw!* I scream. She bolts through the sky, gliding by my side.

A door bursts open. The chief hearth-healer steps outside, holding a gun in two hands. Flanking her are other women, wearing the sign of the crossed brooms. They nock fire-arrows to their bows, draw and loose before Stag and the dredgers can blink. 'You are not welcome in Hearthstone!' they cry as one voice, heart-strong together.

As we run past, the chief gives me the tiniest nod. She hoists her gun to her shoulder and squints down it at Stag.

When I look back, the healers have surrounded Stag and the dredgers. Under the orders of the chief, they start to wind ropes around their wrists.

I whisper a heart-thanks to the healers and keep running, slipping in the snow. I clutch Sparrow's hand tightly.

26
No Hearth-welcome

Higher in the hills, clouds swarm down from the mountain. We disappear under their white skirts, the hems already crackling to ice. Our clothes stick damply to our skin. The back of my neck grows clammy and tiny raindrops pearl on the hairs on my forearms. Hail clatters on the horse-herders' skin tents on the mountainside and thuds against our cloaks.

When Yapok walks too close to Crow, the wrecker boy spits at his boots and veers roughly away, to put more space between them.

'Stag wants to keep the Sky-Tribes divided,' Kes calls after Crow. 'He wants to divide *everyone*. And that starts with manipulating the young, just like at Hackles. But we are going to resist. We must unite, and stay strong together, before we can hope to unite the rest of the Tribes.'

She's desperate to see the good in Yapok, whatever he's done. Her heart-strength steals my breath. I want this girl for crew. 'Aye!' I tell her. 'We won't let him win.'

She nods at me. 'No, we won't.'

Crow freezes, then turns slowly back to face us. 'What've you got to say, then?' he asks Yapok, shoving his hands into his armpits.

Yapok screws up his face. 'I had to protect the Skybrarian. He's the nearest thing I've got to family. I just wanted things to stay the same as they've always been, for us to be left alone with our books!' he whispers. 'But it kept getting worse.' Then he turns to look at us. 'When I met all of you – it was already a snowball I couldn't stop.' He scratches at the burn-marks on his palms. In a flood I picture Stag making the burns. 'He knew I'd do whatever it took.' He looks like he's gonna say more but then his face crumples.

I step towards him and lean onto my tiptoes, gifting him a Tribe-kiss before he can move away.

Crow nods slowly. Then he wraps an arm around Yapok's shoulders and they walk on together. Kestrel struggles along with her skirts twisting around her ankles. 'Still reckon breeches are just for men?' I ask. 'Shudder to think how I'd be faring in a flaming skirt.' She glares at me, then laughs.

After that, the climbing gets harder, and we're often silent. We scrabble, skid, scramble, gulp for air. I slip and land heavily on my side, and Kes gasps, but I'm up again before she can help me.

My muscles scream. Sparrow pulls his hand away and lags behind. 'I can't do it!'

Crow grabs him and swings him onto his shoulders.

'We need somewhere to hide and make a plan. Somewhere we can be safe.' I think about what the map showed us. 'We need to find the Icy Marshes. They shouldn't be too far.'

'Far enough that we'll need to find horses,' says Crow.

Sparrow squeals out a sudden laugh. 'Mouse is bed-wet-frighted of horses!'

'Will you shut it!' I bite, as the others snicker into their hands. Even Yapok chuckles. But just the mention of them skittish beasts has filled my chest with tiny stinging arrowheads, and made my palms sweat.

We pass a herd of horses that are heart-sad skinny, so we leave them be. Then we spy a horse-herder wrapped in a moss-coloured cloak, but he chases us off, waving his stick, before we can get close enough to beg him to sell us a few horses. The next herd is a straggle of beasts with fright shining in their eyes, too wild for Crow to catch. But finally, when we're ready to collapse in the snow, we find a clutch of horses grazing on tough roots. They're tethered, so they ent wild. But there's no herder in sight.

'We might as well take 'em,' pants Crow as he unties four horses. 'For all we know, the owner's not coming back.'

'And we'll pay for them,' says Kes firmly, making us fetch together all the bits of silver we have.

'It'll go to perfect ruddy use amongst a bunch of lone horses,' huffs Crow, eyeing the silver bits as Kes slips them into the saddlebag of one of the horses left behind.

The whole time, I force my spine arrow-straight and pretend my gut ent boiling into a hot frenzy. I wipe my sweaty palms on my cloak.

Before we mount, I stare up at my skinny chestnut gelding and try not to bolt. It watches me with heavy-lashed brown eyes, stamping at the ground and snorting.

Crow makes me step closer and sniff the horse's neck – it's like wood, like someone's warm tunic, solid, and maybe a tiny bit comforting.

'Ain't that the best smell in the world?' he asks. I shrug, biting my cheek.

I try to hold onto the smell of comfort as Crow swings me onto the horse's back, but soon I'm fighting to control the crackle of fright passing between me and the beast, who don't trust me a stitch.

Flighty frighty fearsome two-legs, no trust, wants to run, I want to runrunrunrunrun throw buck rear.

Don't even think about it. Whoa, steady!

The others are all mounted now, watching me. Sparrow is bundled in front of Kestrel. The knot in my belly tightens and tightens, and sickness spreads through me.

'Ready?' asks Yapok. 'We should keep moving.'

'I can't,' I tell them, my voice the size of a krill.

'Told you,' says Sparrow, smug as anything.

My mouth trembles. Even with everything we're running from, I still can't swallow this heart-fright. Feels like I'm wearing my skin inside out. I don't understand horses, and Kes keeps asking me if I'm all right, and I can't answer her. I hate having four legs under me that ent mine and that I can't control. All I want is to jump from the saddle, even if I break my flaming leg doing it, and get away. The horse tosses its head. Painful fright shoots through me.

Thaw sits on a nearby tree branch, spitting insults at the horse, which don't seem to help matters.

Crow watches me. 'Don't flick your fright around like a spear,' he tells me. 'The horse is a gentle spirit – let him guide you. You can't control everything, but you can learn to trust. He can sense all the troubles in you. And he can help you heal them.'

'When did you turn into such a wise-one?' I spit. 'I'm telling you – the horse don't like me, and I don't like him.'

'It's all right to be scared, y'know. Now and then.' Crow bites his lip. 'But there's not much we can do about liking or not liking each other, if you want to find the Marshes.' He takes my horse's reins to help me along, but every time we need to go proper fast he mounts my horse with me and takes over, so I can clamp my eyes shut and cry into the wind. Turns out horse herds are so strongly linked that his horse just tears after us, not wanting to be left behind.

'You know,' Crow says when we slow again and my belly falls out of my mouth, 'it's just like being on a ship. You have to feel the rhythm.'

'Ent nothing like being on a ship,' I spit through clenched teeth. Sparrow – half blind, sickly as anything and seal-pup young – sniggers at me as he and Kestrel canter past. Even flaming Sparrow don't mind horses. Shame bites my bones raw.

After a day's ride I still hate horses just as much as I always did – and I've got a new-found hate for sore backsides, to boot.

Then things go from bad to worse. Even Crow struggles to calm the beasts when lightning zaps at their hooves and trees are torn loose in a storm that tries to gulp us whole. The trees smash to the ground, their roots straggling into the air. One horse bolts when we stop to find water, so we're left with three.

We ride through the storms until we reach the outskirts of the Icy Marshes, where there's a man loaning canoes for a silver ingot each. For extra silver he loans ice picks, veils and gloves – protection from the poison frogs.

'Daylight robbery,' mutters Crow when he strolls back from selling our horses – he's only got enough for a canoe.

I watch the skin boats skudding away down the wandering sea-path to the Marshes. It's proper strange to be back here – the place where Rattlebones helped me escape my ship, before.

''Twill have to do,' says Kes, with a frown.

'We'll be fine.' I stride towards the man renting out the canoes, the others on my heels.

The man takes our silver and slips a canoe from its mooring. We climb in, and when the man sees my scar he smirks a look of amused disgust.

Thaw springs from my hood and bolts into the man's face, hissing and squawking and flapping her ever-strengthening wings. He staggers backwards and splashes into the marsh. I reach down and grab the ice pick from his hand as Thaw spits at him and soars back to me. She smooths a wing-tip gently across my cheek, a habit she's started whenever folks gift my scar hard looks.

Heart-thanks, Thaw.

Fury makes her body tremble, so it takes me a few beats, while our boat gathers speed, to get her to come back to me, out of the beast-world. Then she whisks from my shoulder into the water to catch fishes that dart in the murky shallows.

Our canoe crunches through the frosty water, releasing little puffs of steam. When we reach the end of the sea-path, the marsh widens into a great network of waterways and canoes wreathed in mist, with lanterns swinging from poles at their prows. Finally, I've got a chance to feel a surge of heart-gladness that we found the Sky-Opal, saved it from Stag and all stayed together.

Our canoe crunches to a stop until I lean over and break the ice in front of us with the pick. Crow watches the marsh water, then plunges his hand through the surface and grabs a long-legged insect, stuffing it into his mouth. 'I got hungry,' he says when I stare at him, heat spilling across his cheeks.

We sail until the moon is high, and a mourning-song fills our ears. A township on stilts looms into view, a hotch-potch of skinny-legged stilt homes, swaying in the wind. Heart-sadness wraps around my chest when I see that some of them have been burned by terrodyl blood, too. But the others stand strong and whole, and I won't let my hope fizzle out.

Giant toads with cracked, slimy skin sit in the marsh, urgently calling out.

GlukglukGLOATINGglukglukgloiking!

When they suddenly spring away, showering us with stagnant water, Yapok and Kestrel cower together, cringing with horror.

'I can smell toads,' whispers Sparrow, fear stretching his face.

'S'alright too-soon,' I tell him. 'This is a place of hearth-welcome.'

But he shakes his head. 'It's just like my nightmare.'

A stink swarms close. Folk empty chamber pots from their homes into the marsh, and droplets of slurry pepper our skin as we glide past.

'Urgh,' says Crow, wiping his face with the back of his hand.

'Ever the spoilt land-bab, I see,' I tell him, and he whacks my arm. Then he yells, swerving around a huge column of ice that's sticking out of the marsh. Inside the ice are frozen frogs and fishes.

The air above is thick with fog the colour of rotting meat. I wrap my scarf tighter around my nose and mouth, wondering how to get someone to help us find the Marsh-folks' leader.

Then a rubbery yellow frog the size of a gold piece lands on Crow's bare arm with a muffled wet sound. He glances down at it, his hands stilling on the paddles.

My mind scrambles for Grandma's teachings. 'Don't move!' I tell him. 'The tiniest poison-frogs are the most deadly.' This little one could knock him out cold for days, if not for always.

'Everyone make certain you're covered up,' I call, as my heart pounds, making me dizzy. 'Anyone got a blade?'

'I have not dealt with such foul creatures before!' breathes Kestrel, cowering away from the frog. She kicks a dagger along the bottom of the canoe, and I pick it up. Ettler pokes two dark eyes from inside her cloak.

Whatitwhatit?

'You've never seen a *frog* before?' Crow hisses.

My mind whirrs. Traders squabble on the marsh banks, carrying double-pronged spears like the tails of sand-eels. They watch us pass, suspicion scrawled across their features.

No one else is going to save him, rings a voice in my head.

I reach for my belt and pull free the blade Kes gifted me. 'Don't move,' I tell Crow. He grips his forearm with his other hand, trying to steady the shakes running through him.

The frog sticks out its bone-white tongue. Two curved gold fangs gleam in its mouth. Slowly the tongue flickers out across Crow's skin.

Tastysaltywarm, the frog snickers. *Tangfleshfattysup*.

'My arm's gone numb!' he whispers, barely breathing.

'It's released its numbing medsin,' I whisper.

The frog draws its tongue back into its mouth, waiting.

Bitesoonbitesoonrasptastemeaty!

I bring the tip of my blade slowly closer.

'Just kill it!' wails Yapok.

When the gold of its teeth flashes again I drive the point of my blade clean through the frog's skull, just stopping short of Crow's arm. Careful not to lose any of the venom that's started to seep out, I peel the frog's sucker pads off his skin.

'Argh, you're pulling out all the hairs!' he gasps.

'Want me to leave it next time, do you?' I growl, lifting the frog's tiny body onto my knee.

'Beast weren't mucking about,' he remarks, staring at the bald, still-sticky spots on his arm where the suckers were attached.

'Nor are these others!' snaps Kestrel, shuddering as she stares around at the giant toads. 'How much further must we drift into this place?'

More and more giant toads swarm towards us, and Kes clutches the sides of the boat, knuckles white.

'I reckon they're being drawn by the Opals,' I whisper, nerves jangling as great bulging pairs of eyes watch us pass.

'They are horrible,' whispers Kestrel. We accidentally hit one with an oar and Kes shrieks when it bloats up into the air, muttering and spluttering to itself.

I pinch the shiny gold fangs from the dead poison-frog's mouth. 'They say that rich-as-filth land-dwelling ladies like to adorn their necks with glimmering ropes of poison-frog fangs. We can save these and trade them.'

'Summat tells me this lot of bog-faeries might be sitting on piles of the things already,' snipes Crow, as he sets to covering up every inch of his skin.

Then I remove the tongue, cut loose a scrap of moss and use it to wrap the tongue to preserve it. I feel Crow's eyes on me. 'For its numbing medsin,' I tell him, without looking up. Finally I take the glass tear-vial Kes gifted me and squash the frog's skull with the flat of my thumb, like Grandma once showed me, making a miniature river of black slime drip into the vial, filling it almost to the top.

I stow the teeth and vial of venom in my tunic pocket. What with being on the water and having a longbow and a blade, I'm starting to feel more like my old self with every beat. The rushing of my blood is slowly growing quieter in my ears. I wipe my dagger clean on my breeches but keep it out and ready. 'We should've nabbed one of them nets!'

'How about we just get out of here?' Crow grabs the paddles and pushes our boat away from the bank we drifted into.

'Hang about a beat, wrecker-boy. Think we'd better take a little dose of venom now. Never know when more of the blighters will start sticking themselves to you. This will make us immune for a little while.'

We dab a smidge of the venom onto our tongues. The taste sends a wave of bile and wooziness crashing over me, but I shake my head violently and try to hang onto my wits.

'Where'd you learn how to do that?' asks Crow.

Just then, a shadow falls over us. 'I was going to ask the same thing,' booms a voice. 'That's some mean technique!'

Something hits the bottom of our canoe and instantly I'm engulfed in an angry, biting cloud of green fog. It claws its way down my throat, making me cough and retch painfully. I feel someone grab my boots and pull me up, into the air, until I'm hanging upside down and staring into a pair of buggy green eyes.

'Oi!' yells Crow. 'Put my friend down, right now!'

'Yes,' says Kes, fingering a dagger in the scabbard on her chest. 'Release her at once.'

'If you insist,' says the voice. The grip on my ankles eases and I tumble back into the boat, bashing my head on the struts in the bottom.

I blink to make the trees stop spinning. A long shadow falls across me. I scuttle onto all fours.

A grizzled man stands over us, with long, swaying ropes of viney hair hanging down and getting in the way of his round green eyes. There's a pitted scar beneath one of them, puckering the lower eyelid. His toad-skin coat is covered in a layer of grime, and he carries a sparkling spear covered in fish scales. When a giant toad rises from the water, belching glowing gas, the man lashes it with a whip hooked to his belt, and it vanishes under the steam again.

He looks like he's moving when he's not. Something is swarming, all over him. I know who he is.

'You're the frog man! From my map!' As I blurt the words, I see the poison-frogs leaping about in his hair, in the pockets of his grubby cloak, stuck to his bare chest.

27
One Tribe's Poison

He places a finger to his lips and winks, then unravels a length of netting from his pocket and rigs it to cover our canoe. 'My name is Pike,' he tells us. 'Let me take you to my home. We can talk more safely there.'

As we hack the ice and paddle through the marshes, Pike croaks a throaty tune with the frogs. He looks down at us and winks again. 'A rain charm.'

The gateway to the town above the water is a giant fish-jaw fringed with icicles. I remember when we docked here, right before I escaped Stag's grimy clutches, and Squirrel raced away towards these marshes. What happened to my friend after that?

We glide beneath it and a man on a raised platform lowers a gate in front of us. 'Toll,' he croaks, stretching out a veined hand.

'What've you got to offer to our marsh-gods?' asks Pike, as he kisses a small carving of a frog and tosses it into the rushes.

I try not to grumble as I fish out a frog fang and pass it to Crow. The man lifts the gate to let us pass. We've made a trade of sorts, I reckon. That fang most likely did buy us safe passage and, with heart-luck, Pike might gift us a place to sleep for the night.

On the banks, musicians strum stringed instruments built from the jaws of fish.

We moor at the base of the largest of the houses on stilts. In the boats, on the balconies of the houses, and on the walkways running between them, folks run around barefooted, frogs leaping in their hair. One or two of their stilt-homes smoulder, spewing old smoke. Pike sees me looking. 'Lightning storms,' he explains.

Pike moors the boat and we climb a ladder onto a mossy walkway. The house creaks in the eerie wind that echoes through the reeds. The foul stink of the marsh-fog seeps through the boards and claws into my nose.

Pike pushes open a thin door and we step into the house, dripping onto the black floor. 'I can't wait to get dry,' says Kestrel, peering around.

'Get dry?' says Pike in alarm. 'That can be dangerous. Why should you want to do that?'

Rushlights flicker in the gloom, and a woman sits in a rocking chair by the stove, dipping rushes in kettles of fat to make more lights as the old ones die. 'Hearth-welcome,' she says, dipping her head. Then she stands and pads stickily towards us, gripping a pan and ladle. Pike takes our cloaks from us and hangs them from hooks in the wall. He glances inside the lining of mine and nods to himself thoughtfully.

Then, without a word of warning, the woman starts dumping ladlefuls of thick, clear slime over our heads. I start to complain, then shut my mouth before the slime runs down my throat. I stare down at the woman's webbed feet until the slime stops coursing down my face. Then I wipe the worst of it out of my eyes and mouth, gasping.

Kestrel is fuming. 'You should ask before doing that!'

The woman smiles. 'Slime-dunking keeps us warm and prevents our skins from drying. Now please remove your boots and stockings, and come inside.'

We look at each other. 'Best do as she asks,' I say with a shrug, peeling off my boots. Then I move further into the house, my hair and clothes welded to my skin. Sparrow follows close behind, and the others are still squabbling with the slime-woman. My feet stick to the rubbery black floor. It's covered in eel skin. My jaw falls slack when I see how the main room crawls with huge newts and salamanders. *Ooze*, they chatter. *Drip, plinkplunk, slimeslimeslimesearch, tonguedartsnack?*

Thaw reels away from them into the rafters, where she perches, bristling. *Nonono*, she whispers to me. *Uh no oh no, no heart-thankings from me!*

Don't flaming blame you, Thaw, I tell her, watching the creatures shuffle around the room.

A fire crackles in the corner, stirring up all the strange stinks of the place – fish and frogs and damp. There's a constant *croak-chirp-plop* of frogs falling from the rafters. I jump, brushing them away. 'It's all right,' says Pike. 'The ones in here should have been defanged.'

I don't like the sound of *should*.

All around us, there's a slimy pattering as frogs land on the fish-skin roof.

Pike fetches a tray filled with steaming mugs of broth. 'Help yourselves.'

I take one and sniff the steam – it smells suspiciously froggy. I pinch my nose and drink it down, cos these days we never know when we'll eat again. Kestrel tucks herself into a chair and hides her feet under her skirts, staring round at everything with what looks like a mix of horror and wonder. Ettler wiggles out of her cloak and starts chugging around the room, ogling everything.

'You wanted to know about the great wide,' I whisper.

Kestrel sucks in her bottom lip and raises her eyebrows. 'But so much of it, all at once?'

Pike lights a pipe and puffs out green rings of smoke.

'I saw the symbol of the *Huntress* sewn into two of your cloaks.' Strings of slime plop from the roof into our laps. 'I'm more heart-glad than you could know that you didn't drown when you fled your ship. I'm guessing you learned your poison-frog extraction from Captain Wren.'

'Aye!' Heart-gladness swells in my chest. 'You knew her?'

He nods, drawing in a sharp breath. 'And are the whispers true? The Hunter had her drowned?'

I flinch, watching Sparrow. He curls his feet under him on a chair, watching the space next to Pike's head. 'S'alright,' he says, 'you can talk about it around me, y'know.'

I turn back to Pike. 'Aye, the whispers are true. So I'll be needing your help.'

He strokes his whiskery chin. 'I didn't just know your grandma. I know Fox, too.'

I sit arrow-straight at the mention of Da, brushing a tiny frog from my hair. 'Do you know where he is?'

Sadness floods the crags of his face and he shakes his head. My hopes turn sour. 'I have gathered whispers in the dark. He sent a message to say he hadn't made it back to your ship, that Stag had caught up with him.'

I reel. Finally, someone's said out loud what I've always known in my heart – Stag didn't kill Da!

'Stag left Fox for dead, but he was rescued by a tree-tribe. I was about to travel there when another message arrived from that tribe, telling me he had already left.' Pike stops abruptly. 'Can all of your companions be trusted?'

Crow bristles, glaring at Yapok until he flushes. Pike watches them in bemusement.

'Aye,' I tell him. 'You can talk freely.'

'I helped your da on his quest to get the Storm-Opals to safety.'

'You were *with* him?' My mind races to keep up. That must be why the map showed us Pike.

'Yes. But to complete our quest we had to separate. I trust my parcel reached your grandmother?' His eyes fall to my pocket and a rush of knowing hits me.

'Did you send Grandma the Opal?' I say, voice barely a whisper. 'Was it wrapped up in this?' I pull out the piece of fish skin Crow found.

Pike shutters the windows and we're plunged into guttering rushlight. 'That I did, and yes, it was. Your da and me never intended to split the Opals for long. We had to get them safe from Stag. When Fox wrote to me, he told me to send the Opal I had on to Captain Wren and he would be there to meet it. He wouldn't tell me where the others were, in case Stag caught me. So I tied it to the foot of your grandma's sea-hawk. But I didn't hear from your da again, and I've been sick with heart-worry about it ever since.'

He inhales a lungful of smoke and blows out a thick green cloud. 'I am heart-thankful you found our marshes,' he croaks. 'But I'm almost not daring to hope – does this mean you've found another Opal? I've been searching myself, to no avail.'

I glance at my toes, sticky with slime and slowly thawing. 'Aye.' I look up and grin. 'We've ridden a day from the foothills of the Eastern Mountain Passes, where the hearth-healers had one of the Opals safe. Stag almost got his mitts on it, but Yapok saved it.'

'Aye, after he sold us out,' mutters Crow.

Kestrel shoots him a dark look. 'He made up for it.'

Yapok blushes, squirming.

Pike waits patiently for us to finish our squabbles. Then he speaks. 'We must find out the third Opal, and quickly. I have heard reports of trapped whales being attacked by polar dogs, and whole villages destroyed by landslides. There is talk of a group aligning itself with destruction, against nature. Ancient trees have been felled in the forest of Nightfall. The world is splintering, and Stag is reaping full advantage. And I have a feeling he is not working alone.' He sighs deeply, rubbing his jaw. 'Enough talking, for tonight. All I ask of you for now is to surrender yourselves to sleep. In the morning, we make a plan.' He shows us to a sleeping chamber filled with low mattresses woven from eel skin, moss and reeds.

Curling my knees into my chest, I burrow into the damp, scratchy mattress. My skin is covered in sleeping frogs.

Mmm, warm skin, they chatter. *Sleepy warm-place snoozings.*

I've already stopped bothering trying to scrape them off – but Kestrel sits in her bed, desperately prising them off with the tip of a dagger and flipping them onto the wall. When she's finished in one place, there are more than ever in the next and her eyes bulge in horror. Crow don't like it either, but Sparrow just strokes their backs, giggling.

I shuffle down in my bed and shut my eyes, but too many faces and pictures flood into my brain. I shake my head to try to rid myself of all the mutterings of the frogs and the flickering of all the little beasts' hearts. The Opals are making me feel too much of the world.

I take the green Sea-Opal from my pocket and hold it in one palm, then hold the blue Sky-Opal in the other. Side by side, they glow bright and crackle with power. My palms grow warm and the hairs inside my nose twinge and tickle. Their shapes are curved one to the left and one to the right, so that when I bring them together, curling my palms over each other, the Opals fit together with a *chink*.

Suddenly I can hear all the beast-chatter on the Marshes right inside my head and it pounds like a rotten tooth. I fall sideways, trying to pull the Opals apart, but they're fixed and they send lightning down my arm.

Ettler wriggles out from Kestrel's bed and stares at the Opals. Their light shines in his eyes. Then Kestrel reaches out and places a hand on my arm, making me startle. 'They're trying to heal the rift, for they never wanted to be severed,' she murmurs. I nod, watching the colours play under the jewels' surfaces. Then I realise they're swapping streaks of colour between them, like a gateway has opened from one to the other.

Beyond the Marshes, there's a thud and a *hiss*, a thud and a *hiss*, like booming thunder followed by hail. 'What's that?' I whisper.

'Makes me imagine giants' footsteps,' whispers Crow, eyes gleaming in the almost-dark. 'Remember when the Skybrarian said they've been waking?'

Kestrel watches us. 'I have an idea that I'd like to share with you all.'

'What?' I ask.

She stares into her lap, then draws a deep breath and looks up. 'Oftentimes, the full-growns close their borders and cross their spears against outsiders. They shut their ears to reason. This I have always known, growing up in war.' She uncrosses her legs under her blankets. 'But I'm of a mind that one can be a quiet warrior, using gentle ferocity to heal, to make, to dance. Quiet strength. And I believe that the youth of other tribes could think this way too.' The spark of her passion catches her voice, lighting her whole face up, into a glowing brown. 'We could target the youth of every Tribe. Write to them, visit them in secret. Sneak into Tribe-Meets. Rally them to join us. They will want to stop the creep of this ice and put things right.'

'Every Tribe?' I look up from the Opals, shocked.

She nods. 'I was thinking of starting with the Fangtooths. Yapok's Skybrary isn't far from their Frozen Wastes. We could travel to them easily enough from there.'

I splutter out an angry laugh – she wants to reach out to the most brutal Tribe ever known? 'You want to go to the *Fangtooths*?' In my hands, the fused Opals grow warm.

Sparrow murmurs in his sleep, turning over, and Thunderbolt chatters angrily at me. I lower my voice. 'Are you addled?'

Kestrel blinks at me slowly, membranes slicking up and down her eyes. 'There may be many differences between us, but there are also many similarities. We are in this together.'

'The main thing is that I get Da's map working again and find the last Opal,' I say.

She reaches for me. 'Even if we find the last Opal, we still need to find this golden crown. Who knows how long it will take? At least this way we can talk to people, we can—'

'Heart-luck *talking* with those murderous bone-clatterers!'

'Mouse,' says Crow, touching my knee. 'Let her—'

I round on him. 'Have raw eels poisoned your brain?' I scoot backwards, away from them, my feet tangling in the blankets and the slime of the floor pressing through my breeches, but I don't care.

He scowls at me. 'That's it. Round on anyone who disagrees with you.'

I ignore him. 'Don't you know *anything*?' I spit at Kestrel. Her eyes widen and a frown flickers between her copper brows. 'What that Fangtooth Tribe did to my kin—' I stop, cos I'm in danger of losing grip of my voice. I carry on in hushed tones. 'You don't know what I've seen them do, what they're capable of.'

Ettler chirps at me angrily, and Kestrel flushes. 'It isn't all of them! You cannot blame a whole *Tribe* for—'

'So are you saying my grandma was wrong, then?' I

stand, searching the gloom for my boots. 'You saying that everything I was taught as a nipper weren't true? You got any clue what it's like trying to sail through the Frozen Wastes unseen, while the Fangtooths send their filthy hounds after your kin?'

Sparrow sits up in his bed, carefully stretching out his injured arm. His fingertips crackle and the smell of burning cloth fills my nose. Even in the gloom I can see the bruises on his neck, made by Stag's hands. Stag, who let a band of Fangtooths crawl all over my ship.

'No, I'm not saying that, I'm just saying that a few tyrants do not equal a Tribe.' She crosses her arms and stares towards the window, breath coming too fast. She's getting angry now, and that flares up my own rage.

'Go on, then.' I nod at the window. 'Fly to the Frozen Wastes and see how long it takes them to saw off your head and shove it on a spike!' Thaw notices my tone and *hisses* at Kes, spreading her wings wide.

'Oh, grow into your boots before you start hurling them at others!' she snaps. 'There are good folks among the Fangtooths, just like every other Tribe. You're beginning to sound as unjust as my mother.'

'She's got a point, Mouse,' says Crow.

'It's no surprise to find out where your loyalty lies, *wrecker*-boy. But you're out of luck, ent you? She loves Egret, as well you know.'

He narrows his eyes at me.

Suddenly all I can see is the gloat on Axe-Thrower's face and Grandma's hawk Battle-Shrieker plucked bald and the polar dogs terrorising our deck. A bolt of power lashes into my hand from the Opals and then the sound of Grandma's body smashing into the waves fills my ears with a roar that makes my vision go black and my throat close until I feel like I can't breathe. Stag kneels in front of me, branding me with his mark. Bitterness scorches my throat.

'Mouse?' Kestrel calls to me, and it's like she's stars away. 'Are you all right?'

'Aye, no heart-thanks to you,' I snap, blinking myself back into the room. The Opals unfuse and I realise that a low, buzzing hum that was coming from them has faded away.

I wriggle out of bed and head for the door. Kes reaches for me but I shove past and storm away.

My vision's blurred by tears but I keep moving, sobs twisting my chest. The memories make my hands sweat and my legs shake and my heart feel loud and heavy as a drum pounding in my chest. I stumble into the middle of the room where we talked with Pike, then trip over a lumbering salamander and when I've righted myself the thought strikes me. Me and Sparrow are getting out of here, without any of these so-called friends. I was right all those times back home. I don't need no one else.

'Still think you know it all, don't you,' says Crow suddenly. I spin to face him and he's standing behind me. His breath frosts into the air. 'My loyalties lie with *you*, little fool.'

He steps closer, watching me with kind, bright eyes. It's the first time he's looked at me unguarded. 'So what?' I glance away, confused by the heat creeping up my neck.

'Look, I never had a sister, all right? For so long, I never had anyone. You make me feel like I've finally got family to protect.'

His words make me feel winded. 'So now I'm stuck with you, am I?' I hiss, to cover the flush stealing across my cheeks.

He looks away, his lopsided grin flashing, eyes crinkling at the corners. ''Fraid so.' He looks down, blushing suddenly. 'Listen, rat. I'm so sorry about your grandma. All them attacks of fright and sweats you're getting – that's gotta be hard.'

I stare at my toes. 'Heart-thanks.' Before I can step out of the way, he sweeps me into a proper tight hug that reminds me a tiny bit of Bear. When I pull away, a yawn steams out of my pipes.

'Ready to sleep?' he asks.

'Aye.' I look around at the chairs. 'But I'm not going back in there.'

In the morning, none of us wants to leave now we've found friends. We spend the next two days drinking froggy broth and padding around the marsh-huts with Pike, listening to his stories of Da and his thoughts about the Opals. He tells us he'll help us get the last Opal, but that we're to rest properly first.

I'm heart-glad when I think that we'll be able to look for the last Opal together. And it's proper strange to hear about Da from a friend of his. He tells us how they were two scrawny sea-tribe lads who met at a tribe-meet, and got up to no good together. 'Always singing, he was, even then. Just like you, Sparrow!' Sparrow goes all pink at hearing that.

The only rotten thing about being at Pike's is Kestrel. Since she said her stupid things about the Fangtooths, I can't stand being near her. She keeps creeping up on me and touching my elbow, trying to get me to talk, but I jerk away from her each time, and go to a different part of the house, or out on the marsh walkways. I don't wanna hear a thing she's got to say.

On the third night, I settle down to sleep in my chair, itching to rove. Pike says we can be off at dawn. I'm starting to doze, lulled by the pattering of the frogs, when the peace is shattered by a roar.

'*Pike!*'

I know that voice and my spirit quails against the knowing, but it don't change a thing cos the roar echoes through the marsh again. 'Show yourself. Give me what is mine.'

Stag. He's escaped Hearthstone.

Pike's fish-spear rings against the scaly floor as he makes his way to the balcony of his home. 'Hide!' he hisses as he passes me. He walks on, but when he reaches a gap in the eel skin wall, he presses his lips against it and gives a short, high whistle.

I stop breathing. There's a beat where my legs won't move. What will happen to the marsh-man? I can't let Stag hurt him! But Pike twists back to glare at me. 'Now!'

I slink into the shadows, sinking to my knees behind the rocking chair.

'There you are, good brother. Where have you roved?' Pike calls the sea-tribe greeting calmly.

A distant boom drums across the Marshes, thrumming in my ribs.

'Your ramshackle hovels are in my way,' says Stag, ignoring the greeting. 'And you are harbouring slaves that belong to me.' He coughs harshly and spits into the marsh water.

Shock prickles me. The Marshes are where Squirrel, Hammer and Ermine fled to the day I abandoned my ship. Are they the slaves Stag's talking about? Or does he mean my brother and me?

A door squeals. I flinch and look towards the sleeping room – Crow steps out of it and comes towards me. We crouch together, Thaw in my hair, listening to the gentle *pop pop pop* of Pike's smoke rings. Then I creep towards the gauzy netting covering the doorway and peer out. Crow follows.

Stag stands in a canoe, staring up at Pike's balcony. He turns, hands on hips, and beckons into the darkness. A band of Fangtooths straggle through the reeds.

Around us, from the other stilt homes, ebbs the sound of singing and spear-sharpening.

'You swore you would not return for another moon-cycle yet. We have much to talk about. Will you drink a dram with me?' Behind his back, Pike rolls his spear between his palms.

The boom grows louder, rumbling bones-deep. Across the marsh, lit by the thin moon, stride a line of immense shadows, wearing dented odds and ends of armour. They stand in the middle of the sea-path, feet as long as hunting boats cutting off the flow of water to the Marshes. By their sides hang fists the size of crow's nests. When I crane back my neck, I still can't see their heads.

'You will be drained by daybreak,' shouts Stag, and his followers whoop, beating their chests.

'Sparrow,' I whisper, but his hand is in mine before his name has even left my mouth. 'Told you I didn't wanna come to the Marshes,' he whispers. 'You shoulda listened.'

Yapok and Kestrel stand behind us, clutching each other.

'Marsh-folk, to war!' bellows Pike, leaping from the balcony to his canoe far below. All around us, in the stilt-houses, throbs the war-beat of countless spears pounding the floors.

'Giants, stop the flow to these marshes!' calls Stag.

Sparrow flinches. 'The burning,' he quails, and I try to hold him still but he hops from foot to foot.

'The Marsh-folk have chosen drought. Light me a torch,' Stag calls. 'I will smoke these rats from their waterholes.'

I nock an arrow to my bow as I run to the balcony. But the moon's dipped behind cloud and when it comes out again, Stag spies me and ducks low. My arrow whistles past his ear. I draw another one. Then I'm almost knocked flat by a deafening bellow as lines of Fangtooths and Marsh-folk charge at each other across the Marshes, meeting with a clash of axe and spear that's loud enough to shake the night's teeth from its jaws.

Stag stands straight and stares me in the face. 'The dust has settled. I have won. You can stop fighting.' His voice is flat, though malice seethes underneath.

'The dust won't settle. Not ever!' I picture Grandma's face, and spit into the water. 'The dust is blood and knives!'

Soldiers hulk near him, holding guns, longbows and quivers full of arrows. We're surrounded. The giants pound their chests, making the house shake.

'Come,' says Stag, eyes crawling over my face. 'Give me the Opals.'

Crow stands behind me and I feel the cool touch of his fingertips on my elbow. His friendship spreads ripples of heart-strength through me. 'As if!' I call down. I stick one hand behind me and wave at Sparrow, Kes and Yapok to run – maybe they can get out the way we first came in, on the other side of the house.

Stag fishes in his cloak and pulls out a glowing amber gem. He's got the last one – the Land-Opal! Sickness rises through me. He passes it from hand to hand, and the muttering of the poison-frogs grows louder around him. He screws up his face in disgust. *Shut up or I'll rip the fangs from every last one of you!* he growls. Then he shakes his head violently as though he's trying to get the beast-chatter out of his ears. He looks at me again. 'Is this what you've been looking for?'

I stay silent, chewing my lip.

Stag calls to a Fangtooth. 'The *torch*.' His face lights up all red and cragged and wild-eyed as he grabs the rag-wrapped torch that's passed to him. Then he stoops, touches it to the stilt-legs of the house and hurls the torch at the next one over.

'*Don't!*' I scream. But a roar goes up, and I ent sure if it's the Fangtooths, or the giants, or the fury of the Marsh-folk, or the fire itself.

But I know the fire is hungry. A rich, sharp stink like burning meat and vinegar creeps into my nose. Orange light scorches the backs of my eyes as smoke burns my throat.

A spine-shivering scream goes up, as toads and frogs and salamanders run and jump and dive to get away. Bare feet slap against the eel skin inside the house.

'You dung-mouthed viper-fish!' I leap onto the wooden handrail of the balcony, ready to jump into Stag's canoe and slash his throat, but Crow charges after me and pulls me down. 'This way!' He drags me along the walkway. There's a slap of feet as Kes and Yapok tear down the walkway in the other direction.

Then I panic. 'Where's Sparrow?'

'Here!' I grab his hand and the three of us jump into a boat. There's a shout as Stag paddles after us. 'It's all coming true,' whispers Sparrow.

Flames dance and lick across to the next stilt-house, and the next, until the whole marsh is crawling with flame that crackles, roars and sheds a haze of heat that ripples over the water.

'He's gaining!' shouts Crow as we push along the marsh as quick as a tail-flick, though it's still too slow. He glances around and spots a house tucked behind the others that ent caught light yet.

All around, in the boats, on the burning houses, on the walkways and in the shallows, Marsh-folk and Fangtooths battle, spear against club, axe against blade. We rush through a storm of leaping poison-frogs trying to flee their home, and I shove Sparrow flat in the boat.

'Overturn the canoe and hide under it!' Crow hisses. 'I'll make him think I've got the gems.'

'Both of us go or both of us stay!'

'Think on it – you need to get the Opals to safety! Now go!' He pushes us out of the boat.

I bite my tongue and swallow a scream, as I scrabble to overturn the canoe, tearing my nails. Then me and Sparrow gulp a breath and dive underneath it, the relief at getting away from Stag filling me with shameful tears. The gloopy water is bone-bitingly cold. I know I can't do what Crow said. I ent leaving without the wrecker, Opals or no Opals.

'Stay here,' I tell Sparrow. 'The fire won't get you in the water. Just keep kicking.' He nods, Thunderbolt sitting on his ear.

I swim out from under the canoe and jump into the webbing of wooden struts under the stilt-house. But when I reach for Crow he knocks my hand away and paddles another stray canoe back to face Stag.

'No!' I whisper, watching them from under the house.

'We're alone again, traitor,' throbs Stag's voice. 'Cosy, isn't it? Just like being back in that cabin, with you my scraping servant-bird.'

Crow stays silent.

'Nothing to say? Not even a filthy *squawk* for your old master?' Stag chuckles.

Anger sweeps through me. Flames flicker all around, the reeds send smoke curling into the sky, and boats creak as people paddle away.

'You are a nothing, boy.' There's a creaking of boats as someone shuffles their feet. 'To see you running around after my savage daughter is truly pathetic.'

All the sounds in the world fade in a heartbeat.

I stop breathing.

28
Monstrosity

'Your – *what*?' Crow stutters.

My belly lurches.

'You heard me.' He speaks lightly, like all he's doing is trading for spices. 'And while I may have been soft-hearted before, not even our blood-tie can save that little bow-wielding thug, now. She has sealed her own fate.'

'Mouse is your daughter?'

Crow's words lie buried deep beneath a fug of muffled sounds, as my blood beats hard in my ears. Bile rushes into the back of my throat, but I swallow it down and dig my nails into my palms to keep myself heart-strong.

'She should have been a boy,' says Stag. 'I was *owed* a son, to soothe the loss of the boy who lived for seven sunrises. Then that monstrosity slithered into the world. I wanted to shoot her gloating hunter's moon out of the sky.'

Stag's lying.

He ent my kin.

My kin have open arms and hearts. My kin are proud and fierce and heart-strong, loyal and brave. My kin laugh 'til it hurts.

He ent a thing like my kin.

The house above me catches light with a *woofff* of flame. *But he don't know you're listening,* chimes a treacherous voice in my head. *So why would he lie?*

And what about him having the beast-chatter, like you?

I turn hot and dizzy, can't move a limb. I heave and retch into the water under the burning house, Thaw fussing her feathers and keening sorrowfully. I can't believe it, I won't – cos if he ent lying, then my da ent my da at all.

My mind slows. I stare at a knot in the wood of one of the house-stilts. I feel my eyes going crossed and my spirit thirsting for the dream-dance world. I fight to keep myself in the here and now.

My father is a murderer. No. *No.*

There ent no way I can ever be captain, now.

And I had another brother, who I never knew died. *Shut up.*

Even if I can forgive Da for abandoning us, how will I ever forgive him for not telling me a stitch of the truth, and for not really being my – I push the thought down but it flies at me, all tooth and claw. For not being my da?

Then worse thoughts come, sharp as arrows, punching into my chest. I've always known there's a streak of badness in me. Now I know it's a blood-taint.

I cover my face with my arm and scream, biting hard into the fur of my cloak, shaking, as fire crackles all around me.

I dive into the marsh. Thaw tries to stop me but then I'm under the water and its foul gloop fills my mouth.

Why didn't anyone ever tell me? Suddenly I'm thinking of Ma's brooch and how Stag stuffed it under his pillow. And how Grandma mentioned Ma's name to Stag, just before he killed her. Horror strokes shivering claws up and down my nerves. It can't be true . . . maybe he knows I'm lurking here, listening. Maybe he's just trying to get inside my head. But everything swarms closer now. I think of how Sparrow has Ma and Da's yellow hair, and mine is black as tar.

Dimly, I'm still aware that I need to keep the Opals safe. I surface underneath another burning house, and ash falls into my hair. On the banks, Stag's army crank huge catapults laden with pots of terrodyl blood and unleash the black rain over the marshlands. Folk run, terrorised.

'Why are you telling me all this?' asks Crow, voice

edged with panic.

I can't leave without Crow. And where would I go? Who can I trust?

'Because you won't live to squawk to anyone,' gloats Stag. 'You didn't think I'd let you get away with it, did you? No one turns their back on me and lives to tell the tale.'

Crow's breath is shallow and tattered. I can smell the sour animal-stink of his fright. 'One thing I'm curious about,' he says quickly. 'When you first came round the Orphan's Hearth, you said we was the same. You said you knew what it were like, to—' Crow pauses. 'To be made to smuggle loot through them caves of filth from as young as five summers.' His voice is edged with poison.

I could swim through caves as deep and dark as the tomb, drifts Stag's voice across time. Dead Man's Caves . . . *Stag* was a child at the Hearth?

But Stag's stopped listening. 'You bore me,' he says absently, looking round at the destruction he's making. 'I have territories to claim.'

'Look,' says Crow. 'Just don't go after Mouse. I've got the Opals.'

I'm trying to stay in the waking world but a dream-dance plucks at me, trying to take me away from the pain.

Stag snorts. 'You expect me to believe that?' I hear

a metallic *click* and straight away the image of that gun he used to shoot Grandma floods back into my mind.

I need to save Crow, but my spirit *keeps* popping in and *out of my body.*

Crow-boy is friend now friend nownownow get away! hoots Thaw-Wielder. She bursts through the ash and smoke, into Stag's face. He levels the gun at her.

'You!' rings a strong, sudden voice. Kestrel. 'You cannot tear us apart. That is my friend's sea-hawk. You will not harm her!'

For a heartbeat, my spirit settles in my body and my eyes focus. Yapok and Kestrel are paddling a canoe towards Crow and Stag. Kestrel reaches him and tries to wrench the gun away.

Soldiers laugh, their voices dead-dull, like heavy clubs all around the marshes.

No.

I try to warn her. 'Get away from him!' But my voice is barely a whisper.

Stag rips the gun from her grasp and hits her hard in the back of the head with the end of it. The world fills with a brutal *smack*. Then he shoves her in the back, away from him.

Kestrel crumples forwards into another canoe.

Crow freezes. Yapok bellows her name. 'Neither of you move,' orders Stag. He kicks the canoe away from him and it carries our friend away, downriver.

I slip heavily under the water. My mind is flailing and my body's so numb I don't even feel the cold.

A small figure bumps past me, hair gold in the underwater firelight. Sparrow! Thunderbolt hangs from a strand of his hair, shedding the light he needs to see.

He shoves under the boat and sends Stag toppling backwards into the water, his gun cracking as he falls.

Then he swims to me and tugs me to the surface with his good arm.

Yapok is swimming towards the canoe that's carrying Kestrel, crying out as he tries to keep his face above water. 'Wake up!' he yells when he catches the canoe, reaching inside and shaking something, hard. Then a stillness settles over him that screams louder than anything of the sickening wrongness he must be facing.

Crow drags Sparrow and me out of the water, onto the nearest bank. We spin, looking for anywhere that ent ablaze, as Stag surfaces, spluttering.

'We have to run *away*, fast!' says Sparrow. He and Crow pull me along between them. Yapok clambers out of the water, wiping his nose with the back of his hand. Ettler shivers in the crook of his arm, whimpering.

Crow looks at Yapok, but he shakes his head, once, quickly, then every one of his muscles and bones seems to slump. His teeth chatter and he puts out a hand to stop himself from falling.

'We can't leave without her!' I scream, belly raked hollow.

Crow presses his hand over my mouth. His skin smells scorched. 'Shhh, you can't help her. She's gone. Yapok saw, all right? Breathe. Just *breathe* for the gods' sake.' Anger steams from his mouth, hot, into my ear.

'This way!' says Sparrow, Thunderbolt hovering by his head. 'I seen it in my vision. I can get us out of here.' We run. The houses are crumbling into the water and the marshes stink sickeningly of roasting toad. There's no sign of Pike. A few Marsh-folk still battle Stag's soldiers out on the banks, but most have fled. Or worse.

'Quick, there's a boat!' Sparrow gestures behind a clump of reeds to a canoe, loosely tethered to a mooring post. 'Get in!' We jump into the boat and I wrap my arms around my knees and shake so hard I feel like my bones will snap.

We drift through a haze of burning wood and fizzling fish scales. Stag's destroyed the Marsh-folk's home, just cos they wouldn't join him, just cos they were in his way.

My gut's a sick, hollow pit and shock has splayed my eyes and mouth wide. I know what's happened, but I can't feel anything, and I can't focus on anyone when they try to talk to me. Sparrow takes the lead and the older boys listen closely to him, nodding, faces grave.

Then Yapok curls on his side, weeping for Kestrel. Ettler quivers next to him. I wish I could gift Kes my tears. But there's nothing left of me. There's just a knot in my throat and as I watch the blaze, I realise again how it's all just as Sparrow saw in his nightmare. The smoke makes us wheeze for breath, so Sparrow carefully cuts a scrap of cloth from his tunic, with help from Thunderbolt's glow. Then he presses it over my nose and mouth, and tucks his own face into his sleeve, eyes streaming.

The Opals make the sparks dance in the air and let me see through this world into the dream one – the one where I'd rather be. 'We have to find Da,' Sparrow tells me, gripping my fingers hard and trying to make me focus on him. 'Then we'll be all right, won't we?'

But I don't know if anything will ever be all right again.

The fire spirits dance all night, as we sail. While the others lie in a crumpled heap in the bottom of the boat, snoring, I watch the spirits flicker, feeling nothing, not even reaching up to brush the snow from my face.

There's a wound in the world, left by Kes, that hurts

so much I have to turn away from it. I cradle the Opals as the boat creaks and the wind carries its smell of burning.

Da, I think. *Da. Where are you?* In the depths of my bones, the word *Da* creeps like a sickness. Cos Stag said – *no*. No. I know what Stag said, and I don't know why he would have lied. But it can't be true, can it? I can't be his kin.

I roll onto an elbow and stare at my brother. 'It weren't just a nightmare, about the Marshes.' I don't need to carve my words into a question.

Sparrow shakes his head. 'No,' he whispers huskily. We lie down, face to face. I breathe his sour breath.

'Have you had nightmares – visions – about Da?'

'I think I saw Da in some kind of cave,' he splutters, too much smoke still in his lungs. 'His hands were tied up.'

'A cave?'

He nods. 'In the bottom of a great huge mountain.'

Crow sits up in the boat, wiping his face as he wakes up properly. 'What about the caves at Hackles?'

I sigh. 'But we were there, and there was no sign of Da. Sparrow – could the cave have been on the mountain where we were trapped?'

'I ent sure. It weren't a cave with creatures in,' he says. 'It was another one. There was someone wearing a red cloak.'

I remember the figure staggering towards us as we escaped on the draggles. Where had it come from? 'We have to go back there anyway,' I whisper. 'To tell Egret about—' My throat closes thickly.

Sparrow stares at the space next to my head.

'I'm always gonna listen to you telling me your visions, from now on,' I say.

He grins, but the grin falters quick as a melting snowflake. 'I heard that Stag saying an odd thing about you when I was waiting under the boat, in the water.'

My chest squeezes tight. I wish I could run. I shut my eyes. 'I didn't hear anything. Let's find Da.' I lie back down in the canoe and when Sparrow peers at me, asking me if I'm all right, my eyes seep silent tears.

PART 3

Unity

29

Spirit Battles

I lie on the floor of the canoe for two days. When the others try to slip me crumbs of the odds and ends of food they've saved, I turn away.

Crow grips my shoulders. 'What's happening to you? You said it yourself – we can't let Stag win.'

'Wrong – I can't stop him.' The hopelessness hurts worse than hunger.

'We're going to search for the mountain caves your brother saw.' Crow's mouth keeps moving but I can't hear the words. After a while he stops talking and sits back in the canoe with a sigh.

'Stag got the third Opal from me,' says Yapok.

This wakes me out of my stupor. 'What?' I sway, spots swirling before my eyes.

He pushes himself upright in the canoe and hugs his knees. 'I opened a parcel sent by owl to the Skybrarian – because sometimes he doesn't wake up for days, and no one is meant to know about us. The note was written on fish skin and it said to keep the Opal safe. It was signed by a person called Fox.'

Tingles race along my spine.

'When Stag came, I was desperate to keep the Skybrarian hidden. So I gave him the stone. But it wasn't enough. He still forced me to help him search for the Sky-Opal, and to betray all of you. Now the Skybrarian is alone!' He looks at us, full to the brim with heart-sadness. 'He's the closest thing I've got to family, but if I'd known how important that Opal was I never would have let it leave my Skybrary, I promise.'

I gift him a small nod. 'I believe you. What's done is done.' Now we've got to make things right, for Kestrel.

We leave the boats by the edge of the river far to the north, and trek for half a day across the snowscape, towards Hackles. Doubts pummel me like fists. I can't trust myself to know if we're headed the right way, even though Kes showed me how to read the star-paths. We're heading back towards the place she worked so hard to escape. The pain strangles me again. How will I ever explain any of it to Egret? I wipe flecks of sleet from my eyes. Then Crow taps me on the hand and offers me his snow-goggles. I take them and slip them on, still heart-numb.

When we're nearing the foot of Hackles, a great sky battle rages. In the distance, huge brown scraps dart between the frozen clouds, lunging for streaks of smoky grey with wide toothy mouths and lashing claws. The draggles and the sky-wolves are fighting. Every few beats there's a deep, shocking boom as Hackles' defences spew massive ice boulders. Shouts, snarls, yelps, yawps and cries echo off the rocks, chilling my marrow.

Under the spiny mountain jags of Hackles, there are gaping dark caves in the rock. Sweat trickles down my spine as we struggle higher and higher towards them. My muscles feel torn and my bones weigh me down, but I want to run if there's a chance Da could be here. I watch the sky, sickened at the thought of being captured. When we're swaying in front of one of the caves, Sparrow stops and frowns. 'I think this is the place!' he says. Thunderbolt flits ahead of him into each cave and back out again.

Empty! She sighs a silver cloud of moon-dust. I tell the others.

'Don't worry, kid,' says Yapok, patting Sparrow's arm awkwardly. 'We'll keep looking at dawn.'

We rest in a cave with paintings of rust-brown reindeer on the walls. Crow takes first watch. I slip into *dreams*.

'In between light and shadow, ice and water, sleep and wake, there is another world,' she tells me. 'I have seen you

dive into it before. This time is no different. You can stay true to yourself.' She holds a fist up to her heart.

I copy her. 'Here is the birth of a mountain,' I say, and she covers her mouth as tears fill her eyes. She sweeps me into a hug.

The kestrel-membranes on her eyeballs slick up and down as she peers at me. Her scarlet skirts swirl against the dirty snow. 'Are you ready for your dream-dance?'

Ent I already in one?

I wake, heart pounding, cheeks wet with tears.

When I stumble from the cave, trying to catch my breath, Hackles is a sharp shock in the pale dawn. I can feel the mountain pressing down on us from all sides, staining my mind as it hunches overhead, sneering.

We keep searching for the cave from Sparrow's vision. Thunderbolt swings from a strand of hair in front of his eyes, helping thin the fog for him, but he says he can't remember anything else about the vision and slowly the hope inside me withers to ash.

Ettler squishes through the air, helping us search – though in heart-truth I reckon he's still searching for Kes. *Wherewherewhere?* he chatters sorrowfully.

'There!' Sparrow shouts, jolting me. He points at the base of the mountain that the stronghold of Hackles looms on.

We press close to the mountain, cos I'm frighted that

the Protector will spy us if we linger in the open. The rock is as dark on the outside as the inside, so at first I can't see any cave at all. Then we get closer and see an opening in the rock. Outside the cave lies a tangle of animal bones and empty flagons lying on their sides. 'It's like – someone's brought food here,' shouts Yapok. 'But why?'

Before anyone can answer, there's a movement at the entrance and we duck out of sight behind a boulder. Two figures cloaked in red crawl out of the cave, lugging a lifeless shape under another cloak. Mystiks. How many of the ghoulish slackwits are there?

Then a shriek curdles my bones. A terrodyl dives towards them and carries the shape out of their hands, up and away into the sky. The mystiks brush off their hands and duck back inside. 'What are they feeding to the terrodyls?' asks Crow, turning to me with wide eyes.

'I ent gonna think long on that,' I reply. 'Cos I've got to go in, anyway.'

Crow dips his chin into the thick wool of his scarf. 'We're coming with you,' he says firmly, though Yapok looks like he wishes he didn't have to. Ettler flaps around him, dripping ink into his hair.

'I'll go alone. Can you guard the entrance and keep Sparrow safe?'

Crow sighs. Then he nods reluctantly. *Then* he

329

sweeps me into the tightest hug I've ever known, until I can barely inflate my lungs. When he lets me go, my cheeks are hot and I can't look at anyone.

The cave has wormed a path into the roots of the mountain. I have to stoop to walk inside, and the crumbling roof scrapes the top of my head. Branches snake off the path, into dark corners and passages. I follow the footsteps of the mystiks as they echo towards the heart of the cave. I know I could get lost forever in a place like this.

I follow the snaking path until I'm forced to crawl on hands and knees. Then it opens out into a wide chamber that flickers with dull yellow light. There's a constant low moaning and a smell of dampness and fizzling fat. I stop, then dart to the side, gluing myself to the wall, out of sight. The cave is filled with skinny, grimy folk tied to posts nailed in the ground. Most of them don't move, and suddenly I know for certain what that bundle was that got given to the terrodyl. Sickness courses up my throat. What are they using these poor people for?

To the left-hand side of the cave, a red-cloaked figure hunches in front of a cloaked man tied to a post, pressing bony fingertips into his temples. His eyes are rolled back in his head. Spit froths in the corners of his mouth and when the wind catches his hood, hurling it back from his face, I shudder at the sight of his wind-burned scalp and hollow cheeks.

But the wind's caught the other figure's hood, too. The man's yellow hair is knotted on his head and he's got slender yellow brows and a bushy yellow beard.

His hands are curled in his lap, large and skilful despite the lengths of rope binding his wrists, and his legs are long. His clothes are slack on his body, though, and his breathing comes quick and ragged, like a new-birthed bird. His face is puffier than I remember and the skin around his eyes is crinkled and slack. His cloak and tunic are stained with dark splatters and blood has clotted in the corners of his mouth.

'*Da?*' My breath catches on the word. My hands rush to cover my mouth before I can be stupid enough to speak again. That leech is feasting on Da's energy! Rage needles my skin.

I sink further into the shadows as the mystiks we saw outside the cave pass by me and start murmuring.

'Stag's sent word he has seized control of the Marshes.'

'Fortunate he's so keen to do our bidding, isn't it?' replies a mocking voice.

My gut twists. Pike lost the battle! And Stag's doing the mystiks' bidding? I'd reckoned the boot was on the other foot, and they were doing his. 'Indeed – he wants to prove himself. He'll arrive at Hackles soon and will seem to be saving the stronghold from the mindless destruction of a tyrant. He will easily take over power. Then we can continue our hidden work.'

I pull my cloak tighter in the claw-sharp chill. Little wonder Stag always seems to know so much. I think of the mystiks at Castle Whalesbane, the ship-wrecker Weasel and the Fangtooth Chieftain who are all in league with Stag. Who knows how many other bad-blubbers might be working with him, too?

'And the woman on the throne?'

'We are still maintaining control using the current warm-blood – though his life-spirit fights the leeching, his energy is potent enough for us to possess her while Stag strikes, and beyond.'

I remember the trapped spirit that tried to steal my body, that hollow-eyed face that's been haunting me, and almost jump out of my skin as I begin to understand. The Protector is locked out – she's been possessed by these mystiks!

My mind wheels faster and faster as I listen. This rotting at Hackles isn't the Protector's fault. I need to get to her. If I can free her from this gruesomeness, maybe she can help my da in return. I'd better do it quick, though, cos each beat that passes might be bringing Stag closer to Hackles.

I start to back away, on my hands and knees. I let the

murk suck me into its folds. I won't look back at Da – I only want to see him when he's free and safe again.

Outside, I scramble upright and gape at my friends, hardly knowing where to start. Crow puts his hands on my shoulders. 'Calm down, and tell us.'

'Where's Thaw?' I ask, casting around for my hawk.

'She must've gone off to hunt,' says Crow impatiently. 'Come on!'

I gabble it all so fast I ent heart-certain they've understood. But Sparrow starts to cry when I finish.

Yapok clutches fistfuls of his hair.

Crow whistles.

'I reckon that if I go into a dream-dance, maybe I can find the Protector's spirit and pull her back to herself, breaking the possession,' I say.

'Sounds like a good enough place to start,' says Crow.

'Crow – can you and Sparrow stay close to Da and help him when I've freed her?'

He nods.

'What can I do?' asks Yapok.

'Keep watch, and make sure none of you are spotted.'

'Wait,' says Crow. 'Can't you dream-dance from here? It's too dangerous to sneak in to the fortress!'

I shake my head. 'The Protector's spirit tried to possess me last time I was here. My body is bait. I have to get into the same room as her.'

I climb through the snow towards the stronghold and pause below the courtyard, listening. The mountain is deserted, and an eerie wind whistles past the long-hall and swoops over my head.

'Mouse, there's an avalanche brewing – you might get stuck inside!' calls Yapok. I whip round to face him, Crow and Sparrow.

'I thought you were all waiting at the caves!'

'We ain't letting you go up there alone,' says Crow, eyes blazing.

'All right, but I *have* to go in!' I tell them. 'I'll be arrow-swift, just – look after Sparrow!' I swallow. 'And if I don't come out, find another way to free my da?'

Without waiting for an answer, I turn and scurry up the steepest part of the mountain, lungs wheezing in the thin air. The endless storm-barrier rages high above, snatching clumps of my hair and trying to rip it from my scalp. I reach the entrance to the draggle cave and the others catch up. 'I'll go in through here and climb up!'

Crow shakes his head. 'Remember the trapdoor!' he yells in my ear. 'You can't climb up!'

I wrack my brains, frustration snaking through me. Every beat wasted is another beat that Da's in danger. Then I spot a thin path upwards through the mountain, towards the fortress at the top. It looks like a place where mountain goats have trodden to reach the toughest plants for grazing.

'Please,' I beg the others. 'Don't follow me up there. I need you to stay here with Sparrow, and be ready to help Da.'

Crow never agrees to let me go alone, but he forces himself not to follow.

I climb until my arms and legs are numb and I feel like the storm's gonna snatch me off the mountain. Every time I have to stop and rest, I struggle to move again. Then, finally, the grazing path leads me to a tiny gap below the storm-barrier – is that how the sky-wolves breached? I slip through and climb down to the courtyard. Then I stare around warily. The wind drags frozen fingers along my spine.

I duck behind rocks and peer out, clutching my longbow, and gasping for breath. Inside the courtyard stand soldiers with walrus-hide coats and mail forged from bloodied merwraith scales.

There's no clear route to the long-hall so I edge around the settlement, crouching behind the armoury and drifts of snow, until I reach another door in the mountain. I hurry over to it and creep inside. The passageway is empty, so I seize my chance.

I sprint along it, bearing in the direction of the

long-hall. Suddenly the passageway ends and I reach a platform of rock at the back of the fortress and teeter there, putting out my hands to stop myself plunging over the edge. Just in front of the platform is a door, coloured dark blue and patterned with golden stars.

I'm behind the Star Door.

I stretch forwards, grab the edge, and it swings outwards. I clutch the inside handle as the wind catches the door and I'm swung out over a void far below the fortress. I kick my legs and swing the door back towards the long-hall with all my might, then leap off and land on the platform where the thrones stand.

The cauldrons are empty and the hall is cold. A sickly, wasted creature sits curled tight on the throne. She startles when I step closer, turns to face me and snarls, dripping spit down her chin.

Suddenly, a pair of spears are crossed over my chest and Lunda and Pangolin stare down at me. 'You again!' hisses Lunda, face weary and smudged.

'What's going on?' I ask.

'You don't get to ask questions,' she says. Then she glances around fearfully, eyes shining with tears.

'I think I can help you all,' I hiss. 'None of this is right. She—' I point at the Protector's wizened form. 'That ent her in there.'

Lunda splutters an outraged laugh. 'What are you

336

talking about?'

'She's being controlled. You've got enemies closer than you think.'

'You're right there, sea-creeper.' Lunda bares her teeth at me.

I shake my head. 'Wait – I'm going to try and free her!'

Lunda laughs but Pangolin utters a groan. 'Stop, Lunda! What have we to lose?' she asks. She lifts her spear off my chest and points it at Lunda, who gasps. Suddenly I realise how much taller Pangolin is than either of us.

'Pang, think about what you're doing!' shouts Lunda. 'The soldiers forbade anyone to enter!'

'I am sick of everything about this place!' snaps Pangolin. 'Including *you*. We let the girl pass.' She holds Lunda back.

I stare at Pangolin in amazement for a heartbeat. Then I stumble forwards. Lunda spits and curses.

I step closer to the throne. The Protector swivels her half-closed eyes onto my face. I stop next to the throne and stare at her.

Her mouth falls open. 'Get down from here, wretch,' throbs her vicious croak.

Ignoring her, I lie down on the platform. The Protector stares down at me. 'Guards!' But Pangolin don't take her spear-tip from Lunda's throat. I think about the spirit that tried to claim my body in my cell and know that I have to dream-dance without a binding if I'm gonna coax her near.

My fury for Kes and what's being done to our kin pushes my spirit *against my skin and I rise into the air. Where are you? I know you!* The Opals buzz in my pocket, clicking together. *I look down at my own slumped body and the Protector of the Mountain on her draggle throne.*

'Protector of the Mountain!' I call, mouth dream-dance clumsy. 'Where are you? I know you're locked out! I can help you!'

Suddenly, behind the throne flits the trapped spirit. It sees me, and its face stretches wide with gut-clawing yearning.

'You!' *I float closer to her, even though dread shivers through me the further I get from my body.*

The spirit don't look at me. Instead, it dives for my body. 'Warm-blood!'

I spin and catch its ankle. 'Wait!' *I call.* 'I know what's happening to you! I know you! You have a daughter called Kestrel, don't you?'

The spirit stops pulling against me and spins around. Its mouth starts to form clumsy words. 'Kestrel?' *She cocks her head.* 'Yes. My darling little girl. She hurt herself so badly. It was all my fault.'

'That was long ago. Time's been thieved from you. You've been shut out of your own skin. I can help you get back in!'

She looks at me then, like she's seeing me for the first time. 'Can you see me?'

'Aye,' I tell her. 'That's your body, ent it? You're stuck outside of it.' I flick my dream-fingers towards the creature on the throne.

She nods, terrified, blurring apart at the edges and buzzing back together again as I watch. 'I don't know how long I've been stuck out here. I was only dancing for a moment.' She shivers, and rubs her arms like she's cold.

'What can we do?' I ask. 'Can we force the spirit out of your body, so you can get back in?'

She presses her fingers to her mouth. 'I don't know.' She begins to sob.

I drop lower in the air and flit towards the thing on the throne, peering into its sunken face. Now that I'm in the shadow world I can see the gritty outline of the mystik's face within the slack shell of the Protector's skin. 'I know all about you,' I rasp, making my voice as mean as it can go.

'Stay back!' it screams. 'Lunda!'

I move closer. 'You ent who you say you are!' I roar. 'You thieved someone's body!' And now her daughter's dead and she weren't there. I believe in my heart-strength again. I know my love for Kestrel has gifted me the strength of a hundred full-growns. Suddenly I yelp, and my glance flits to my body on the floor. The Opals are shining through the cloth of my breeches. When I look down at my spirit, the same light is dancing on my leg in the dream-world.

A foam of Sea and a fragment of Sky. As I think it, green light touches my back with the strength of a wave and shoves my fingers through the false-Protector's skin. The blue light gifts me the strength of a hawk's wings and talons, making me stronger than the creature's hate as I search for a thread of its spirit, then pull the spirit all the way out of the Protector's body, quiver-flickering with the effort. In my bones I know that this might kill me. But it's for Kestrel, and I have to do it.

The mystik's gnarled, pock-marked spirit pings free and flicks towards my body. It's like a storm-wrecked tree stump, barren, full of rotten pits. It tries to slither down my throat but the Protector's spirit rushes over and pulls it back, screaming sudden fury. I jump back into my body as the other two fight, clamping my mouth tightly shut. I watch in the in-between world as the true Protector spirals towards her body, chased by the mystik's spirit. I open my eyes. My head throbs and my bones ache, as I fight to pull my mind back from the dream-dance.

The Protector of the Mountain is slumped at the foot of her throne, motionless, blood trickling from a cut on her forehead. The struggle between the spirits must've made her fall. 'Remember who you are!' I shout, grabbing her shoulders and shaking her. 'You are the Protector of the Mountain!'

I remember Kestrel stitching my wound, her chatter keeping my spirit from slinking into the dream-world for ever, and I lift my head and howl my sorrows for her and her ma into the sky.

A silvery slip brushes past me – I can almost see its face as it rushes up towards the throne. I flinch, remembering when she tried to get into my sleeping body, but then she's already slipping into the Protector's slumped form – she takes a huge, ragged breath, wakes up and climbs unsteadily to her feet.

Lunda breaks away from Pangolin, thunders towards me and grabs my arm. 'What did you *do?*'

Pangolin steps between us. 'She brought our Protector home.' Out on the mountain, there's a twisted scream, inhumanly loud. It muffles her words. She jumps, sucking in her breath. 'What was that?'

'P – Protector?' asks Lunda, shoving past me towards the platform.

I stagger away from them and burst from the long-hall. I scuttle over the courtyard, squeeze through the breach and clamber back down to the cave. 'Da!'

Then there's a shrill cry that echoes off the rocks. Thaw-Wielder bolts proudly across the snowy sky, leading a blizzard of streaking sea-hawks in her wake. I'd know them anywhere. They're the sea-hawks I freed from the *Huntress*, so long ago. My heart thuds into my mouth.

They drop lower and begin to swoop a wide circle around the cave mouth.

Yapok and Sparrow are hiding outside the cave. 'Where's Crow?' I pant.

'Inside,' says Yapok. There's a smear of blood on his cheek. 'With Egret and Pika. The mystiks tried to climb to the stronghold but we held them off and they fled. Now we're trying to move the prisoners out, but most of them are already dead.'

Inside the cave, Egret and Pika are helping survivors to their feet.

Crow stares down at the mystik that was feasting on Da's spirit to keep possession of the Protector. The mystik's body has buckled and lies bent over at an odd angle on the cave floor. Crow prods the mystik with the toe of his boot, but he don't stir.

Da sits opposite him, cheeks hollow and lips tinged with blue. He's slumped to one side. I drop to my knees by him, a sob wrenching my chest. 'Is he alive?' Horror stops me from touching him.

'Aye,' says Crow, dropping into a crouch by my side. 'Look at his chest – see it moving?' He gently saws away the ropes on Da's wrists.

I nod through my tears. Now Crow's said it, I can

feel warmth coming from Da's arm, so close to me. I tug his sleeve.

Da's eyes flicker open groggily, and he looks up at me blankly. But then, just as a drum beats hard in my chest and the world stops moving, his eyes clear and widen and shock splays across his face.

I'm in his arms before I know I've moved.

I squint up into his faraway blue eyes, eyes like the sea, and touch his face gently with the ends of my fingers. I take one of his hands in both of mine, feeling for the roughened pads on his palms and checking the lines and scars and freckles that I know so well, then press my face into the folds of his tunic and breathe him in. It's him, all right. He's got that smell, like honey and parchment, but I keep checking him over, suspicions crawling over me like spiders, until he takes my shoulders and holds me still.

'My *girl*,' he whispers, voice cracking. 'Hair black as pitch and eyes grey as a storm. Am I lost in a dream? Where is your brother? Is he safe?'

'It's you,' I say stupidly, through my tears. 'It's really you.' I stare at him and then I'm shuddering against the tangled nest of horrors in my brain. I never wanted to take my hurts out on Da, but now I'm hailing them down on him like little fists of spite, and all he does is gather me in his arms and let me.

'Tears are one with the sea,' he murmurs into my hair. 'And salt water heals all wounds. Let it out.'

'I *am*!' I bellow into his chest. Then I sag limply against him, my face a storm of tears and pain. 'You left us,' I whisper hoarsely.

His long fingers wipe the hair from my forehead. Then he kisses me and holds my chin while he studies my scar. 'You know, all the most fearsome captains have scars,' he whispers, but his voice is tipped with sadness.

'Da, I ent seven moons old,' I tell him, cos somehow, after everything, it's more than I can stand to be safe and held.

'No,' he says, eyes clearing as though he's seeing me proper for the first time. 'No, you are not.'

'So much for coming to find me when you can, eh?'

'Aye.' He dips his head, tears brimming. 'I am sorry, Little-Bones. More than you could know. I was on my way – I tracked you as far as the Bony Isle, but before I could reach Castle Whalesbane, the mystiks surrounded me and took me prisoner.'

'You went that far, for me?'

'Mouse, I would go to the ends of this world and beyond, for you and your brother. And when they caught me, I fought – oh, I fought as hard as I could.'

'Shall we get out of here?' asks Crow softly.

Da lets Crow help him to his feet, then drapes an arm around both of our shoulders to walk.

We slip outside, into icy mists and dagger-cold. Sparrow and Yapok are waiting. Ettler wriggles into my cloak pocket. Da falls to his knees in the snow and I drape my cloak over him and help him up, checking the shadows for movement. What if there are other mystiks close by?

'Just a rest,' he whispers, eyelids fluttering. 'Not for long.'

'But look, Da!' I tell him, pulling at his arm. 'Sparrow's here.'

Thunderbolt buzzes round his head in a cloud of moon-sparks. He stops dead still in front of Da and holds his fingers before his face as though tracing a shape in the air. Thunderbolt flits to his fingertips, touching each one in turn, then she drifts in a haze of moon-dust before his eyes, and he squints. 'Da?' he calls.

'*Sparrow*,' splutters Da through his exhaustion. 'My little one. Come to me?'

Sparrow dithers, twisting his cloak shyly, making Da cry. Then he barrels up to him and snuggles his face into Da's filthy cloak. That makes Da cry harder. A treacherous voice snakes in my ear. *He loves Sparrow more than me, cos I'm not really his.* I dig my nails into my palms and banish the voice to the back of my brain.

Pangolin tears down the mountainside, clutching her ribs. 'Here you are!' she gasps. Then she looks at Da and her face falls. 'Quick, to the draggles – the Protector says we're to get all the casualties to the hearth-healers – she's opened all the cells and let the prisoners go. Even the moonsprites!' She laughs, brushing a giddy sprite out of her thick dark red hair. 'And you won't believe it – she's ordered the storm-barrier to be stilled!'

'Heart-thanks, Pang,' I tell her. 'But can you take an urgent message to the Protector for me?'

She nods, brown eyes bright.

I fish Ettler out of my pocket and pass him to the startled Spearsister.

'Tell her that her daughter is dead.'

30
Da

Outside the tiny mountain settlement of Hearthstone, the draggle sets me and Da onto the frozen ground. The Protector scans the sky. 'We'll never be far away,' she calls down to me. 'We will rid these hills of mystiks and keep Stag away while you get your father to the healers.' Then she hesitates, her draggle's wings circling.

'How did my girl die?' she whispers, watching me brokenly.

'It was quick. But I know what it's like, not being able to stop the pictures in your head,' I tell her. 'If you get the chance not to know too much, take it.'

'Wise thing, aren't you,' she says, with a deeply buried hint of a smile that never appears. Then she turns her draggle around, leaving us.

Tears crowd behind my eyes. What I'd give for Kes to have the chance to see that her ma's a good person, after all.

The wind shoves against our backs, helping us along, but when it dies for a heartbeat I feel the suffocation of the thin air. My feet hit the mud and send thick globs into my face but I don't even wipe them away. I can feel eyes peering out of dark doorways and my heart hammers harder and harder against my ribcage. What if they keep their brooms crossed, and won't help us?

But another feeling, full-blooded and bold, sizzles across my nerves like a shooting star.

He's with us, now. And he's going to get better. And when he does, I can tell him I've found two of the Opals.

My heart rises gladder than it's ever been, into my mouth, making me grin though I gasp for air and my earth-slapped feet ache. Cos now I know I have to be what Grandma always knew I could be. The fire spirits know me and my kin, and I have to trust them. I will find the last Opal, and one day, I will be captain. Maybe I'll find crew that measure up to Kes. Maybe I won't. But I'll never forget her.

'C'mon, Da. Not much further.' He gifts me a weak smile.

Something golden snags my eye, hovering at face height. It's a dragonfly, the colour of my brooch, with delicate scarlet wings blurred by speed. Sparrow laughs aloud, slowly raising his fingers to try to brush a cobwebbed wing. Then he sneezes in the damp, dark snow.

Thaw sweeps wide circles through the air, watching tensely. *Hurryhurryhurryquick!*

We hobble into the home of the chief hearth-healer – one of the only houses undamaged after the black rain attack – and she bustles up to us, cheeks rosy, eyes strained. But when she sees Da, resolve settles over her like a cloak and she starts shouting orders. 'Hot water, please! Plenty of it, and prepare a fresh bed in the sick chamber. I'll need warm bricks in his bed and fresh linen and the herbs I gathered last night. Someone come and help me cut this crusted garb off him.' I try to heart-thank her for helping us escape Stag but she brushes me away kindly. 'There are no thanks needed among friends.'

A healer stands behind Sparrow and peels him away from Da, ignoring his shrieks of protest. 'That's enough for the time being,' she coaxes. 'Your father needs to get well.'

'Heart-thanks, sky-sister,' murmurs Da, the warmth of his smile lighting up the moot-hall.

'Save your thanks for when you're better, young man,' she scolds.

After the riders have set off for Hackles, the hearth-healers won't let us in the room with Da, whatever threats I make. 'He needs to sleep,' they keep telling me.

I'm about to storm away when their chief catches me by the wrist and peers into my eyes. 'How old are you, child?'

I shake her off. 'That's none of your blubber's concern,' I tell her. Then I feel a stab of guilt, cos she's the one that helped us get away from Stag the night of the black rain.

'No, it ent,' agrees Sparrow, scuffing his foot against a doorframe.

'Is that so?' she asks, looking from one of us to the other.

'Yep,' says Sparrow, nodding vigorously.

I kick his foot. 'But – heart-thanks, for taking care of our da,' I add.

'What about you? I'd say you need some care, and urgently. Why don't you tether your bird and break evening bread with me?'

Thaw leans down and we frown into each other's eyes. Her bright yellow ones are full of merriment. *Tether?* she asks. *Feather?*

'She stays with me, until it's time for her to go and hunt,' I tell the healer. '*She* chooses where she goes and when, not me.'

The meal is small and the stew is thin, but I sup

it gratefully and pretend I'm full so the healers don't feel bad that there ent enough. When Sparrow starts to whine that he's still hungry I jab him in the ribs 'til he shuts up, then sneak him some of my own bread under the table. I think of the Wilder-King, keeping so much food and riches to himself, and my blood boils.

One of the healers leans back in her wicker chair, peering at Sparrow's fingernails. 'Have you been playing with fire?'

'Might be you could say that,' replies my brother. Then he starts up giggling and I join in, 'til my ribs ache.

But then a memory of laughing with Kes pulls at my heart and I feel my grin collapse around me, dragging me down. I miss her so much it's like a chunk's been bitten out of my side, and nothing can heal the wound.

I leave Sparrow having the ash scraped out from under his fingernails with a quill. 'Don't fuss!' I call over my shoulder, when he squeals for me to stay put.

By the time they finally let me in Da's chamber, I'm oddly tongue-trapped. I scuff into the room.

'Mouse!' says the old, deep voice of my home. When I look up he's propped on his pillows, the sunlight coming over the mountains and streaming through the shutters, touching all the gold in his hair.

The bones-deep horror slams into me again, when

I think of Sparrow looking so much like Da, and Ma having fair hair 'n all.

Now I know who I take after.

'What is it?' he asks, reaching out for me. I go to him and let him haul me up onto the bed like I'm a nipper again. He smooths my newly brushed hair. 'Tangles won't stay away for long,' he says. The warmth of his big hands on my head makes me want to blub all over again so I suck in my lip.

'I know something, Da. Something about me and—' I bury my face in my hands and he rubs my back, singing softly to me until I can speak again. 'My birth.'

His hand pauses on my back. I listen to the rush of his breath, like waves on a stony shore. 'Mouse. I will always be your da. Whatever it is that you have learned in my absence, I am here now and nothing need have changed.'

I look up, nerves flaring. 'But something *has* changed! My da ent you. He's a murderer!'

'No,' he says simply, and I stare up at him. 'That man is not your da. It is true that he and your ma brought you into this world, but he disappeared the moment he set eyes on you. It couldn't have been more different, with me. I came along when you'd just had your first Hunter's Moon, and I could never have left you after that – you stole my heart, as fiercely as your ma did!'

I lock my eyes onto his blue ones and drink up the warmth spilling out from him. I know he's telling heart-truth, and it eases the hurt a smidge. But then I realise something else. Once again, it's gonna fall to me to tell my kin that Grandma's gone.

After the telling's done, and we've shed enough water to fill a well, Da takes hold of my shoulders. 'Your grandma stitched thunder into your heart. Did you know that?' I nod, shuddering with tears.

'That thunder will always rage on. It'll gift you all the heart-strength you need, and more.'

'Aye.' I dredge a grin from my bones, then wipe my nose on my sleeve. 'I know.'

We swap stories of Grandma until our eyelids grow heavy. We sleep for a while. When I wake up I find I'm brimming to tell him scraps of my adventures.

'I've got to tell you everything!' I shout.

'Shhh, the healers and the patients are still sleeping!' Da whispers with a grin.

'So?' I whisper back. 'Did you know that Captain Rattlebones still prowls?' I'm gleeful as I watch his smile broaden.

He presses his forehead to mine and makes his eyes go crossed, then sticks out his tongue. 'Nooooo, really?'

'Aye. You do believe me, don't you?' I poke a finger

into his chest.

'Course!'

'Well, you'd better! Cos you know what else? *She* was a woman captain! And I met her, more than once, and she saved me!'

His face has turned serious. He clasps my hands. He gives a startled laugh and his smile breaks again. 'She *was?*'

'Aye!' Then I can't stop the words spilling and I'm telling him every last drop of what's happened. When I tell him about being swallowed by a whale his eyes widen like Wilderwitch platters.

'That is proper gloriousness, Bones! The things you have seen!' There's a sadness to the way he says it again, so I reach up like I used to and gently press his eyes closed.

'Da, you sleep now,' I say, like I did when I was four moons old. And he does, 'cept he ent pretending.

When he wakes again we haul reindeer skins outside and sit wrapped up warm with our backs to the stone of the hall, sipping the strong, sweet tea that the morning healers brought us.

'How could I not have been there to protect my family,' says Da to the mountain, eyes questing the sky.

I reach over and take his hand. 'You were trying to protect us. You stopped Stag from getting the

Opals from them mystiks at Castle Whalesbane. That would've been a thousand times worse than the trouble caused by the scattering.'

'It's true that Stag was on his way to collect the Opals from the mystiks at Castle Whalesbane. Pike and I stole them before he could claim them, and scattered them, because he was gaining on me. He caught me the day I was supposed to come home, and he almost killed me because I refused to tell him what I had done with them. He thought he *had* killed me. But none of it is how I had it planned in my mind's eye.' He shakes his head.

'Ent that how life works?' I ask him. He opens one eye and peers at me. 'That's one thing I learnt while you was gone.'

He laughs. 'How did you get so wise?' Then he shakes his head again and laughs. 'No, wait. The story of your wisdom is famed among our Tribe. Your grandma used to say that when you were new-birthed, you would look at her with such calm grey eyes that she knew you'd seen much more of the world than she.'

I have to wait a few beats before I can speak, but Da carries on, wrapping an arm around my shoulders so we're snuggled under the warmth of the skins, watching the dawn. 'Before you found me, Bones, I was having dreams of merwraiths.'

My skin tingles.

'I don't know about you, but I've a sense that your grandma might be biding her time beneath the waves, especially cos she once turned—'

'Half to merwraith,' I finish, my breath steaming in the frozen air. Da's right – Grandma already started the process of becoming wraith, once before. So what if, this time, she became one good and proper?

I try to brush away the hope, cos what if the wound got her before she could change, and what if the sharks came? But hope sticks to me like a glob of honey, too bright and sweet to resist.

The pain of hope squeezes my chest and fattens up the lump in my throat, but then, for the thousandth time I'm back on the deck and Stag's firing that gun and the waves shatter as Grandma hits the water. Da fades and I'm back on the storm-deck, clear as day, with the stinks of polar dog and fish guts filling my nose. The wind batters me and the shadow of Battle-Shrieker, bald and lifeless, dances over my head. Sick fear clamps my gut and I'm running for Grandma and she's toppling from the plank, bloody water jetting into the sky. I feel again how strongly me and Grandma reached for each other in that moment, and now that yearning to stay together, with our ship, is a connection between the worlds of the dead and the living, the worlds of above and below the sea. But I ent got that connection with Kes – *she* won't become a wraith. In painful-slow motion I watch in my mind's eye as she topples backwards into the canoe again. How many times will I have to watch that in my head?

Da pulls me back to him, stroking my hair and whispering soft comforts in my ear until the room appears around me again and I can see where I really am, know I'm not really back there. When I can see Da's hand holding mine, I realise how much I'm trembling, and how sweaty my hand is in his.

'We need to save the wraiths, Da. Them, and the whales. We need to get the last Opal back and find the crown.' I glug my tea, wrinkling my nose cos it's so bitter. 'Have you got any clues where the crown might be?'

'Well, I've been studying every legend I can find, but I'm far from finding real clues, Bones.'

'When the whale spat me out he told me that the crown can't "adorn any man's head". What sort of crown is that?'

Da drifts into thoughtfulness.

After a while, I sigh. 'Can we let stories and legends and mysteries alone, for now, and just be in the here-and-now?'

'Aye, Little-Bones. There's a wondrous idea, if ever I did hear one.'

31
Naming Ceremony

When the hearth-healers finally proclaim Da well enough to leave, three days have passed and we're proper rested. His wounds have started to heal, though he walks with a limp.

A draggle comes to get us and zooms us back up the mountain to the stronghold. We pass a flock of draggles leaving their cave at dawn, dodging frozen clouds.

At Hackles, Pangolin bursts from the long-hall, red-brown hair flying everywhere in her haste, and stands in front of us, grinning, until I step forwards for a hug. 'Good to see you again!' She points to the draggle flock, now a distant smudge against the sky. 'They're off to the Wildersea, to smash the whale-hunting and wraith-dredging boats into firewood, and make breathing holes for the whales by dropping goat-skull bombs,' she tells me. 'Your ship is the *Huntress*, though?'

I nod.

'We won't be hurting that one. The Protector just wants to scare it off.'

'Thank the sea-gods for that!' I blurt, making Pangolin grin. Then I frown. 'Did the Protector find Stag? Was he as close as the mystiks said?'

Wear your armour close to your heart and your enemies closer.

Her eyes harden. 'We found no trace.'

Then she shakes the snow from her hair and smiles at me. 'Will you come into the long-hall? Our Protector is desperate to meet your father!'

But before we reach the steps to the long-hall, Crow bounds up to me and grabs the back of my cloak. Yapok races after him. 'Mouse!' they both yell at once, making Da chuckle.

'Crow and Yapok, I presume?' he asks. 'But which of you is which, I wonder?'

'No time!' says Crow roughly, knocking the hair from his eyes.

'Ah,' says Da. 'You have answered my question.'

'You have to come and see this!' shouts Yapok, dancing on the spot.

'What?' I ask. But they pull at my sleeves, bundling me through the snow towards the gap in the rock where the storm used to rage.

'Look!' says Crow. There's a wide opening now, and

my breath catches in my throat when through the gap and a few feet below I see a swirl of red and gold. I hurry away from Crow, my blood jolting hard enough to make my heart twitch in my chest. I run to the gap in the rock and squeeze through and a sob bubbles into my throat when I see that below me a girl with a bundle of red braids climbs towards the stronghold, with a seahawk flying high above her.

It can't be. My chest expands wider, wider, wider. I blink, waiting for my hope to explode to ash. But then the braids bob closer, and Thaw calls out for me.

Two-legs! Healing girl! She hereherehere! She breathes!

I run. I slip. I whack my hip on a rock and Crow's fingers are under my armpits pulling me to my feet though I never knew he was with me. We pause on an outcrop of rock and stare down and – 'Oh, my gods!' I exclaim.

'Told you, didn't we?' says Crow. When I meet his eyes, his grin is wide and bright and full of golden warmth, like his eyes.

Egret staggers through the snow in Kestrel's wake, and behind them – wonder spreads through my chest. Behind them hike a long, snaking trail of Tribesfolk. As they grow closer, I can't stop yelling her name.

'Kestrel!'

She gets close enough to hear and looks up, a proper

sunbeam-beautiful smile cracking like an egg over her wind-burned brown face.

I race down the mountain trail towards her, ignoring Crow's warnings about eagles and snow-cats and breaking my bones. I don't care a jot about any of the risks. I need to be with this girl, in this heartbeat, right now.

When I reach her she sweeps me into the tightest, warmest hug, and I press my nose into her neck and breathe her sweet smell. 'I thought I'd lost you.'

She puts her fingers under my chin and makes me look at her. 'That Stag knocked some sense into me,' she says, wiggling her red eyebrows mischievously. 'When I woke up, leagues from anywhere in that canoe, with a *very* sore head, I knew I must waste no more time putting my plan into action. The youth will unite, whether the full-growns like it or not.' She looks warily up at Hackles.

'Kes, I've got proper good news,' I say, taking her hands in mine as Egret catches up, grinning at me. 'Your ma, she . . . weren't herself before.' Then I explain how I got her back in her body and Kestrel picks me up and swirls me around, kissing my cheek, which has healed pretty well since she stitched it.

'You wondrous girl,' she tells me, over and over 'til I flush painful-red.

'Kes, I was wrong before, about the other Tribes. I thought I'd never have a chance to gift you my sorry.'

'Hush.' She takes my hand. 'Walk with me?' And she leads her army of kids up the mountain towards her home.

We keep ahead of the trail of youngsters, talking in low voices about all that's happened. 'Once Stag and the mystiks discovered the Sky-Tribes they must've guessed they could strengthen their power by making the war last until the Tribes destroyed each other,' says Kes.

'Aye. That's why he didn't kill your ma – her being Protector of the Mountain makes her proper important and powerful. They twisted her power and made it his own.'

Kes takes up my thread, nodding. 'He could see that our Hackles was a place he could use to rule over the mountain-folk, a place of ancient power.'

I nod, churning through my thoughts. So could Stag and the mystiks be trying to gather strongholds? My ship, to rule the seas. Hackles, to preside over the Sky realms. They've already got a foot wedged in the door of the Wilder-King's domain. What about the Land?

'And the thing is,' mulls Kes, 'both he and these mystiks seem to think they're the ones in real control. Which way round is it, I wonder?'

When we reach the long-hall, Kes brushes down her torn and stained dress, wipes her face with her hands and ties her braids tighter on top of her head. 'I can't go in,' she whispers, stunning me again cos this strong-limbed girl says she can't do stuff and then challenges the whole world to battle.

'You said you couldn't leave, either,' I remind her.

'Mouse, I haven't told you everything,' she says, warmth making her freckles glow. 'My mother didn't just burn books.' She lifts her eyes to my face and they're scorched with pain. 'She burned Wilderwitches, too. How will the witches ever truly forgive us? How will she forgive herself, if she remembers what she did? Part of me wishes she'd never woken up, into a world where she's going to know all the terrible things she's done.'

'You've gotta deal with that later,' I tell her. 'It weren't really her, don't forget.'

She tightens the laces on her fur-trimmed snow-boots and counts each dagger pommel on her circular scabbard for heart-luck. Then we push open the double doors to the long-hall. The thrones have been taken away and windows have been cut into the shallower rock near the entrance, letting light in. Tribesfolk chatter, helping former prisoners to bowls of soup. The Protector glances up and when she sees us she catches hold of the back of a chair for support. She steps towards us, staring at Kestrel as though she's been gifted a second chance at living the life she ought.

As they reach for each other, I'm already slipping away.

I spend the gloom-time before dawn talking with the Protector and her closest riders and Spearwarriors. Lunda eyes me suspiciously, but when I pass her a mooncake before taking one for myself she blinks and risks a small smile. I gift her one back and look away. Might be we'll never be real friends, but I know what it's like not to trust anyone outside your own Tribe. Now that the Protector's spirit has come home, Lunda's gonna have a lot of learning to do about unity.

'It got in while I was grieving,' the Protector tells me, eyes as green and gentle as Kestrel's. 'When my husband's ghost worried these walls and I lost myself.' She shudders, staring round her. 'You have restored me to my people. I will do whatever I can to help you, and you and your kin will always have a place in my long-hall.'

'Heart-thanks,' I tell her, beaming.

'Now it's time I earned my title again,' she announces. 'I'm flying to battle. I must seek revenge on Stag and all those land-lurkers helping him. Not to mention the Wilder-King.' Her jaw sets. 'And I must regain the trust of the mountain-dwellers; the shepherds and villagers.'

'No!' I cry, and Kestrel nods. 'War is exactly what Stag wants! He is the one driving home the bolts to keep the witches out! Please, for all we have fought for already, let us foster unity with witches!'

'I have brought two young Wilderwitches here to the meeting,' says Kestrel, lifting her chin proudly. 'It is a start, huh?'

I remember the Wilder-King and how his forest is descending into just as much chaos as Hackles was. But I gift her a grin and squeeze her hand. 'Aye. A proper good start.'

'Very well,' says her ma with a sigh. 'I need to regain my strength, in any case. We will test out your plan.' She smiles broadly.

I glance around the long-hall. You don't earn trust easy with these Sky-folks. But as their suspicions fall away like rain, their eyes grow lighter when they look at me. Still the question rises in me. What am I, without my ship? But now my own voice answers, heart-strong. I am something, wherever I am in the world, because of my kin and the friends I have made along the way. If I'd never left my ship, I wouldn't be who I am now; a girl looking at all these eager Sky faces, searching for unity.

Now I'm heart-certain that Grandma was right about what the fire spirits saw for me. That I will be captain.

That's why I have to go home and set things right, once I've taken the Land-Opal from Stag and gifted it to the crown along with its kin.

When the last of the trail of people have reached Hackles, there's a feast cobbled together from the snippets of food everyone brought. While I'm eating, Sparrow comes to find me. 'I've had another nightmare,' he tells me, rubbing his eyes with the heel of his hand.

I pull him to one side. My heart clamours. 'A vision? What did you see?'

Dread nips at my bones. He opens his mouth to reply when a heavy hand touches my shoulder. I spin to look. 'Pike!' I can hardly believe the heart-luck that he survived the battle with Stag and his cronies.

'I'm a tough old boot,' he tells me, eyes twinkling. 'I've brought some friends to meet you.' He beckons, and a small girl with a thick red braid flowing over her shoulder comes to his side, followed by a tall boy with short black hair and a smaller one with a shock of white locks. I blink, gasping at the grinning faces in front of me. My heart riots. 'Squirrel! Hammer! Erm!'

Squirrel leaps for me and wraps her arms round my neck and we're laughing and weeping together, sharing memories of home without needing to say a word. Then she and Sparrow start babbling to each other. I turn and Hammer's swept me into a hug before I can breathe and Erm looks around awkwardly, until I step closer. Then we're pressing our foreheads together in a Tribe-kiss without a second thought.

'I can't flaming believe I'm seeing you again!' I tell them. They tell me their stories – how Pike and his kin sheltered them until the great burning, when they all had to run again. When they see Da, they jump around him like crazed beans, heart-glad to see a full-grown from our Tribe. They beg him for stories and he sits on a bench with them, bundling them into his arms. 'So you're finally back from your trade, then?' says Ermine, in his usual grumpy way. Then Da musses his white hair and he breaks into a toothy grin. 'Heart-glad to see you, Fox,' he says.

Before Da can reply, Pike steps in front of him and the squirming bundle of kids. Da's mouth falls open. 'Friend,' he says, voice thick with feeling.

'Yes,' says Pike, stamping over to sit on the bench and eyeing the long-hall. 'We've heaps to talk about. But first, shall we eat?'

As I watch them, the Protector pushes through the crowd to find me. 'It's time for your Sky-naming!' she tells me. I wanted to talk to Sparrow again, but now he's playing with Erm and it'll have to wait.

Yapok and Kestrel lead me to the platform where

the thrones once stood. I sit on a goat skin and two Wilderwitch kids push bronze bracelets onto my wrists. They paint a rune onto my forehead and feed me sugar-dusted mooncakes. I try to gift them my heart-thanks but that makes them try to feed me more so in the end I stay quiet, cos my belly's swelled near to bursting with cake.

'Your sky-bow keens for a name,' Egret tells me, mountain tattoos silvery bright on her cheeks.

I stare at the longbow, and the rune staves Egret etched into the wood, ones that I hope she'll teach me. But why do Sky-folk name their weapons? I stare around at all the keen faces and let my eyes rest on Da. My da – his love is stronger than any blood-taint. My blood will not define me, and I will choose who I become. 'I will call it *Kin-Keeper*,' I tell them.

'I am sorry for the mistreatment of you and your kin,' says the Protector, stepping forwards. 'Also for the behaviour of the so-called Wilder-King. My daughter is right about the need for unity – but perhaps the witches need a new leader. You have done a better job than any of the full-grown leaders of the Tribes. I believe Stag wants to destroy them and bring about war for all time. If it had been left to me, he would already have won.' She looks away, eyes bleak. I climb down from the throne and take her hands.

'What happened weren't your fault, Protector,' I tell her. Then I remember something and give a sudden shout, startling her. 'The dream-dancing! You are the first one I ever met who could do it, too – I mean, some of the younger ones in my Tribe could do it 'til they turned about six, but no one else ever kept dream-dancing as they grew up.'

'Do you know something?' she replies, leaning closer. 'I have *never* met another! When I was about your age I tried to tell my mother about it, but she told me never to speak of it again. Thank you for giving me the chance to accept myself openly, sea-sister.' She smiles. 'You should know my namesake. It is Leopard, but you may call me Leo.'

Next day, Yapok leaves for the Iceberg Forest, to check on the Skybrarian. Two days after that, Kestrel and Egret prepare their draggles. I swallow away a lump in my throat. I've grown close as a sister to the sawbones girl, and now she's off to Nightfall to start secret talks with the young scholars there.

'Then we'll aim for other Tribes,' she tells me, around a mouthful of snowy mooncake. 'Ah, take heart, sea-sister! We'll see each other again soon.'

'Dunno what you're on about,' I grumble. But to make her heart-glad, I hold up a tear-vial and use it to catch a tear inside.

'There you go,' she says. 'By the time I see you next, the air will have drunk your tears and all will be well.' But when she sweeps me into a hug, she holds me so tight it's like my bones are gonna snap and I know she's gonna miss me as much as I'll miss her.

'Time to go,' says Egret gently.

GogogogogogoHUNT, mutters one of the draggles, while the other snaps its teeth at Ettler, who squeals.

Kestrel pulls away and holds me by one shoulder. Her wide green eyes look into me, down to my bones, and sudden as lightning a picture of a merwraith flashes behind my eyes. A merwraith with one blind white eye, and one gaping, empty eye socket. I gasp, but Kes don't notice cos she looks down and takes a scroll from her pocket. 'Whoops! Almost forgot. Will you give this letter to my mother? I know she wouldn't want me to leave so soon, and if I tell her in person I won't want to, either.'

I nod, taking the thin scroll from her and rubbing my fingers over the wax seal.

Then she and Egret climb onto their draggles and I stand and watch them soar through the sky. I stay there, clutching Kestrel's letter, long after I lose sight of the draggles' orange fur.

I ent ready to head back to the shindig. Da's there,

with Sparrow and Crow. And the Protector wants to break hearth-bread with me. But I need some time to myself, to gather close the threads of my thoughts. I still feel numb. Even though we've done so much, we've brought the Sky-Tribes together and freed the Protector and found Da and claimed another Opal, I still feel too drawn to the shape-dancing world, and I can feel my spirit thirsting to fly.

I feel drawn to the shadowy other world where Grandma waits, beneath the waves, maybe – just *maybe* – slowly remembering the truth about who she is. The distance between us stretches taut as a bowstring.

I go to the courtyard, as the full moon rises and spills her milky light over the edge of the mountain. The weight of everything we must still do presses my shoulders, and my bones are weary.

Cos the rare times I sleep, I can feel the merwraiths pulling at my nerves, plucking my hair 'til it waves like seaweed. When I dream, I see the faces of Grandma and Rattlebones, blurring into one ancestral spekter. I can feel them stirring beneath the distant waves.

I bring my fingers to my face and, for the first time, trace the shiny, thick scar that runs from my right eye to my mouth. It's only just stopped being too raw to touch. And I've realised how heart-proud I am of all the scars that mark my days and nights of adventure for the world to see. My scars are a map of who I am and where I've roved.

The clouds thin, and between them is a bright white beam like the fire spirits are searching me out on the mountain. A white streak like Grandma's hair, waving in the sky. Grandma knew I could do this – all of it. Now comes the time to believe her.

When the moon is high, I turn to make my way back to the long-hall, but then I freeze. 'Sparrow!'

My brother is curled on the steps of the long-hall. He must've followed me outside. There's just enough moonlight to see his foggy eyeballs twitching here and there, like he's watching another vision. 'No!' he mutters, tossing his head.

All the hairs prickle along my spine like needles, as purple fire kindles and then splurts violently from his fingertips. He didn't get the chance to tell me what his vision showed. How long have we got until whatever he's seen comes true?

Acknowledgements

Huge thanks to the amazing Liz Bankes, for shaping and shining this story into the best book it could be. Thank you for letting me know that you were a big fan of *Sky*, and that you also loved *Sea*. That 'also' meant everything during those famous book two nerves. Thank you for your thoughtful edits, warmth, humour and patience. And for inventing 'best wish-teas!' It's been the best fun getting to know you.

Endless thanks forever to the wonderful Ali Dougal, for another expert edit and for continuing to be such a joy to work with on this trilogy. I'm profoundly honoured and grateful to have met a person as magical as you.

To Jodie Hodges for your initial very enthusiastic email to say that you loved *Sky*! Phew! Thank you for your continued support and guidance on this rookie author's journey. You are the most poised-but-fun agent ever and also an unparalleled style queen.

To *Sky*'s incredible illustrator Joe McLaren, together with Laura Bird, Janene Spencer and the rest of the immensely talented design team at Egmont – you knocked it out of the park again with another stunning cover and more gorgeous internal artwork. Thank you!

To Alice Hill for guiding me through the world of PR and accompanying me on my first tour for the series (also thank you for having identical tour priorities, aka Train Snacks). Every one of the lovely Egmontees for giving me the best ever publishing experience and promoting *Sea* so expertly whilst *Sky* was finding her wings. Special mentions to Amy St Johnston and Selina Holliday for your expertise and close attention to detail on all things editorial and digital strategy, respectively.

Thank you to the many wonderful members of the children's books community who have championed book one from the rooftops, especially Robin Stevens, Katherine Woodfine, Abi Elphinstone, Kiran Millwood Hargrave, Lisa Heathfield, CJ Skuse, Emma Carroll and too many amazing booksellers to name.

Thank you to my awesome workshop crew 'The Offenders': Becca, Alyssa, Annie, Lindsay, Carlyn, Jess, Irulan and Emily. Thank you for easing my panics, inspiring me, being amazing early readers of the first chapters of *Sky* and for believing in me. Thank you for helping me celebrate the launch of my first book in serious style!

Becca, thank you also for being a great 2016 research trip buddy – for walking the Giant's Causeway with me, showing me around your beautiful Northumberland,

and taking me to your workplace – Lindisfarne Castle has to be the coolest office ever, with the best crooked corridor. Thank you also to the National Trust, for everything you do.

Thank you to my NHS colleagues for being so supportive and so excited for me, and buying copies of *Sea* by the armload!

Thank you to the Natural History Museum, London, for being one of our finest institutions. Visiting your exhibition 'Otherworlds' was a pivotal moment of inspiration during early drafting of *Sky*. We are incredibly lucky in the UK to have world-class museums that are free to access. Long may these places be protected. Thank you also to Leeds Royal Armouries and Hull Maritime Museum.

To Lucy Christopher and Melvin Burgess for an amazing writing retreat set amidst the stunning scenery of Mexico. Thank you for your invaluable advice and support.

Thank you to Bryony and Elvie for meeting up with me as often as we can, sharing hot chocolates (and babycinos) and listening to my melt downs.

Thank you to Reuben for being understanding and sharing my thirst for adventure.

Thank you always to Mum, Dad, and Nick, for everything.

Join Mouse and her crew
in the epic, thrilling conclusion to . . .

THE HUNTRESS

trilogy

Mouse and her friends fight to unite
the warring Tribes, forge new
friendships in unexpected places and
save Triannuka from the creeping ice.
But time is running out . . .

STORM

COMING SOON

EGMONT